Summer of Love

A TIMELESS AMERICAN HISTORICAL ROMANCE BOOK 3

SUZANNE RUDD HAMILTON

HHH PRESS

Copyright © 2023 by Suzanne Rudd Hamilton

This is a work of fiction. Names, characters, places, and incidents are products of the author's imagination or are used fictitiously. Any resemblance to actual events or locales or persons, living or dead, is entirely coincidental.

All rights reserved. No portion of this book may be reproduced in any form without written permission from the publisher or author, except as permitted by U.S. copyright law.

ISBN: 9798397288385

Contents

1. Chapter One — 1
   Peggy
2. Chapter Two — 12
   Two Doors
3. Chapter Three — 22
   Sheep vs. Wolves
4. Chapter Four — 43
   First Romance
5. Chapter Five — 60
   Door Three
6. Chapter Six — 74
   Finding Yourself
7. Chapter Seven — 93
   The Village

8. Chapter Eight An Irish Lad	104
9. Chapter Nine Exploration	121
10. Chapter Ten Friends and Lovers	136
11. Chapter Eleven Peace	154
12. Chapter Twelve Blackout	163
13. Chapter Thirteen Family Roots	175
14. Chapter Fourteen Beginnings	189
15. Chapter Fifteen Endings	199
16. Chapter Sixteen The Farm	207
17. Chapter Seventeen Rainbow Studios	225
18. Chapter Eighteen Woodstock	243
19. Chapter Nineteen Grandma Piggy	267

About the Author	276
My Other Works	278
Acknowledgements	282

Chapter One

PEGGY

The attic in her family home was little Peggy's favorite playground. Boxes, trunks, and chests of long-forgotten memories left behind by generations of McIntyres filled the days of her youth. It was like a family museum echoing the history of her ancestors.

Family lore was important in their clan, as the Scottish call it. Starting with the history of her Irish great-grandmother Maggie and her Scottish great-grandfather Mac, she heard many tales of their Irish and Scottish homelands and how they came to America. Imbued by the legacy of all the McIntyres who came before, her mother Suzy and father Red filled her impressionable head with their bigger-than-life legends.

Her father often said, "With an Irish grandmother and Scottish grandfather, I have the best of the Old World pumping through my veins."

Even though they passed before she was born, through the stories of her heritage and her attic inheritance, she always felt a strong connection to Maggie—the backbone and spirit of the McIntyres.

Little Peggy often spent hours on the attic floor surrounded by boxes of hidden gems. Wearing Maggie's yellowed straw hat with its faded silk flowers, Peggy's orange-red hair and gleaming green eyes were nearly hidden by its brim. She pushed it up out of her face and buttoned up the vest she found in an old box and tied the Clan McIntyre Scottish family tartan kilt around her waist a few times until it fit and cinched it with a green leaf pin. Then she carefully slipped on some long aged satin gloves that had clearly once been white.

From a tot, Peggy's fiery green eyes and red hair made her a striking twin of her namesake great-grandmother. She loved to pretend that she was the spunky seamstress her father revered and never stopped talking about. He told her all the yarns about Ireland that Maggie spun for him when he was a wee lad.

When Peggy herself was a bern, her father Red would read to her from an old Irish storybook he had as a child and sing her to sleep with songs of the Emerald Isle and especially the tale of Tír na nÓg. He said Maggie used to tell him the story of the young Irish warrior Oisín, who fell in love with the flame-haired maiden Niamh, the daughter of the king of Tír na nÓg. They crossed the sea on Niamh's white mare together to reach the magical land, where they lived happily for three hundred years.

"I always thought she made up the story about herself, but later I found it was a common Irish folktale. I still see her as the flame-haired maiden Niamh—after all, she made her own journey here to America," Red told her when she was a small girl.

The attic was a treasure trove of endless possibilities for adventures, one that could be held back only by her burgeoning imagination. It was truly a wonderland for her creative mind.

An invaluable find of an old Victrola transformed a cane into a conductor's wand, waving pixie dust of musical notes in the air, dancing to the symphony of her heart and mind. In spite of the awkward crackling sound of the high-pitched records, little Peggy only heard the melody of beautiful music.

She twirled the cane around while pulling the satin gloves up her tiny arms and hummed a sweet tune as if she were a songbird on the long-gone vaudevillian stage.

And as she grew, she combed the scrapbooks and letters she found, daydreaming about the lives beyond the attic that her parents, grandparents, and great-grandparents made for themselves. The narratives combined to become her own personal storybook; she read of the girlfriends who came to America and parted, betrayed and hurt, never to be reunited. The love stories of her parents and great-grandparents spun a tapestry of romance that wrapped around her young imaginative senses.

Musical gifts came easily to Peggy—another legacy from the past. Her mother, Suzy, showed her postcards and scrapbooks from her days in the USO and sang her songs, day and night.

Suzy taught Peggy to sing like her, cook like her grandmother, and sew like her great-grandmother Maggie. Peggy loved to don costumes from the old steamer trunk and play her mother's recordings from when she was a USO singer during the war. She treasured the few reels they kept of Suzy's appearance in a movie and some of her shows. Gifted with Suzy's talent, Peggy learned every song and emulated her mother.

And when she was eight, her father bought her a guitar and taught her how to play. Many nights he would play as Suzy sang to Peggy, eventually turning into a family sing-along tradition.

As she grew up, Peggy honed her skills and came by her families' talents honestly. Though one family trait that her family regretted was her restless soul.

She embodied the spirited personality, Red said mimicked his grandmother. The spitting image of his grandmother Maggie inside and out, Peggy inherited Maggie's driving passion for what could be, never accepting the status quo, spending many school days in the corner as punishment for marching to her own drummer—something teachers deemed disruptive.

Growing up, her hereditary Scottish stubbornness and Irish temper were trademarks of her ancestry, but made her feel she was moving away from the fabric of the McIntyre line. Peggy rarely agreed on anything with her parents. Many of her friends thought their parents were old-fashioned and didn't keep up with the times, but for Peggy it was worse. She always sensed her true self was being hinged and constricted just like the corsets and bustles in Grandma Maggie's trunk by her parent's well-meaning, but narrow and predictable view of her life.

A budding musician with a rich alto voice, like her mother, Peggy relished the attic as her fortress of solitude away from her parents and the world. It was a place to write poems and play music in peace.

She picked through her family's possessions to create an eclectic wardrobe and quilt bits and pieces to craft her own style, replete with rainbows of colors and free-flowing bohemian skirts, tops, and dresses.

She despised the constricting oppression of the day's fashions for proper ladies—tight skirts and buttoned-up jackets over binding girdles and torpedolike brassieres, tiny pillbox and doughboy hats, and pointy kitten heels. And everything came in a limited palette of hueless pastel blues and pinks, white, or beige. It was like her life. Uncomfortable and conforming, she felt like she didn't belong.

With only the streaming daylight of the sole window of her family's Chicago bungalow and the bareness of a single bulb in a terrible old tacky wooden log lamp that her great-grandfather Mac made when he first came to America from Scotland, she spent endless hours in her attic sanctuary, singing, playing music, reading, writing poems and songs, and dreaming.

Family legend said tradesmen had to prove a skill to enter the US, to show they wouldn't be a burden, so Mac made a lamp out of a log from a small tree chopped down in a forest near the tenement camps where he was housed. It was ugly but it still worked over a half-century later and won him his ticket to America, freedom, and the hope of a better life.

Just like the stories her parents told of her great-grandparents, Peggy considered herself confined to the place and time she was born into.

With her restless heart, she felt like a round peg trying to fit a dozen square holes around her, but nothing fit. She wasn't satisfied with anyone or anything. She wanted a different life.

In high school, her sparkling green eyes, fair freckle-kissed skin, and light orange-red hair made her popular with the boys, but her bohemian ways often kept them at length from her, worrying her parents about her future.

Graduating with honors in 1963, Peggy finally saw the light at the end of the tunnel. She was an adult and could be free to embrace her music and explore life. But the problem was she didn't have any money, and Suzy and Red wouldn't relinquish a small nest of bonds Maggie left for her before she died.

Trapped, Peggy toggled between furiously voicing her objections and clasping her lips in silence, refusing to speak until she was liberated, retreating to her attic. As Red predicted, she had inherited more fire from Maggie than her red hair.

One day in her attic oasis, she was looking for a screwdriver to repair her guitar when she came across a small green fabric box that she had never seen before. It looked delicate and special, and when she opened it, she found a lovely lime green broach that looked like a leaf, a lace handkerchief, and a small leather-bound book.

The pin shimmered in the daytime sunny glow of the attic window. Peggy recognized the lace handkerchief as the Irish lace she knew from many of Maggie's possessions in the attic and the tablecloths and linens Maggie gave her mother when she got married.

This handkerchief had Maggie's initials and was beautifully embroidered... *May you never forget what is worth remembering, nor ever remember what is best forgotten.*

It was another personal message sent directly from Maggie to her. She often felt Maggie's presence around her, imbuing her with wisdom and strength from the great beyond. Peggy believed in their spiritual, familial connection because of their similar appearance and often kept Maggie's heirlooms around her for comfort. It was as if she held a mirror into the past and saw Maggie looking back at her.

The white leather-bound book was filled mostly with blank pages, but the first one contained an inscription.

To me darlin' lass. May the road rise to meet you, May the wind be always at your back. May the sunshine be warm upon your face, the rains fall soft upon your fields.

And until we meet again, May God hold you in the palm of his hand. May God be with you and bless you: May you see your children's children. May you be poor in misfortune,

Rich in blessings. May you know nothing but happiness from this day forward.

May the road rise up to meet you; May the wind be always at your back; May the warm rays of sun fall upon your home; And may the hand of a friend always be near.

May green be the grass you walk on, May blue be the skies above you, May pure be the joys that surround you, May true be the hearts that love you. I love ya, and now be free, me daughter.

Your loving mother, Katherine.

Peggy remembered that Red once told her of Katherine's bravery, raising Maggie herself in service as a maid, after her lover abandoned her.

The book was a journal and a sign. She could use the blank pages to tell her story to Maggie and contribute her own piece to the generational legacy of McIntyre women. She takes the attached pen and thinks of how to begin.

Dear Maggie,

I'm told we are alike. To me, that's my fabulous inheritance from you and an unbreakable bond between us across space and time.

I don't understand why my parents won't let me be free. They did it. Mom was a USO singer and in a movie. She moved to New York when she was only eighteen to be a singer. Dad toured the Pacific on his own at the same age—the same age I am now. But every time I ask them why I can't go and find myself, all they say is that there was a war. And it was different.

And that's the point. I am different... than them, than everyone. I see all the colors of the world through a kaleidoscope of texture and light. Not just what's there but what it can be. Music is my passion and I want to find my way, just like they did. Why won't they let me?

They want me to follow in their footsteps with a family and a home. But I hate the constraints of four walls. I want to put my feet in the oceans, run through fields, see the pyramids, and bring my music to others. I'm so frustrated!!!!

Peggy sighed and put everything back in the box and took it back to her room. She would write to Maggie again. When she walked down the attic stairs, Red and Suzy were waiting for her in the hallway.

"Honey, we know you don't see things the same way we do, but we want you to be safe and well in life," Suzy said.

"Then let me do things the way I want. I want to go to New York and become a folk singer. It's my calling, just like you wanted to be a singer," Peggy pleaded.

"It's a dangerous world out there now. Your mother wasn't alone and there was a war on... people were friendlier and more considerate. It's a grittier, meaner place now and you'd be on your own. We don't want something bad to happen to you," Red explained.

"So becoming a wife and a mother is my only option? I'm not you. I don't want the same things. And what's my guarantee that I'm going to have a whirlwind romance like you two did? It doesn't happen for everyone, you know," Peggy argued.

Red and Suzy glanced at each other and smiled. They did have a special romance that began in a tornado of love and war and lasted forever, and they wanted the same wonderful life for their daughter.

"It could happen to you too. Mr. Right could be out there waiting for you," Suzy said.

"Then let me go find him," Peggy urged.

Red handed her a brochure. "We have a proposal for you—Fox Secretarial School. It's downtown and will teach you skills to get a job."

"I have skills. I'm a musician," Peggy insisted, folding her arms in opposition.

"These are skills that can earn you money," Red said. "Your mother had to wait tables until she got a job as a singer. This offers you a strong foundation to earn money and then if you want to play music on the side, you can."

"And there are lots of successful men in offices, so you may find someone, even if you're not looking," Suzy added.

"Do it our way and we'll release the bonds your great-grandmother left for you," Red promised.

Peggy had no choice.

With the deal in place and seeing no other option, Peggy reluctantly enrolled in the Fox Secretarial School in Chicago, where she would learn shorthand, typing, and dictation.

Week after week, she trudged through each boring day in the stale windowless classroom listening to the incessant tap tap tap of 20 typewriters in the same room, all keying the same thing.

While musing one day, she listened to the musical cadence of the keys. It permeated her senses until it became the soundtrack in her mind on a never-ending loop.

At home, she found herself unconsciously clicking her fingernails with one hand on the Formica kitchen table, creating a musical symphony with her fingers.

"What are you tapping?" Red asked. "Is that a new song on the radio?"

Peggy looked down, not realizing what she was doing.

"Nah, it's just the noise I hear every day of all the typewriters in the classroom. It's persistently playing in my head and now I guess on my fingers," Peggy said. She stopped the clicking.

"Do it again," Red urged.

Puzzled, Peggy thought hard, listening to the sounds in her head, trying to replicate them on the tabletop.

Suzy smiled as she heard the rhythm and began humming. Red grinned and joined in. Peggy added her other hand and got into the beat. They all laughed and created beautiful music together. It was a fantastic family moment that reminded Peggy of the nightly sing-alongs of her youth.

That night, with the music still circulating in her head, Peggy went to the attic and picked out the beat on her guitar. She loved playing syncopated jazz beats mixed with soothing folk melodies and lyrics.

The rhythm cycled through her, so every fiber of her being was electrified to the beat. She didn't just play with her fingers, but with her whole body. She worked on the song all night until she got it right, then fell asleep in the attic and awoke abruptly to the blaring sound of her alarm in her bedroom below.

Music was in her body, her blood. No matter how she had to get there, she was going to be a musician. She'd have to play it their way first, but her destiny was music and she knew without a doubt her path was New York.

Chapter Two

Two Doors

Summer, 1963

The whole idea of secretarial school seemed like a dead end to Peggy. Every day she sat in the room and watched all the other girls her age dutifully rat-a-tat tapping on the keys while repeating the same phrases. Now is the time for all good men to come to the aid of their country. The quick brown fox jumped over the lazy dog.

Most of the girls were there to earn an MRS degree in secretarial work so they could find husbands. They figured the office was the best place to find them and get on track to become wives, mothers, and ladies who lunch.

Even though that wasn't her goal, she liked the camaraderie of the girls and appreciated them for their fortitude. They knew who they were and what they wanted.

Peggy wanted to make music and be free, but she never talked about it, because that bohemian lifestyle was not appealing to most people and certainly not her friends. She just went along day in and day out, playing the part she thought everyone saw for her life.

On their lunch half-hour, Peggy and her friends Cherry, Laurie, and Shirley always went to the Automat across the street from their secretarial school.

For just a few nickels and dimes and in a very short time, they could get a full meal—main course, dessert, and coffee—from walls lined with human vending machines where armies of people inserted freshly cooked food from behind tiny individual glass doors. The variety of fare offered the opportunity to eat different home-cooked delicacies each day, depending on your mood.

Peggy liked macaroni and cheese with chocolate cake, especially when the weather or her attitude was grim. Comfort food warmed her up inside and made her feel cozy. But some days, tuna salad and lemon meringue pie or pie à la mode were her fancy, when she felt light and wanted something tangy. Sometimes the girls would make different choices and trade, like a tasting smorgasbord. There were so many choices—something for everyone, every day.

The Automat served up another special menu too; a runway assortment of men in uniformed office suits on their lunch breaks. Tall ones, short ones, rich ones, poor ones, old ones, and young ones all paraded by each day. It was like window shopping where they could pick their favorites, trying to guess what lay beneath their starched shirt and Brylcreem surface.

Cherry, short for Cheryl, was a gorgeous glamour girl. Confident in her curvy shape, which she enhanced with tight angora sweaters and skirts, she puffed up her blonde bouffant hairdo with bangs to accent her azure eyes. She displayed every tool in her toolbox with precision to present her best assets and attract her prey like a hunter. And her prize catches were usually handsome older men with money. She sat in profile anytime she saw graying temples, so they would notice her best side.

Demure Laurie was nothing but proper, from her low kitten heels to her tightly bunned hair. She wore her Chanel suits like a badge of honor and a calling card.

Describing her perfect man, she said, "Handsome is a bonus, but I'd trade looks and personality for a decent bank account. I just want to be taken care of."

She clearly saw her future as a wife and mother, but with a housekeeper, so she could be a lady who lunched.

Shy Shirley was the girl next door. Clad in sunny dresses, she wore her mousy brown hair long with a bow in the back. Her clean pale complexion was untouched by makeup. And she looked for young men with pale rosy cheeks and sweet smiles.

"I want a young man with a good disposition who I can go on picnics and long drives with and bring to church and home for Sunday dinners. Someone I can make a home with," she explained of her Prince Charming. She didn't have the highest expectations for an epic romance… just a nice guy.

Cherry and Laurie enjoyed their man shopping and directed the daily selection by labeling each man a wolf or a sheep.

Queen Cherry definitely wanted wolves. She said they knew how to treat a woman; she also liked the excitement of a man who recognized what he wanted and would take her for a ride, not a silly love-struck boy. But that ride better be in a limousine or Rolls-Royce, dripping with diamonds and pearls. Cherry only went first class. Her prerequisite for attractive worldly men didn't particularly require if they were married or not, as long as they kept her in the lap of luxury, so she didn't have to work.

Laurie couldn't care less if they were sheep or wolves. She'd even settle for a wolf in sheep's clothing, but she looked out for wedding rings with exacting precision. No married men for her. And at six feet tall, she needed a tall man and used the Automat's doorjamb to see if a man measured up in every way.

Shirley had to have a sheep... an easy-going man who would follow along or fall in with the flock. Cherry and Laurie helped her spot them by making a "baaaa" noise and laughing when a likely candidate walked by. Shirley bashfully lowered her chin when any man passed but when she heard the sheep sound, she'd perk up to look.

While Peggy enjoyed their lunchtime game selecting men for the others, she was different. To her, marriage felt like another kind of restraint, just like the straight-jacketed suit uniform for office men and women. She didn't want to be put in a pretty blue box with delicate white tissue paper and a bow like something with sweetness, fragility, or beauty to behold. And she didn't see a life cooped up in an office either.

She craved freedom. A life where she could pursue her music for fun or for a job, letting her long red hair down to wave in the breeze, free from the stiff ponytail and bow she had to wear in the office. Somewhere she could walk in her bare feet through a field of flowers and never have to worry about tight skirts, heels, and hose or being locked in the pretension of a life that would imprison her, like her parents wanted.

But she knew it all may be beyond her reach. She was trapped in a societal situation that forced her to pick a door. She could have a respectable office job or she could have a husband.

"Oooh, there's a good candidate." Laurie discreetly pointed to a young man who seemed to be staring at them from a few tables away. "He has a nicely tailored suit on, and the wave of his coiffed hair shows immense attention to grooming. I like that. Does he look tall to you girls?"

"He's handsome, but too young to have accumulated any wealth," Cherry said dismissively and redirected her attention to her apple pie.

"Does he look nice?" Shirley lifted her head up to take a quick peek and then immediately lowered her eyes.

"I don't know how you can tell if someone is nice by their appearance, but I wouldn't classify him as a sheep," Laurie sniped a bit, tired of Shirley's meek demeanor.

"I don't think it matters, girls. Looks like he's gazing at Peggy." Cherry shot Peggy a sideways grin.

Peggy barely paid attention, focusing on eating her chocolate cake. Her unusual red hair often attracted unsolicited gazes, so she learned to ignore the intermittent stares.

"Oops, we need to go anyway; our lunchtime is almost up," Peggy said, noticing her watch and shoveling the last rich bite of cake in her mouth.

As the girls grabbed their coats and purses and scurried back to secretarial school, Peggy was grateful to have been saved by the bell. The last thing she wanted was to be dragged into a discussion of her type of man.

The next day of school was typical, mining the typewriter keys for hours on end. Peggy watched the clock for their breaks and lunch. Even though she wasn't looking for a man, it was fun to help the others.

Since the Automat was a constantly revolving door, when you saw an empty table, you had to grab it. At times the girls had to stand while eating until empty tables came up, but it was also a good opportunity to look for eligible bachelors and sit with any who had available seats. But most of the time, the girls used their system of taking turns to get food while the others held the table.

That afternoon, Peggy sat at the table earlier and was at the food machine wall when a handsome man came up to their table with a tray of four coffee cups and addressed the other girls.

"Ladies, I thought you might like a cup of coffee with your lunch," he said in a soft, polite voice.

It was the well-groomed young man from the day before. He was tall with deep ocean blue eyes and slicked-back dark brown hair. His voice caused Shirley to perk up her head to see him. She smiled and shyly hung her head low again.

"Well, thank you, sir—how considerate of you," Laurie said coyly. She and Cherry locked their eyes on him, reviewing every aspect of his appearance while summing up his character in their minds.

"Do you always serve coffee table to table?" Cherry flirted.

"No, only to the most attractive and thirsty women in the Automat," he said with a sly grin.

Then Peggy approached the table with her lunch.

"Look, Peggy, this nice gentleman brought us all coffee," Laurie said.

Peggy flinched at first, then proceeded with unwavering ambivalence and sat down.

The man straightened his back and pulled out her chair for her. "My name is Michael Brett," he said, reaching out his hand to shake hers.

Peggy didn't even look up, but out of courtesy shook his hand and thanked him.

"You're very welcome, and I hope to see you ladies in the future," he said. Getting no more engagement from Peggy, he excused himself and retreated to his table.

When he was out of earshot, the girls descended on Peggy like hawks descending on their victim.

"What's wrong with you? That nice man was intrigued and you disregarded him," Laurie scolded.

"He's definitely interested in you. His stare lingered even though you ignored him," Cherry said.

"It's a free country. He can look at whomever he wants, but that doesn't mean I have to reciprocate," Peggy said, trying to end the subject by digging into her pot roast and potatoes.

"Don't you like when men look at you? I wish they'd look at me that way," Shirley asked quietly.

"He's just not my type," Peggy answered quickly between bites, trying to move away from the line of questioning.

"It seems to me no one's your type," Laurie retorted.

"You never look at any men, ever. Why?" Cherry curiously alleged.

Peggy took a deep breath and put her fork down, staring at her friends.

"You girls are lucky you know exactly what you want. All I know is I want more out of life than a suit in an office or a picket-fence home. I just need to be free to find it, and I know I haven't seen it here," Peggy confided.

"You don't want a husband?" Shirley asked earnestly.

Peggy glanced up at the ceiling for a moment and blurted out. "I don't know that I do. I want to be a musician and I'd love to travel around and see things and meet different people, like my mother did when she was with the USO during the war. Even though she hated to be away from my father, she said it was one of the best times of her life. I think I'd go crazy constrained to one house and one man. I just think I was made to be more of a free spirit."

The other girls glared at Peggy with amazement. This was the first time she confessed her true feelings; the concept was so foreign to them; it was difficult to comprehend.

"Well, I don't see how that will work. I can't imagine living like a nomad without a home and nice things around you. No, that's not for me," Laurie stated delicately, munching her cake in proper small bites.

"Do you really think you can make money as a musician? And would you want to work all that time? I don't necessarily want one husband—I'd be happy with anybody's husband or a few of my own. I see it like an elevator right to the penthouse. A stop at each floor gets me something until I can accumulate enough wealth to get to the top and stay there. I'm not made for working," Cherry concluded, sipping her coffee.

"I want a home and family, like my mom and dad have. I'm not picky, just a nice man is all I ask for," Shirley sighed.

Listening to the others, Peggy gazed aimlessly into space. Maybe she was delusional thinking she could live a different life. While the girls' plans weren't the right fit, she started to believe she was on an endless search to nowhere. In her mind, the two doors loomed, husband and a home or the workaday world. Her parents and friends all thought she should open one of them and walk through. Neither was the life Peggy aspired to, but they seemed to be the only options available.

After lunch, as the girls hurried back to the secretarial school, Peggy realized she forgot her jacket on her chair at the Automat.

She frantically dashed back to get it, hoping it was still there. As she stepped inside, she saw the table was occupied. She asked the new diners if they had seen her jacket and looked on the back of each chair. To her dismay, it was gone.

Defeated, she headed toward the door, where she saw Michael Brett standing and holding her pale blue waistcoat.

"I thought you'd come back for this. I saw you left it, but I don't know where you work." He beamed at her holding up her jacket.

Peggy was relieved to get her jacket back, but felt awkward toward the man who was coming to her aid two times in the same day.

"Thank you. It's my fault for leaving it on the chair all the time. It's a bad habit," she said, politely distant. "I thought it was lost."

"That would be a tragedy," he said. He chivalrously draped the jacket over her shoulders.

Peggy couldn't help but smile. "Thank you."

"Well, I'd like to take you to lunch tomorrow and you can thank me again," he hinted with a gleam in his twinkling blue eyes.

Peggy felt trapped. He was so nice. She couldn't turn down his offer—and she really had to get back to school.

"Ok," she quickly agreed. "I'll see you here tomorrow at noon. I'm sorry to run, but I'm already late."

He said goodbye and opened the door for her as she hurried across the street. Being careful not to look back, she thought about his polite and helpful manners and wondered if lunch with a man in a suit may not be the worst thing in the world.

After she returned to school and relented to the girls' grilling, explaining every detail of the brief event, she felt less resistant to the idea of the date.

"This is a nice man," Shirley said.

"He is obviously interested, so have an open mind. What can it hurt?" Laurie added.

That night, she couldn't get it out of her mind. Listening to the girls talk about men every day reverberated in her head again and again. So she wrote about it in her journal.

Dear Maggie,

How do you know what kind of man to pick? I thought when I met the right man, there would be fireworks. But maybe I've been listening to my parent's love story too long. Everyone doesn't get fireworks. I think I need to be realistic. I'm never going to live up to the relationship my parents have. No one can—it haunts me. Maybe that's why I've resisted adult dating.

Married men are for Cherry, not me, but I like the idea of danger and excitement. Older men, however, seem less adventurous. And I don't care about money, so Laurie's ideal doesn't check my box either. The image of endless martini lunches complaining about housekeepers and husbands seems mind-numbing.

Maybe Shirley has the right answer—a sheep. He could be easy-going enough to let me pursue my music in some form and could be a friend. But the picture of a white picket fence and PTA meetings leave me screaming.

I'm like a perpetual Goldilocks; nothing fits me the right way. But the girls are right. It's only lunch. What can it hurt?

Chapter Three

SHEEP VS. WOLVES

Dressing the next morning, Peggy found herself primping a little more than usual. She teased her hair up at the crown of her head with a barrette to hold it and let some of her hair cascade down. And she picked her prettiest pink tweed suit with a crisp white shirt and collar bow.

As she glanced in the mirror, she thought she looked appealing, but then realized she was wearing a mask and the costume that a man like Mr. Michael Brett expected. She stared down at her vanity table and smiled as she reached for the green leaf broach she found in the attic. She would take Maggie with her, or at least a part of her, to give her strength.

All morning she contemplated about how the lunch date would go, watching the clock even more intently as it moved incrementally through the first few hours of the day. She didn't know if she was anticipating the date or terrified of it.

She'd been on some dates in high school but very few. Peggy didn't get a lot of offers, but then she didn't really care. Either she wasn't interested in boys or they weren't in her.

The girls were staring at her while she was staring at the clock. Finally at noon, the bell tolled—it was time to meet Michael. She had hesitations about meeting him at her friends' regular gathering place, especially if the date didn't go well, but the Automat was also a source of security for her. It would be full of people and her friends would be nearby the whole time, examining every facial expression and movement. That was both comfort and a curse.

The girls excitedly teased and combed her bangs as they walked across the street. Peggy didn't know who was more anxious, them or her. As they got closer to the door, she was enveloped by a cold feeling of terror that overwhelmed her.

"Remember, it's just a lunch," Laurie said, seeing Peggy's obvious hesitation.

Peggy took a deep breath and entered. Michael was already sitting with two cups of coffee in front of him. He was prompt and prepared—she'd give that to him. She stopped a moment, her feet frozen in place, until Laurie gave her a shove.

"Just a meal," Cherry encouraged.

Walking forward toward the table, one foot in front of the other, Peggy tried to muster a gleeful smile to cover her terror and falsely appear pleasing. She felt her teeth grating against each other. When she approached, he stood up smiling and took out her chair.

"So glad you could make it," he said as Peggy nodded and continued her fake toothy grin. "What would you like to eat? I'll get it while you enjoy your hot coffee."

"I can get it myself," she said and started to get up.

"Oh, no, my mother would never forgive me if I let a lady get her own food," he insisted.

"Macaroni and cheese and chocolate cake…please," she blurted out before she knew what she was saying and then remembered her manners. That was her favorite meal when she was feeling uncertain, like today.

Michael's smile expanded to the sides of his face. "I love macaroni and cheese. I'll have that too."

Peggy eked out a smile as he left. She wondered if he really liked mac and cheese or was just trying to gain points with her. It didn't matter. Although she was usually a free spirit, Peggy had a head for sums and when he was gone, she sat there calculating how long it would take him to get the food and how long it would take to eat. Of her half-hour lunch hour, she surmised she only had to talk for maybe five to 10 minutes, if she was lucky. She sat back in her chair, a little more at ease. She could do a 10-minute date.

As he walked back to the table with two trays, Peggy really looked at his face. It was a nice face with luminous blue eyes. He had a tall stature with great posture, which showed confidence. She liked that, although she felt his suit and hair were a little too overgroomed—he clearly paid attention to details. She even saw the little wave in front that Laurie mentioned before.

Then she noticed a small vase with a rose on the tray. That was impressive. He really did think of everything.

"Milady, lunch has arrived." He placed the macaroni and cheese and chocolate cake in front of her, sat down, and then leaned in earnestly. "Let's go crazy and eat the chocolate cake first," he whispered.

Although that was a silly notion, as the macaroni and cheese could get cold, Peggy knew she could wolf down the chocolate cake quickly and loved the whimsical nature of his suggestion. Despite his meticulously primped exterior, maybe he did have a bohemian heart.

She smiled and nodded quickly, then dug into her cake with a big forkful. She took too big of a bite and ended up with the sumptuous chocolate encircling her mouth.

Michael looked at her and laughed. She realized she didn't have delicate lady table manners, but he seemed amused by it.

Taking a tip from Cherry, she thought if she started the conversation, maybe he would talk a lot about himself and she could eat.

"Michael, which office do you work in?" she asked.

"I am down the street at Price Waterhouse. I am an accountant," he answered. He began to tell her about how his family members were all accountants and he fell into it right after college.

Peggy was a little disappointed about his occupation. Accountants were notoriously conscious of numbers and clueless about people. It sometimes happened when a person stuck their nose in a ledger with a pencil all day and used a calculating machine. But then again, secretarial school wasn't what she wanted to do, so she knew she should be careful to not judge him by his occupation. After all, he suggested eating cake first. That wasn't beancounter-like thing to do.

She continued eating while he spoke, making sure to look at him often, while taking care not to get food all over her shirt.

He talked about his family, longtime Chicagoans from the North Side. He had two brothers and one sister.

Peggy noticed how assured he was talking about himself. He had an impenetrable aura about him. He knew who he was and what he wanted. She admired that.

"Look at me going on about myself, and not even asking anything for you. My Irish grandmother would say the devil took hold of my tongue."

The words "Irish grandmother" made Peggy instantly perk up.

"You had an Irish grandmother? I had an Irish great-grandmother," she gleefully grinned.

"How about that? Molly Anne O'Hara, she was," he said, imitating an Irish brogue.

Peggy felt a rush of warmth come about her. It was silly, but somehow his Irish ancestry made her feel friendlier toward him.

"My great-grandmother was Mary Margaret Katherine Donnelly. I'm named after her except mine is Peggy, for short."

Suddenly the floodgates opened. She told him all about Maggie coming to America and her father and mother during the war. Talking about her family came much easier than lowering the wall, revealing herself. As she continued, she noticed he was listening intently. Whether he really cared or was just displaying good manners, he at least pretended to listen. That was a good thing too.

Looking down, she realized she had shoveled through all her macaroni and cheese without knowing. Uncertain if she had eaten like a pig, she put her fork down and smiled with closed lips to make sure she didn't show any food stuck in her teeth.

"I'm terribly sorry. I can't believe I took over the conversation like that," she said. And she meant it. According to the clock, she had gone on for 10 whole minutes straight. "Oh, no—I think my lunchtime is almost over. I apologize."

He just stared at her and grinned in silence, puzzling her even more. Then he chuckled.

"Don't worry about it, Margaret. That will give more time for me on our next date."

Next date? He wanted a next date? She thought, noting that he called her Margaret. She wasn't sure if she liked that. She always considered herself a Peggy.

She mindlessly nodded, still baffled at what happened.

He got up and pulled back her seat so she could get up to leave. Then he put her jacket over her shoulders.

She was so nervous. She hadn't even realized that she had taken it off.

Finally, he smiled again, took the rose out of the vase, and handed it to her. "How about dinner Friday night?" he asked.

Still in a state of shock and uncertainty, Peggy aimlessly nodded and walked toward the door. The girls were waiting for her right outside with the most inquisitive looks on their faces. As soon as they crossed the street, they impatiently pounced on her for information.

"Well?" Laurie asked. "How did it go?"

Peggy took a deep breath and answered with a slight grin. "Good, I think."

In the short walk back to the secretary school, she narrated the full details of the date.

"He's from the North Side—that's good. He probably comes from a family of money, especially accountants," Laurie said.

"Not necessarily," Cherry chimed in. "Accountants don't always bring home the bread, but you're right, North Side is promising."

"He sounds like such a gentleman," Shirley said with her head dreamily tilted to the side and her eyes lit up.

"I agreed to dinner on Friday," she exclaimed, met by an eruption of excitement in unison.

Back at her typewriter, Peggy didn't even listen to the syncopation of the keys around her. For the first time since she started the program, the melodic mechanical symphony hushed as her mind raced.

Dinner Friday night. She saw the words in her head as big as a marquee. Dinner Friday night. The words haunted her. Dinners were long, sometimes two hours. She'd already talked about her family. What was there left to say? Maybe he could talk about himself for a while, but that wouldn't take up that much time.

Now those words glared in her mind. Two hours.

For the rest of the day and into the evening, she was paralyzed by the thought of filling that time.

At dinner, she told Red and Suzy about the date. By the satisfying smiles on her parents' faces, she could tell they were pleased.

"That's wonderful. He sounds like a very nice boy. You know, your father always brought me flowers for every date. That's a good sign," Suzy said enthusiastically.

"Price Waterhouse. That's a prominent firm. He's got a good stable job," Red added.

Lying in bed that night, she thought about Friday, only a few days away. Breaking it down, she figured she could probably be responsible for less than half of the conversation, as he did seem free to speak. And, in this case, the convention was that women were quieter and spoke less, so she could probably get away with a half-hour or a little more. But that was a lot of time. During her monologue at lunch, she didn't remember how much she said about her family, so she may have crossed to the other side of the bridge on that topic. The only thing she had left was to talk about her.

The last thing she wanted to do on a second date was talk about herself. She had tried to be on her best behavior for lunch, but she wasn't ready to truly be herself, not yet.

Facing up at her ceiling, she decided to write a note to Maggie.

Dear Maggie,

I went on a date today. At first, I was horrified merely by the idea of the date, but he was nice and put me at ease, as much as possible. I'm going on another date with hi, but I'm still scared. If I talk about myself, my music, my thoughts, will that push him away?

But then again, doesn't he have to know the real me? Do I have to play the quiet young lady everyone expects? Does he want that? And do I really care if he likes me or not? And if he doesn't like the real me, what's the point?

You should've seen Mom and Dad's faces. For the first time in a long time, they looked at me in agreement. Lately all I've seen are concerned looks and despair reflected back at me. It was nice to see them content for a change.

That was the answer. She was swimming in unknown territory. Maybe, she thought, her parents and the girls were right this time and she should defer to their wisdom and experience. Until she knew better, she would play the game their way.

Friday came sooner than she anticipated. For days, the girls and her parents buzzed around her with smiles and suggestions on wardrobe, hair, makeup, everything. She felt a little outside herself, looking in like a doll whose clothes and coiffe made up the entire image.

Dazed at school, she made more typing mistakes than ever—10 incorrect words for every 50, and she was down to 50 words a minute. Playing the piano and guitar made her fingers nimble and she was comfortable not looking down at the keys, so her score was usually a good clip of 125 words per minute. Now she was lucky she even knew her own name.

Even worse, Michael would be picking her up at home this time. That meant he would meet Suzy and Red and they would meet him. She loved her parents and they were great, but she wasn't ready for them to begin planning her wedding. It was only the second date.

After school, she changed for the day, taking all the suggestions from the girls and Suzy, adding none of her own. At this point, she felt they knew better than she. She wore a pale green sheath dress with an overcoat, slid on tea gloves, and put her hair up in a pillbox hat. She completed the look with a string of pearls that Suzy lent her.

Gazing at the mirror, she didn't see herself in the reflection—she saw a proper lady who she didn't recognize.

She took a big sigh and looked again. She did look respectable, and for now, this was the mask she would wear.

Looking down at her vanity, she grabbed Maggie's broach for good luck and strength. It was the only thing that fit with the outfit and that made her feel like her. Maybe it was a bridge. Just as she affixed it to her coat, the doorbell rang. She tightened up and gasped. The sound echoed ominously—and it tolled for her.

She heard Red open the door and greet Michael, followed by Suzy.

It was time. She walked down the stairs and into the parlor of their bungalow home like she was walking the last mile. Before she went into the room, she paused in the hallway, took a quick breath and pasted on a smile in keeping with her role.

"Hello Michael." She said and silently sat on the edge of her chair with her ankles crossed and gloved hands neatly resting on her lap, as Red and Suzy conversed with Michael.

Blankly disconnected, she watched as if she were viewing a television program of a scene... boy meets parents. It was typically scripted, with Michael making a couple of small jokes to Red and Suzy. She returned the obligatory chuckle. They liked him, but the courteous pretense was fake, leaving her cold and colorless. But it made her parents happy, so for now, she would try to be the good little proper lady, suppressing her inside voice screaming to be her authentic self.

But she had to pick a door. She hoped Michael could be a way to walk through the door and not regret it every day after. He was a bit quirky, but also stiff. She needed more time to figure him out until she revealed too much of her eclectic nature, which could scare him off.

When they left the house, Michael escorted her to his car. It was a sleek convertible with the top on for the evening. It was a nice car, but a sporty model was predictable. But she felt a little at ease since a convertible meant he had a little adventure in him. A sedan would've meant he was steadfast and stolid as his ledgered job.

He grinned and chivalrously opened the door for her. After she was seated, he slipped a rose corsage from the dashboard onto her wrist. He didn't miss a trick. Flowers were a nice touch, she thought, remembering what Suzy told her about her father's penchant for giving flowers at each and every date.

She neglected to factor the car ride into her date conversation equation, but she opted to escape into the ladylike role of demure silence.

"You'll like this restaurant," he said, breaking the ice. "It's tops, and they have excellent desserts, including a devilishly delicious chocolate cake."

For the rest of the ride, Peggy imagined what stuffy restaurant they might be going to. Maybe Palmer House or The Pump Room, some of the swankier places she'd heard of downtown.

Her whole body tightened. She was going to have to watch every move she made, from dainty eating manners to sitting straight and erect in her chair. Most men didn't relish women gulping their food down their gullets, as her mother told her.

Suzy taught her all the proper ladylike ways, of course. Between that and what she had picked up from Laurie, she felt equipped to pull off the façade, but she dreaded it. It wasn't her.

When they pulled up to the restaurant and the valet let her out, she looked up at the sign: The Greek Isles. She let out a breath of pleasant surprise. Everything she heard about Greeks indicated they had a notoriously joyous and free nature, very bohemian. She glanced over at Michael; he took her hand and led her to the front door. Maybe there was more to him than she expected, she thought.

Upon entering, she felt immediate relief. The music from the live band was loud and boisterous, and people were laughing. It was her kind of place—an atmosphere of joy. When they reached the table, Michael pulled her chair back for her.

She started to take off her jacket, as usual. It was very constraining and strangled her body. But then she hesitated, searching her mind for Suzy's lessons on whether ladies leave their jackets on in restaurants. Then suddenly, she felt a tug on her collar.

"Here, let me help you with your jacket. I know you like it on the seat," he said, gracefully removing it and putting it on the back of the chair.

Peggy exhaled, thinking maybe this wasn't going to be so difficult. After all, he remembered she puts her jacket on the chair.

When the waiter came to the table, Michael took over as usual.

"Please bring us some wine and Saganaki," he said assuredly. Then he turned to Peggy. "I'm sorry—have you ever been to a Greek restaurant? I should've asked your preference, but I love this restaurant so I just ordered what I like without asking."

She shrugged, as she didn't know anything about Greek food anyway. It was a little presumptive of him, but she tried to be an adventurous eater, so she didn't object. Adventure in everything exhibited a slice in the pie of life Peggy wanted.

The wine and food came quickly and Michael thanked the waiter kindly.

"I hope you like this appetizer. It's one of my favorites." He smiled as the waiter squeezed a wedge of lemon in the pan, poured a bit of brandy on it, and then lit it on fire. After a few seconds, he put a lid on the searing gold flame and left the table.

Peggy waited in wide-eyed anticipation. Michael removed the lid, stuck some bread in, and scooped up what looked like a glob with whitish strings of cheese.

She leaned in to smell the sharp aroma of the fried cheese. It looked delicious, so she grabbed some bread to imitate Michael, but again paused, wondering if it was appropriate to dig in or instead put a spoonful on her plate.

Michael smiled and nodded at her. "It's ok, go ahead. That's the way it's done."

Peggy gladly dipped her bread in. It was delectable, like nothing she ever tasted before.

"My father's business partner is Greek, so I kind of grew up in a restaurant like this. Let me tell you about the menu." He sweetly explained the different types of foods, carefully asking her opinion and taste on any selections. In her head, she wanted to joke that it was all Greek to her, but instead she went the demure route.

"I like all kinds of food," she said. "I've never had any Greek food, so I would be very happy for you to order for us."

When the waiter returned, Michael comfortably and confidently ordered like a native. She didn't understand a word, but it all sounded delightfully interesting. The ease of the language on his lips was alluring.

After the waiter left, the band began playing. Michael smiled and clinked his wineglass with a fork in time with the beat. It was a mathematical melody that sped up and slowed with a whimsical lack of precision.

Then a group of people gathered in a line and shouted "Opa!"—and started to dance. It was remarkable how everything looked choreographed, like the Rockettes on TV at Radio City Music Hall. It was perfect and once more, it wasn't, and they were laughing, singing, and having a good time. It was wonderful.

Michael must've noticed her eyes on the dancers. "Would you like to dance?" he asked, holding out his hand.

Eagerly nodding, she waited for him to pull out her chair and lead her over to the dancers. Holding hands with her and others in a giant line of people enjoying themselves, Michael was a pro. He followed along as if he'd been doing it his whole life, swaying back and forth with the group, kicking their feet out and ending in a big circle all the way around the restaurant. It was an incredible display of unabashed joy.

Peggy was in her element; even though her hair was tightened up in a bunch of pins, she felt as if she was clad in a flowing floral dress with her hair cascading down like a waterfall. She looked around at everybody and instantly felt she was among friends.

She found she was picking up the dance without much trouble.

"Hey, you're good," he said.

"Well, I am a musician. It comes easy to me."

As soon as she said it, she clamped her mouth shut and silently admonished herself. How could she have blurted that out? No man wants a musician for a wife, unless it's in an orchestra, and now she said it, she thought. She closed her eyes tight for a moment and then looked over at him. He didn't make any acknowledgment of what she said.

Maybe he didn't hear me, she thought. I'll just keep going. They danced and sang until the song ended and then happily retreated to their table a little winded.

"That was so much fun," Peggy said.

"Yes, you can't beat a Greek dance. That's one of the things I love about this place. You don't have to know anybody here to feel like you belong. It's like a universal family." He smiled and took a big gulp of wine.

Just then, the waiter brought their food. On the table lay an astonishing array of culminating scents filling her nose and giving her an immediate feeling of warmth.

"This is Greek comfort food," Michael said. "Moussaka, Manestra, Chicken Souvlaki, Fasolada, Spanakopita. It's served family style here—so would you mind if I gave you an assortment?" he asked.

Peggy anxiously nodded and smiled as he filled her plate with food.

She was thrilled to continue her international cuisine lesson and try everything, so she immediately dug her fork in. It was a festival for the tastebuds with different flavors and textures she'd never experienced before. She couldn't help herself and audibly uttered. "Mmmm."

Michael laughed and continued eating. "I love that you have a good appetite. So many girls eat like little delicate birds picking up their food on dates when you know they're hungry. That doesn't work with Greek food. That's why I brought you here. I thought you'd like it. You're different."

Peggy stopped mid-bite, uncertain she had heard him correctly. Did he say I was different, and he liked that? Maybe I did judge him a little by his cover and there's a little bohemian underneath that starched suit, she thought.

Relieved, Peggy sampled more of the food. Everything she tasted was a delicious departure from normal American fare. The whole place had an atmosphere that set her at ease, somewhat releasing her inhibitions.

They were both enjoying the food so much that conversation was at a lull, mostly just comments about their dinner. As soon as they finished, the waiter approached and asked about dessert.

Michael glanced at her with anticipation. "I know you like chocolate cake, but do you trust me? I'd like to recommend something."

She agreed, excited at what fascinating delicacy was next.

Michael nodded to the waiter and without a word, a few minutes later, the waiter brought coffee and a yellowish-orange dish called Baklava.

As soon as her fork delivered the flaky pastry to her mouth, she tasted a full sensation of sweet flavors of honey, orange, and chunky walnuts with the light taste of the crunchy phyllo layers.

After dessert, they sipped coffee. Despite her constrained exterior, inside Peggy relaxed as if she was basking in the free-flowing sumptuous aromatic breeze of the Greek islands.

"Did you say before that you were a musician?" Michael asked.

There it was. One question and she was immediately whisked back into her stiff shell, uncomfortable and panicked.

The topic was out there she couldn't take it back. The words hung in the air between them, lingering like sticky grease that wouldn't come off a stovetop.

She had to say something, so she quickly concocted a half-truth to move the conversation along.

"Oh, I play piano. My mother taught me. Remember I told you she was a singer in the USO during the war?" Peggy said nonchalantly and immediately took a sip of her coffee.

"I really like music. I can't sing or play an instrument, but I would say I'm a connoisseur." He said and sipped his coffee, so she thought she was home free.

Since he liked music, Peggy desperately wanted dip her toe in the water and tell him about her songs, but she was guarded. She needed to keep it cool. She didn't know what kinds of music he liked. There were very different camps between the top 40 radio songs and the rebellious jazz, blues, rock and folk music she was drawn to. Mustering her best posture, she daintily tipped her coffee cup up with her pinky out and took a quick sip.

"Really—what kind of music do you prefer?" she asked in her best matter-of-fact, unemotional way.

"I don't know that I have a preference," he said, staring frankly at her. "When I was little, my parents would play big band music. I thought I'd like to be a drummer because I liked the beat. Then they moved on to Perry Como and Pat Boone. I don't really care for those, although some of them have beautiful melodies. I like Elvis and the rock beats, but I also like harmonies like the Everly Brothers. I guess I just like music; does that make sense?"

Peggy was dumbfounded. She wrongly assumed he was a Lawrence Welk type. Proper people don't like rock 'n' roll, as it's too messy and controversial, but now she thought maybe there was some danger in him and wondered how far away from conventional he would go.

Intrigued, she wanted to delve into his musical preferences more and tell him hers. But she was afraid to let her hair down for real. She needed more time. So to avoid any more slip-ups she just smiled and nodded, sipping her coffee.

"That's nice that you like all kinds of music."

He gently took the hand that she accidentally left on the table. Listening to him talk about music, she forgot about the faux pax of having her elbows on the table. But surprisingly, she felt a little tingle when he touched her gloved hand. It was like a buzz tickled her hand. It was little, but it was there. Maybe, she thought, this was her subconscious telling her that she might like him, even a little.

On the ride home, he tuned in a dreamy ballad on the radio. Peggy sat there letting her imagination soar into the world of romance. Could he be someone she would be interested in? There seemed to be more to him than appeared. Maybe he could be somebody who would bridge the gap between respectability and Bohemia? A perfect balance she could accept.

Catching herself, she didn't want to get too carried away when the Everly Brothers song All I Have to Do Is Dream came on.

"This is a great song," he said and turned up the volume.

Just as in the song, Peggy mused if her dream of a man who could love her and let her be herself was within reach. The song was about believing in something that could happen despite reservations. She slightly let herself go and unknowingly started humming softly with the music.

He looked at her in surprise. "Hey, that's pretty."

Peggy smiled and couldn't help thinking he could be Mr. Right, maybe.

Once they reached her home, he walked her to the door with his hand in hers. As they stood staring at each other on her porch, she panicked a little. Was he going to try to kiss her?

He leaned in and she held her breath. "Good night, Margaret," he said, kissing her on the forehead.

The house was dark and her parents were asleep, so she immediately went to bed with her head reeling. In the darkness with only the glow of the moon, beaming, she took out her journal.

Dear Maggie,

Now I'm not sure what to feel. He likes me, that much is true, but does he like the real me? He doesn't even know who I am, but then again, I haven't given him the chance. He complimented to my humming, but that was still all prim and proper. So far, I've let him in a little and he is still interested, so there's hope.

And he keeps calling me Margaret. While I'm proud to carry your name, it's so formal. Even you didn't use it. I'm Peggy. Why doesn't he call me Peggy?

I just don't know what I'm doing. I'm afraid I can't be standing on this bridge all the time between the world my parents and friends want me to be in and the one that I want. But if someone were standing alongside me, maybe it would make it easier. He does seem like a nice man.

There's still too much to understand and so much I don't know. I guess I'll just have to wait and see what happens.

She planned to have lunch with the girls the next day, as they were unsatisfied with the prospect of waiting until Monday to get the details of her date. So they met at a small diner near the El train, so they could converge without having to go into the city loop area. Still full from the feast the night before, Peggy ordered a small salad. She knew as the subject of interrogation she wouldn't have a lot of time to eat.

Once the waitress left, the girls immediately demanded a full recounting of the date.

"All right, tell us everything. Don't leave out any detail," Cherry said.

"Where did you go? What was he driving?" Laurie asked.

"Answer one—it went well. Answer two—a convertible. Answer three—a Greek restaurant," Peggy replied with few words.

Shirley sighed satisfied, but Laurie went on the attack.

"Wait, did you say a Greek restaurant?"

"Yes. There was vibrant music and dancing and the food was incredible," Peggy said.

As Peggy described the food in detail, Cherry and Laurie were astounded.

"Why did he take you to a Greek restaurant?" Cherry asked, bewildered.

"I think it's nice," Shirley said assuredly.

"What's wrong with a Greek restaurant?" Peggy asked confused, as Cherry and Laurie looked at each other, astonished.

"Where a man takes you on the first dinner date says a lot about him. He takes you to someplace like the Palmer House, you know he has money," Laurie said.

"Is he Greek?" Shirley asked.

"No, he said his father's partner is Greek and he spent a lot of time in Greek restaurants as a kid. It really showed another side of him," Peggy smiled.

The girls all pursed their lips and glared at her.

"Is that a side that you really want to see?" Cherry laughed.

"I'm very surprised. I thought he'd take you to a nice steakhouse. He's from the North Side, after all." Laurie shook her head.

There was a silent pause as the girls looked down and ate their food for a few minutes. Peggy didn't know what to think. She thought things were going in a good direction, but her friends didn't.

"Did he at least kiss you good night?" Cherry said.

"Not on a first date!" Shirley objected.

"Oh please," Cherry rebuffed. "And it was technically the second date."

"Only evening dates count, not lunches." Laurie puckered her face in disapproval.

Peggy smiled, recreating the kiss in her head. "He walked me to the front door holding my hand and kissed me on the forehead."

"The forehead?" Cherry objected.

"No, that's good. Respectful," Laurie said in a matter-of-fact way.

"I think that's wonderful," Shirley said.

With that, the conversation shifted into a lot of chatter. Later, Peggy left the lunch feeling even more confused, but walking home she realized that she and her friends didn't like the same things anyway, so why would they like the same men and same dates?

She stopped cold. Her head must've thought of this before her mouth did. She liked Michael.

When Peggy got home, Suzy rushed to greet her at the door with a bouquet of roses.

"Look what came for you from Michael!" she gleamed. "He must really like you."

Gazing at the flowers and the enclosed card, Peggy beamed.

The card read, Keep dating me and you'll sleep on a bed of roses every night. How could you not like a man who sends flowers?

Chapter Four

First Romance

In their romantic notions, Suzy and Shirley were right. It was the start of something wonderful.

Michael planned every aspect of their courtship—romantic walks around the ponds in Lincoln Park, tickets to the movies and the theatre, boat rides on Lake Michigan, dinners at various restaurants, and one lunch at the Automat per week, so she could eat with her friends the other four.

Every time he picked her up, there was a rose corsage or a beautiful single rose, followed by a bouquet of roses sent to the house the next day. Peggy started to wonder if he had a florist relative, but he was making good on his promise to keep her sleeping on a bed of rose petals.

In the dining room, the overflowing vase of flowers sat atop a runner of Irish lace that Maggie made. Suzy beamed every time she passed it. And in the few months since she and Michael began dating, life was easier with Suzy and Red. They were content and so was she. Michael was smart, attentive, polite, courteous, and fun to be with. And each day she liked him more and more.

He told her about the people in his life, both his family and at work. And slowly, she spoon-fed him little bits of her real personality, while still keeping guarded about her musical goals and bohemian proclivities, waiting for a clear signal of prospective acceptance.

Still playing the part of a proper lady, she felt the most comfortable when they were sharing music. They attended prestigious dance venues to listen to up-and-coming top 40 radio artists that he liked. It bonded them in her favorite subject, but she never suggested any artists she preferred for fear he wouldn't appreciate in the folk and alternative rock music she liked. Her music was in the beatnik and hippie clubs of the underground culture. But as a fan of all music, she seized every piece of common ground.

At their weekly lunch date, they experimented with different foods, tasting and sharing desserts and dishes like food critics, determined to eat their way through the entire menu.

They talked about visiting cities across the country and exploring the food, art, architecture, and music in glamorous places like London and Paris.

Reading about history and art was another commonality between them. Peggy loved the renaissance of art and music in 1930s Paris. It was one of her favorite topics of conversation. The City of Light was the ideal balance between refined European elitism and an eclectic array of culture. She had picture postcards on her bedroom wall of the Eiffel Tower and the Arc de Triomphe. They discussed strolling arm in arm through the arc and along the Champs-Élysées, stopping at every café and artistic venue.

Every week solidified her belief that he could provide a balance between the respectable life her parents wanted for her and the style of life outside normal boundaries she craved.

But she wasn't completely sure about their relationship until he took her on a moonlight dinner cruise on Lake Michigan. With close-dancing orchestral music and candles flickering under the warm night sky, a romantic mood filled the air. As they stood under moonbeams that mirrored in the dark lake water, they gazed at the shimmering reflections and he leaned over, gently put his hands on her cheeks and kissed her.

His kiss perfectly embodied his personality. It was strong yet tender and gave her a little tingle, leaving her satisfied that he could be Mr. Right. It still wasn't fireworks and trumpets, but as she laid her head to sleep on fresh rose petals that night, Peggy thought she might be falling in love.

At their lunch gabfests, she kept the girls kept up to date on Michael and listened to their love escapades. Everyone was moving toward their individual goals.

Cherry was dating a few men, collecting baubles from them all. She didn't discuss their marital statuses and Peggy and the other girls didn't ask—but with Cherry's curious insinuations about the men, they all certainly wondered.

"Roger is a banker and we go out for happy hour. Then I have a very late supper with Edward—he's in advertising and used to many late nights," she explained coyly.

Laurie was seeing a Harvard lawyer, a man she thoroughly vetted, and enjoyed going to the country club for tennis, golf, and dinner dances.

"We're the envy of everyone at the club. It's just a matter of time until he proposes; I'm already picking out china patterns," she boasted.

And Shirley began dating a boy she met on the El train. He gave up his seat for her and she was so humbled by his gesture she had no choice but to talk to him.

"He's a very kind man with rosy cheeks and a cute smile. He makes sure to ride the El home every night at the same time as me, so he can walk me home. And he's Presbyterian, just like me," she giggles.

"But he's a plumber," Laurie scoffed.

"That's good enough for me. Our home will have the best plumbing in Chicago," she smiled confidently.

It seemed like everything was in place for the girls as their secretarial school graduation approached. Peggy suspected the looming requirement for employment kicked the girls into achieving their marital targets sooner rather than later to avoid the daily office grind.

Peggy wasn't aiming at the matrimonial bullseye, but her relationship with Michael made her calm and happy. For the first time, she wasn't prone to bouts of restlessness and discontent, which Red and Suzy took as a good sign, and so did Peggy.

For their lunch at the Automat on the four-month anniversary of their first date, Peggy wanted to take the reins for a change. She planned a lovely spread for them to surprise Michael; she called it "Paris in Chicago" and tried to convert Automat American delicacies to simulate French cuisine.

Shirley and Laurie gathered all the dishes, while Peggy prepped the table with a bud vase with a recent rose from her collection and a checkered tablecloth, like in a real Parisian café.

Cherry offered a bottle of French champagne she received as a gift from one of her admirers. As Peggy was spreading the tablecloth out, Cherry ran in, excited.

"Guess who I just saw coming out of the jewelry store?" She could barely contain her excitement.

"Who?" Peggy asked, anticipating it was one of Cherry's beaus buying her another bracelet or necklace.

"Michael!" she shouted and then, realizing her volume, she looked around to see if anyone was staring.

Peggy nearly dropped the vase she was placing. "What are you talking about? Are you sure?" Her expression went from doubt to confusion to glee all in one minute. "Do you think he's getting me jewelry for a four-month anniversary?"

"Or maybe it's a ring!" Cherry exclaimed and hurried over to tell the other girls.

Peggy plopped down in the chair in disbelief. A ring? She went through the wheel of emotions all over again. Her eyes grew big as the image of a ring flashed in front of her mind and she took stock of her feelings. Was she ready for that?

Before she could process how she felt, Michael came through the door smiling, as if he owned the world. He instantly focused on Peggy and his eyes gleamed at her and Peggy held her breath.

At first, she was terrified, but as he walked toward her with his big, beaming smile and indigo blue eyes, her veil of fear slowly dropped and a rush of calmness flowed over her.

"Wow, Margaret, thanks for going to this much trouble. I love it," he said as he sat down and held her hand across the table.

"The girls helped me. It's just a little gesture to make today special," Peggy said, sitting on the edge of her seat with anticipation.

In remembrance of their first date, they ate the dessert first. It was a combination of chocolate pudding and chocolate cake to simulate a French chocolate mousse.

Laurie talked to the manager and convinced them to make a specific meal for the occasion. She could be very forceful and persuasive when she wanted to get things done. It was hard to say no to her.

The Automat employees also made a loaf of bread to go with the chicken dinner cooked with wine in the gravy to imitate coq au vin. Luckily, the Café du Monde coffee, which was always served at the Automat, was already French. Paris, via Automat.

Even though it wasn't truly French cuisine, they ate and drank as if they were sitting in a cafe on the Champs-Élysées, barely noticing the hundred people shuffling around trying to eat during their lunch hour.

As Cherry, Laurie, and Shirley looked on from afar, Michael and Peggy created an oasis unto themselves. And as they ate, Peggy found herself steadily getting more nervous, anticipating the moment he could strike with a proposal.

She tried to stifle her nerves, but they kept manifesting in the worst ways. She drowned them with a little more wine, then she dropped her fork and knife a couple of times. Michael just smiled and chuckled.

At the end of the meal, when they were drinking coffee, Peggy began to doubt her information. He seemed completely at ease. Maybe he wasn't going to propose. Maybe Cherry was wrong.

Suddenly, Michael finished his coffee and stood up. Peggy held her breath. This was it.

This was her first proposal, so she wasn't sure how she should react. And of course, she wasn't supposed to know anything was happening, so at least she needed to look surprised. He walked over to her and pulled out her chair.

"This was great, Margaret. Thank you for making everything so special, but isn't it almost time for your lunch to be over?" he asked.

Peggy felt deflated. It wasn't going to happen today. But then she experienced some relief. A proposal is an exciting thing, but was she ready for that? She stood up in a fog of confusion and disappointment and went to grab her jacket off the back of the chair, but Michael took it and draped it around her shoulders. And when she looked to her side to pull the jacket tight, there it was—a ruby red velvet box sitting right there on her shoulder.

With one svelte move, Michael was on one knee in front of her, holding the velvet box up to her hand. In an instant, the busy Automat was dead silent, except for a few giggles; everyone froze, laser-focused on Peggy and Michael.

"Margaret McIntyre, will you do me the honor of becoming my wife?" he asked.

This was it! She felt suspended in time, and a wave of panic enveloped her. Was this what she wanted? This was forever, no turning back. But then she looked down at his handsome gleaming face again and remembered the fun they had had together and the kindness in his eyes, and the moment of hesitation passed.

"Yes, I will," she said, and uproarious cheers and applause erupted in the room. Michael stood up, put the ring on her finger, kissed her on the cheek, and hugged her. They were engaged.

People all around rushed toward them. The men shook Michael's hand to congratulate him. And Laurie, Cherry, Shirley and the other women in the restaurant surrounded Peggy, oohing and aahing over the ring.

"Not bad," Cherry said.

"It's a classic," Laurie said admiringly. She held up Peggy's left hand to closely examine the diamond.

Shirley beamed at Peggy. "I'm so happy for you."

When Laurie let go of her hand, Peggy looked at the ring on her finger for the first time, wiggling it a little. With a slim silver band, a round solitaire in the middle, and two small diamonds on either side, it was a classic style, befitting Michael's impeccable taste.

Caught up in the sea of congratulations, Peggy and Michael were eventually swept over to the door and landed outside. Peggy took a deep gulp of fresh air, feeling she hadn't been breathing since he went down on one knee.

"Are you happy, Margaret?" Michael smiled.

Before she could formulate an answer, he spoke again. "Me too. I bet you're gonna have a hard time working for the rest of the day." He kissed her on the cheek. "Don't forget—we're having dinner at the club with my parents tonight," he said. Then he walked away down the street, leaving her alone in front of the Automat.

As soon as he left, the girls came through the door and encircled her, whisking her across the street to the secretarial school. They were buzzing and chattering about the proposal, the meal, the excitement, everything.

Laurie immediately announced the proposal in class and the rest of the day no one thought about typing, shorthand, dictation, or any other secretarial work. Instead, fancies of love filled the room. Peggy was captured in the merriment of the envious gaggle of secretaries-to-be, who were fawning over the ring and mooning about the proposal story, daydreaming of it happening to them next.

Peggy was going to be a bride and her friends were going to help make it a monumental event.

A few hours later, Peggy walked home from the El train alone in her thoughts. For the first time in hours, her mind cleared and the excitement ebbed. She wondered what her life would be like married to Michael. Would she be able to pursue her music? Would he expect her to have babies right away? Where would they live? An apartment in the city or a house in the suburbs?

Then she remembered the dinner at the country club. She briefly met Michael's parents before. They were nice people—a little stiff for her taste, but pleasant. But she'd never been to their club before and was worried she wouldn't fit in.

With each accelerated step toward home, her doubts and nerves reached a boiling point and she fell short of breath, thanking God the moment she reached her front door. She sighed in relief—she could go to her room, play her guitar, and relax from the day's events.

She recalled a song her mother used to sing a lot: Que Sera, Sera. She thought about how maybe the future really wasn't hers to see, but could evolve naturally.

As soon as she opened the door, Suzy and Red were waiting on the other side.

"Congratulations, honey," Red said, kissing her on the cheek.

"This is wonderful news." Suzy smiled and embraced Peggy.

"How did you know about this?" Peggy looked at them, confused.

"Michael asked me for your hand in marriage," Red said. "He's a fine boy with good manners. I always regretted that I couldn't ask Suzy's father until after we married, because of the war. I just couldn't wait to marry her."

"It will be a joyful celebration with his parents tonight. We're looking forward to it," Suzy said.

Peggy was in shock. Not only did her parents know about this before her, but the fancy country club was a setup engagement dinner?

She feigned a smile and made an excuse to her parents about needing to get ready, just so she could escape. When she was in her room, she picked up her guitar and quietly plucked the strings, strumming a bit to soothe her nerves. Looking down as she played, she truly saw the ring for the first time. It was very pretty, but was it her? Was any of this her? She pulled out her journal to mark the event.

Dear Maggie,

Michael asked me to marry him. Everyone's happy—Michael, my parents, my friends... and I thought I was too. I am, but it's all happening so fast.

Maybe I'm just getting cold feet already or everything is just sinking in. This is very confusing. Do I have to give up part of me in order to be Mrs. Michael Brett? Can't I be Peggy Brett? I give up my name, my home... what do men give up?

I'm probably just being silly and nervous about going to a fancy country club. Michael is a good man. We have a good time together. And he loves me. Like Mother sings, Que Sera, Sera.

She put down her journal and picked up the guitar again. She played a few verses of a song that echoed in her mind, humming along, as if ordering herself to go along with things and not worry.

Suzy popped in the door, humming and singing along with her, just like when Peggy was little. She sat next to her, stroking her long orange-red hair.

"I know you're nervous, but I promise this will be great." She grinned and opened Peggy's closet door. "I can help you get into your teal and gold party dress. With your gold kitten heels, it will look very elegant."

Suzy took the dress and matching belt from the closet.

"With that dress, I need the crinoline for the flared skirt. It's so scratchy. I'd rather wear the green sheath dress and jacket," Peggy said.

Suzy laughed. "No, honey, this is a fancy country club. We'll need gloves, hats, wraps, and girdles—comfort is not an issue."

Peggy hesitated, but then agreed. She'd never been to a fancy country club before and felt Suzy knew best.

An hour later, Michael arrived in a black tuxedo carrying identical red rose corsages, placing one on Suzy's wrist and one on Peggy's.

"Are you making me look bad, son?" Red laughed and gently slapped Michael on the back.

It was picture postcard perfect. Happy fiancé and ecstatic parents go out together dressed to the nines. Peggy sighed and smiled at the glowing look on her parents' faces. They were so happy.

The Bretts' country club was one of the most exclusive clubs on the North Side.

Judges, mayors, senators, and the owners of the biggest companies all dined and danced together there.

Decorated with floor-to-ceiling dark wood grain paneling and regal navy and burgundy carpeting with gold swirls throughout, stepping into the country club felt like crossing the threshold into another world they never dreamed of.

Peggy was raised in middle America, through and through. Suzy and Red owned a home and loved their daughter. Suzy was a happy homemaker and mother who sang in the church choir and volunteered at every school, church, and town event. Red continued the airplane mechanic trade he learned in the Navy. He did well, but was not a rich politician or company president. This posh life was foreign to all of them.

As soon as they walked in, Michael's parents greeted them, shaking Red and Suzy's hands and kissing Peggy on the cheek.

Edward and Carol Brett were nice people, but slightly snobbish and aloof. When she met them in the past, they were cordial to Peggy, yet she always felt they were distant.

After they greeted Peggy, Michael, Suzy and Red and all congratulated each other on the upcoming nuptials, they sat down and engaged in some mindless preliminary chitchat about sports, the weather, and the excitement of the engagement. Meanwhile, as news of the betrothal spread through the club like a virus, their dinner was interrupted at every interval, when one of their fellow country club members passed by to congratulate them.

No one seemed to mind—it was fairly expected. But the pauses gave Peggy openings to pan around the room, looking at people jovially clinking glasses and silverware, seemingly chattering about everything but at the same time about nothing. It seemed empty. Everyone was playing their part like they were all actors in a movie and she was sitting there, feeling as if she'd forgotten all of her lines.

Peggy pasted on a smile and faked her way through dinner, but more and more she began to notice the condescending compliments, phony laughs at bad jokes, and undertones and innuendo in the remarks of the people stopping by the table to greet her future in-laws. They were friendly at the table and then changed faces when they turned their backs. Nothing seemed genuine and it bothered her.

When the orchestra started, Michael dutifully jumped up and offered Peggy his hand to dance. The floor quickly crowded with couples twirling around to a prescribed waltz. That and the Fox Trot were the only dances permitted at the club.

Michael was a good dancer; his mother had made him take cotillion lessons before high school. His stance was firm and powerful. Peggy felt his hand on her back leading her around with a gentle push to indicate where to go.

Despite the constricting girdle and starched dress, she felt more at ease alone with Michael, waltzing to the sway of the music. They were in sync.

But the parade of passing congratulations on the dance floor by other members gave her a sinking feeling in her stomach. They didn't even talk to her. Every compliment was to Michael, about her.

"Good job son. She's very pretty," a man said, patting Michael on the back.

"What beautiful red hair," his wife commented as they spun by.

It was as though she was invisible and they saw right through her, like a trophy on the mantle. Seen but unseen.

At the end of the evening, Michael brought them all home. In the backseat of the car, Peggy stared out the window dismayed, wiggling in her seat as the crinoline under her dress became more uncomfortable and scratchy.

Soon they arrived home. Suzy and Red thanked Michael and walked into the house. Michael helped her from the backseat and gave her a come-hither look, guiding her to the front seat.

"I wanted a little alone time with you. I know that dinner was a lot all at once. To be honest, that crowd has a learning curve, but my parents insisted, and I try to please them. The club is really not my scene. Thanks for being such a trooper, Margaret." He leaned over, pulling her close to him, and deeply kissed her on the lips, rendering her mind blank and sending her head swooning, forgetting all her worries and trepidations of the night.

After a few minutes of kissing, he went around the car to open her door, took her hand, and strolled to the front porch.

"I'm so glad you said yes. I'll be proud to have you as my wife." He smiled, kissed her on the forehead, and winked at her as he left.

As soon as she opened the front door, Suzy and Red started raving about the country club, the food, the dancing, the whole experience.

"That was the most beautiful place I've seen," Suzy said in awe and wonder.

"And the food was good. The prime rib was so tender I cut it with my fork," Red remarked.

"I'm still swaying to that orchestra. I haven't heard a band that good since I was in the USO. I was tempted to jump up on the stage and sing," Suzy laughed.

"Well, at least we got to dance like the old days—right, Babe?" Red grabbed his wife and twirled her around as she giggled.

Watching them warmed Peggy's heart. All her life she envied their connection, their inherent bond that kept them deeply in love for 20 years. She didn't know if it was the unique majesty and intensity of their whirlwind wartime romance that kept them happily together, but admired their timeless youthful love and for the first time thought maybe it was possible for her.

With her head reeling and her legs still itching, she said good night, leaving them laughing and dancing to the music in their hearts.

When she reached her room, she spent no time shedding her stiff clothing and settled into bed, picking up her journal to tell Maggie about the night.

Dear Maggie,

I'm so confused. When Michael kisses me, my head empties and I feel drawn to him. That's love, right? But the country club dinner was disconcerting, bordering on horrifying. Observing Michael's mother was like a mirror peering into the future Mrs. Brett. I pictured myself in her seat laughing and complimenting people, martini in hand, and then stabbing them in the back as soon as they turned. And they did the same to her.

Is this going to be my life? So in genuine and two-faced.

Michael said the country club is not his scene, but he seems so comfortable there. Everyone knew him. Such an odd, cloistered place and even stranger people. It was like they were on a carousel just going round and round, never stopping, never getting off, never going anywhere.

But then Michael kissed me and it was the magic pill to make me feel better again. He's a really good kisser.

And Mom and Dad are very happy. They liked the dinner, the place, the people... they liked everything.

Sometimes I think they're in their own world. When they're together, they act as if they're in a bubble for two with romance and love emanating all around them, infecting others. They danced the night away, holding each other in their arms. Michael and I were dancing too, but it didn't seem the same.

When I was younger, I thought they were silly but fun. Their love was inspirational, something to aspire to, but also something I feared I would never get and doubted it was something I even wanted. Maybe someday

Michael and I can be like that. I guess it takes time, but the way Red and Suzy talk, their chemistry was instant. Mom always said she heard fireworks and trumpets playing when they first locked eyes. Although she was on stage with a big brass band, so that could have been it.

All my life their love story has been like a fairy tale. Maybe a soulmate is too much to ask for—it can't happen to everyone. Sometimes marriage is just marriage, but I hope not. Maybe it just takes time.

Chapter Five

Door Three

The following weeks were spent in a tizzy of planning with Suzy, Cherry, Laurie, and Shirley—dress shopping, cake tastings, browsing invitations samples, and selecting china, silverware, and glass patterns. Peggy didn't know what she was doing, so she was glad to have some learned opinions.

At first, playing the part as the blushing bride was fun and exciting, but it soon led to her breaking point.

Standing in the store with Suzy and her friends discussing and debating glass patterns and the options for red wine, water, and white wine glasses, Peggy had an out-of-body experience.

"You need at least six complete sets. You'll have six places at your dining room table for dinner parties. Michael will have clients and business associates over for dinners," Laurie instructed.

"I like the pattern with the flowers," Shirley said meekly.

"You would. This is chic," Cherry said pushing a geometric patterned glass at Peggy.

"I think they're all very nice," Suzy added.

She watched herself going through the motions over the tedious decisions, which all appeared similar and unimportant. It all seemed so programmed and impersonal. And most of all, not her.

Time with Michael was her only escape from the bridal grind. Two weeks after the country club dinner, he took her to their favorite Greek restaurant. She welcomed the chance to relax and enjoy a meal with him. He showed very little interest in wedding planning, so for a couple hours, she was free.

Then out of the blue, he proclaimed, "My parents reserved the 25th for the wedding at the country club. They really wanted to host the wedding there."

She was in shock. They weighed several venues around town, but hadn't made a decision yet. So when he dropped that bomb in passing, she once again felt like an outsider in her own life, with no choice in the matter.

The rest of the night, she tried to summon the words to object, but decided it was likely pointless. Obviously, the country club was his parents' opportunity to laud it over their "friends" and it was likely an obligatory gesture to keep their favor, but it hurt that he didn't even consider her feelings or discuss it. It was a command.

But she shelved her disappointment in her mind's bookshelf and kept going, thinking the marriage was more important than the wedding. And her parents would like the wedding at the country club too. It was her gesture of understanding to everyone.

Two weeks before the well-planned nuptials, Peggy and Michael walked along the lakeshore hand in hand. The lake was a beautiful calming presence at a stressful time. With her hair loosely flowing in the breeze, she breathed in the peaceful air.

Michael suddenly stopped to sit on a bench. "Margaret. I have some news," he said solemnly.

She felt a distinct lump well up in her throat and drop to the pit of her stomach.

"My firm wants to transfer me to New York."

It was as if rays of light descended from the sky accompanied by a heavenly choir singing "New York!"

She hugged him with glee. "Really, that's fantastic!"

He stared at her curiously, expecting a different response.

"You're ok leaving your friends and family? I thought you'd be upset."

"Not at all. I love New York. I've always dreamed of going there. Everything in music and culture is happening there right now. It's the place to be," Peggy said, clutching his hand tightly with excitement.

He squeezed her hand in return, but the demeanor on his face showed less relief and more concern.

Peggy was elated, with ideas flooding her head. She threw her arms around his neck and kissed him, not noticing the change in his mannerisms. While she would miss her family and friends, to her, it was a dream come true… a way for her to spread her wings and explore a new life.

When she got home and told Suzy and Red about their moving plans, they were sad to see her go but happy for their new opportunity.

"I have so many cheerful memories there. New York is a very special place to your father and I. We fell in love there. It was a wonderful place to be young," Suzy said with enthusiasm.

"We'll miss you, but we understand. Michael's job is important and it will be an interesting new place to start your life together," Red added.

Peggy was confused and a bit offended by their about face on New York, but hid her feelings. Thanking them, she excused herself and told them she was tired so she could gracefully exit to her room and open her journal.

Dear Maggie,

Some exhilarating news came today. We're moving to New York! I'm beyond thrilled at the prospect of a new start in this mecca of everything today. I read about it constantly. The beatniks, the folk music scene—everyone who is anyone is playing in New York now. It seems like the coolest place to be.

But I'm a bit slighted by Suzy and Red's immediate approval. A few months ago, New York was a dangerous place. Now it's perfectly fine because my husband is taking me there? Suzy traveled to New York on her own and you moved from New York to Chicago all on your own. I thought we were supposed to be evolving past these kinds of stereotypes.

Why can't I do something you did over 60 years ago? I don't want every idea or action to be tied to someone else's approval or ideals. I want to be me, whoever I am.

But this is a light at the end of the tunnel. In New York, I will find myself.

Peggy ignored the rest of the wedding planning completely, leaving the last details to her friends. She was planning to live in New York. With Suzy's help, she narrowed down the area they wanted to live in and combed potential listings from a real estate agent she contacted over the phone, ringing up the long-distance phone charges.

There was so much Peggy didn't know about New York and what she would need to find an apartment perfect for a young couple and a budding executive.

With her knowledge of the sprawling New York landscape, Suzy directed Peggy to an affordable area in Manhattan that was near Michael's new office and close to public transportation, so she would have a chance to explore.

Peggy recruited Suzy's friends and former singing partners, Kate and Jane, to review their choices in person and make sure they were suitable. After Suzy quit the USO to have Peggy, Kate and Jane went back to New York.

Laurie and Cherry offered opinions on what kind of space Michael would expect and need if he wanted to bring colleagues, his boss, or even clients home for dinner. They were the experts.

After making a few selections, Peggy and Suzy sat by the phone with bated breath, waiting for their call.

Finally, the phone rang; Peggy held the phone up so both she and Suzy could listen.

"Suzy, this is Kate. And Jane," a distant voice said. "We looked at all three places and we like the one on Central Park West in Manhattan best."

"It's adorable and so swanky," Jane chimed in.

"Yes, it has high ceilings and big windows so you can see the city. Plus, it has every modern convenience, just like in Harper's Bazaar."

"Wow, just like Harper's Bazaar. Thanks, girls. We better get on the phone with the real estate agent to send the lease right away. I'll call you later to chat," Suzy said.

She hung up the phone and handed the receiver to Peggy. "Now it's your turn."

Peggy took the receiver and dialed the agent to put in an application and send the lease for Michael to sign. The whole thing was daunting but thrilling. A new city. New apartment. New husband. New life.

She couldn't wait to tell Michael about the apartment the next day at their Automat lunch date, laying all the advertisement information on the table.

"According to my aunties, it's close to everything. The theatre, museums, restaurants, and of course only a little walk away from your office. It's even close to Central Park. I've always wanted to go there—my great-grandmother lived right across the street and used to walk by the lake and in the gardens all the time. I can't believe I'll be walking in her footsteps. Plus, it's near public transportation so I can go explore around the Village music scene. My aunties say the apartment is adorable and has a great view of the city. What do you think?" she asked, breathless from exhilaration.

Michael glanced down at the advertisements, but barely acknowledged them. He was pensive and didn't make eye contact with her.

"Margaret. I don't want you to get the wrong idea here. My wife will not work or be a musician. You can sing in the church choir or play the piano. That's final. Maybe we won't go to New York after all," he stated, pushing the advertisements away and angling back in his chair, nonchalantly took a sip of coffee.

It was like a one-two gut punch. A shiver went down her spine and she stared at him in silence with no words to speak. Just like a prizefighter and a boxing ring, she was completely knocked out.

For the rest of the meal, she sat quietly eating, but slowly envisioned the life she wanted slipping out of her fingers.

. When they were done, he kissed her on the forehead and went back to work, leaving her at the table.

For a few minutes, she sat there stunned, unsure of what happened.

It was like a switch suddenly turned on in her head. Michael was different since the proposal, more commanding and insistent. Everything was different.

A few minutes after Michael left, the girls excitedly came over to the table to find out about the apartment.

"So did you get the apartment?" Laurie asked.

"You look sad. Didn't you get the apartment?" Shirley said.

Peggy didn't say anything or look up.

"Did he want to keep looking for something else?" Cherry asked, trying to elicit a response.

Peggy was still stone silent.

"What's wrong, Peggy?" Shirley asked with concern.

"Nothing—it's all going to be fine. Let's go," Peggy masked her feelings and said softly, gathering the papers on the table and putting them in her bag.

The rest of the day, the usual melodic syncopation of the typewriter keys was unusually taunting.

Normally, their rhythms soothed her, like the many songs she heard in her head. But today they grated on her thoughts with each keystroke, like a woodpecker, pecking her head and repeating You're a wife, not a musician. Women stay in the house and plan dinner parties. Country Clubs! Mrs. Michael Brett. Mrs. Michael Brett!

Peggy's head swelled more and more with doubt. She wouldn't be Peggy McIntyre anymore. She wouldn't even be Margaret McIntyre. She would be Mrs. Michael Brett. Not only would she lose her name, but she would surrender her very identity and become a wife. She would be somebody else. That's it.

Ever since the engagement country club dinner, she realized there were signs. He seemed more rigid. He no longer wanted to listen to music, go to dance clubs or go to the movies. She finally felt comfortable to share some of her music with her and even played a song and sang for him a couple times. But now, every time she brought up music or sang aloud, he abruptly changed the subject.

The dates became fewer and fewer and were usually cocktail parties with his friends and workmates or dinners at a nice restaurant or at the country club with his parents.

Suddenly the reality of her impending life flashed before her eyes. Endless dinner parties and martinis schmoozing with clients and executives while making mindless drivel conversation with their wives boxed in the four walls of a chic apartment that would be her prison.

Aimlessly typing different exercises, she caught the glare of her engagement ring. A ball and chain handcuffing her to a life she didn't know if she could live.

Michael was a sheep in wolf's clothing. He pretended to be someone she wanted to get her to marry him and now that he shed his kindness hide, she can see the real man. Her first instincts about him were right, but she got caught up in the idea of romance and meeting everyone's expectations.

Feeling lost and despondent, after class Peggy trudged down the city streets with no destination, just thinking.

Michael was going to decide if they went to New York or not and apparently would make all choices for them, but he would allow her to play piano and sing in the choir. And it was clear whether in Chicago or New York, or anywhere else, she would no longer be her own person. That was devastating.

She didn't know what to do, except walk with one foot in front of the other, blindly staring ahead.

After a while, she happened upon a bridal store and saw a gaggle of women laughing and giggling as they exited. Peggy stopped and looked into the store window. She could still see her reflection in the day's ebbing light and the image of her head lined up with the wedding dress on the mannequin inside. She unconsciously stared at the mirrored image, noticing how she was just an interchangeable bride, stripped of all her personality, color, and life. Just a bride, then a wife.

Her whole body shuddered as she crouched on the ground bent in half to her waist and held her arms around herself in panic. She felt sick, gasping for short breaths.

Then as if on cue, she heard music in the distance.

She stood up slowly, listening to the melody like in a dream. With an involuntary reaction, she was drawn to the music. Walking toward the sound, she found a street musician with long blond hair and a fringe leather vest over a tie-dye shirt. He was playing a guitar and had a harmonica holder around his neck.

He was outside one of those beatnik clubs she heard about, but, discouraged by convention, never knew where to find them. She was immediately entranced by the aura of the room. It was dark with black walls and small bistro tables flooded with people, who were drinking coffee and listening to a poet up on the stage.

Looking around, she felt like an outsider with her hair in a bun still dressed in a stiff office uniform. Everyone else wore comfortably loose, flowing clothing in all different colors and styles.

Intrigued, she sat down at the nearest table.

After the poet finished, everyone snapped in unison like a wave of happy sound across the room. When the snapping subsided, she heard the lone beat of a bongo drum, echoing one solo thump at a time. Then a woman with long brown hair down to her waist appeared in a flowing floral dress that reached to the floor.

Without speaking, the woman danced freely to the rhythm of the drum. As it slowly increased in pace, her bare feet glided across the floor like a butterfly, spreading her wings with her hair cascading up and down with each movement.

Peggy held her breath as she intently watched every magical step.

Without realizing it, she took the pins from her hair and shook out her long red mane, untied her bow, and unbuttoned the top buttons of her shirt.

Her breathing was slow and steady as her gaze was affixed on every shift the woman made. She felt the freedom of her dance uninhibited by anything around her.

When the woman stopped and the snapping crowd showed their appreciation, Peggy jolted back into consciousness and scanned the audience.

They were smiling. They were happy. It all felt right, like a shower of peacefulness rinsed her panic away. She was free.

For the next two hours, she stayed and listened to an array of musicians, singers, and poets. With each performance, she felt a warmth inside her, something she never wanted to let go.

Looking toward the club door as it opened and the city lights shone through, she saw a vision of door number three illuminate in an astounding revelation.

No matter how hard she tried, she couldn't make herself choose a life that wasn't her own. She had to be free to find something that fit and enriched her. She knew she had to choose freedom.

Arriving late in the night, her home was dark and hushed in silence. Suzy and Red thought she was out with Michael, so they didn't worry anymore. She went to her room and looked at herself in the moonlit mirror.

She tore off her tight pencil skirt, kitten heels blouse and constraining undergarments and shook out her unbridled hair. Gazing at her natural naked form, she inhaled a deep sigh. She saw herself again.

She knew her mission and her time was now. If she spoke to anyone—her parents, the girls, Michael—she knew they would confuse her and try to change her mind or even worse, stop her.

She had to leave in secret. The only way out was to bravely walk through door number three and escape to New York.

Carefully tiptoeing up to the attic, she grabbed her mother's suitcase with all the stickers of the places that she went while in the USO and filled it with Maggie's vest, flowered straw hat, and delicate Irish lace gloves, the Clan McIntyre Scottish family tartan kilt and the clothes inside the steamer trunk that Maggie made.

Then she packed the old Irish storybook Red used to read to her, Maggie's embroidered handkerchiefs, a scarf, some hair combs and vintage jewelry her mother wore in her youth, and a small album of family pictures. Her family would go with her.

She took the suitcase back to her room, gathering the few non-constricting clothes she owned, her journal, and the old coffee can of money she had saved, her guitar, and the pillow Red gave her when she was small that Maggie had made for him. She'd slept with it since she was a little girl.

Then after changing into some jeans, an old oversized shirt, and Maggie's vest, she wrote brief letters to her parents telling them she loved them and not to worry, she would contact them soon and one to Michael, explaining...

I know you won't understand or agree, but I have to be me and I need to be free.

She left the letters in two envelopes on her bureau with her engagement ring on top.

Quietly walking through the house, she looked back one last time and wiped a tear from her eye. She was sad to leave everyone like this, but saw no alternative.

Then she opened the door to the streaming light of the sun rising from the horizon. She walked through and closed the door on her old life and opened all the possibilities that lie before her.

She took the El to Union Station and bought a one-way ticket to New York on the first train leaving that morning.

Nervous but determined, she boarded the train and found a window seat. As the train left the station, she saw the Chicago River and all the unique buildings she'd admired in her youth.

Passing the rows of old brick buildings, she was reminded of the street in her neighborhood lined with the same brick bungalow homes that housed her family and the families of the people she grew up with and thinking of Michael and her friends, wondering if she would ever see them or her home again.

Regretting not telling her friends about her abrupt exit, she knew they would never understand. Their paths were different and they wouldn't comprehend how she could throw it all away. But in her heart, she knew what was right for her.

Closing her eyes, she began to hear music in her head. The soothing music of that street musician strumming a pretty melody on his guitar filled her head with peace and she drifted off to sleep. When she awoke a couple hours later, she looked out the window to see streaming yellow fields of flowers, corn, and wheat, rising to meet the new day's sun and be bathed in its nurturing light.

Peggy remembered a letter she read that Maggie wrote about her train ride from New York to Chicago, and how she was comforted by the rolling fields, which reminded her of Ireland.

Knowing she was following in the same path as her great-grandmother gave her a sense of tranquility and warmth, believing she was on the right track.

Taking a deep sigh, she fell again into a peaceful slumber, hearing her father's voice read her of the land of Tír na nÓg. Tomorrow she would be in New York and awaken to a new life.

Chapter Six

FINDING YOURSELF

Summer 1964

New York's Grand Central Station bustled with busy people quickly walking to and from their destinations. Peggy instantly noted the pace was quicker than in her urban hometown and there were many more people.

She had the address of her auntie Jane, who had always been her favorite. When Peggy was little, Jane would send her bits of music from the musicals she danced in and candy you could only get in New York and would play with her when she visited Suzy. Since she never had any children of her own, she called Peggy her little orange pumpkin.

Peggy knew Jane was a free spirit and would understand her need for autonomy to pursue her musical interests. Jane moved to the East Village and opened a dance studio, after retiring from dancing on the stage and marrying Tony, her dancer husband. She hoped she could stay with Jane until she got her feet wet in the big city.

But first, Peggy wanted to connect with her roots in New York and took a bus to Central Park. For weeks, the thought of Central Park would not leave her mind.

In Maggie's letters, she wrote about her daily treks through the park to walk in the grass, see the water in the ponds, and commune with the peaceful land she loved as a child in Ireland. She called it her oasis that helped calm her Irish temper, center her thoughts, and listen to her heart.

Driving on the bus, she saw the bustling metropolis with seemingly more people than space. Buildings lined the streets without a sign of nature between. Then she saw the vast blanket of green grass and knew she arrived. Just as Maggie described, it was an oasis.

Exiting the bus, she grabbed her guitar and suitcase and gazed up and down at the vast park and admired its beauty. Peggy smiled, sitting on the lush grass looking out at the pond. She drank in the stillness of the water, where only a ripple or two broke its glasslike plane.

Suzy talked about the Central Park lake where Red proposed and imagined her parents as two young lovers in the boat pledging their undying love and devotion.

She took long deep breaths, inhaling the rich heavy air, feeling the atmosphere. Then she got up and walked around, following the paths and bridges, and immediately understood why Maggie sought sanctuary there. It was every bit the haven in the middle of the urban landscape that she portrayed.

Peggy felt a deep connection with everything around her, standing at the top of the bridge, looking down at the water with her eyes closed to fully experience the flora and fauna.

Without looking, she backed up a few steps to reach toward the sky and was startled by the loud neighing of a horse avoiding a collision with her, interrupting her dreamlike state.

"I'm so sorry. Are you all right?"

Peggy opened her eyes to see a man with moplike cornflower blond hair bounding from the steed, reaching his hands down to her.

"I'm fine," she said, confused.

"I thought I hit you with my horse," he laughed. "But I guess I was wrong if you're fine. If I hit you, you wouldn't be fine."

Peggy chuckled, amused by his smile and circular thinking.

"I'm Liam," he said, extending his hand to hers.

"Peggy," she said, shaking his hand.

"Did you say Piggy?" he asked.

Peggy looked at him and pursed her lips in defiance.

"I said Peggy. It's short for Margaret," she fired back.

Liam laughed.

"Ok, ok, don't get your ire up. From your suitcase, I guess you're from out of town. I live right across the street here at The Dakota," he said, pointing to the dark imposing apartment structure on the other side of the park.

"Yes, I just arrived here from Chicago. I'm going to see my aunt in the East Village," she said.

"Well, the East Village is kind of far away, but I can take you there if you'd like," he said with a kind smile.

"On your horse?" Peggy quipped in retaliation, cracking a sideways smile.

Liam laughed. "You're clever. I like that. No, not on my horse. I'm not doing anything today, so I'd be happy to take a drive. It's a nice day."

Peggy looked at him curiously, trying to judge his motivation.

"Honestly, I'm perfectly normal. Well, my father certainly doesn't think I'm normal. But I'm harmless and a ride would be easier than the series of buses or subways you would have to take," he smiled.

She looked deeply into his clear sparking blue eyes, trying to assess his status as a sheep or a wolf. As he petted his caramel-colored horse, she decided anyone who was that kind to a horse or someone he nearly ran down couldn't be a wolf. She didn't understand it, but somehow she felt in her soul that she could trust him.

"Ok, thanks. I'd appreciate a ride," she said.

"Groovy, Piggy," he mischievously grinned. "Let's take this horse back and get you to the East Village."

As they walked through Central Park, the atmosphere seeped into her skin. The soft, timid lake waves and the rolling green grass were a mere postage stamp of flora amid the surrounding urban jungle, but they were everything to Maggie. Peggy could see how the beautiful landscape made her feel at home and gave her a respite to rejuvenate her spirit.

"My great-grandmother Maggie loved this park. And now I can see why. I have letters that she wrote to her mother in Ireland describing the park and how she used to walk her charges every day. One was named Moira and the other actually I think was your name, Liam," Peggy mentioned as they walked side by side.

Liam stopped and glared at her in shock. "Did you say Moira and Liam?"

"Yes, I'm going from memory, but that's what I think they were," Peggy said.

Liam stared at her with a Cheshire-like smile. "My grandfather Liam tells tales of the nanny they had when he was little who sang Irish folk songs to him and his sister every night. There was one particular one he used to tell me when I was small about the land of Tír na nÓg."

"Did you say Tír na nÓg?" Peggy asked as they both looked at each other in amazement and spontaneously recited the story together…

"And so they lived happily together for 300 years, in the land of Tír na nÓg, the land of eternal youth and beauty."

They both looked at each other and laughed.

"My great-grandmother used to tell my father that story. When I was little, he told me that tale every night and said 'Grandma Maggie kisses you from heaven and watches over you.'"

Liam gasped with excitement. "Piggy, I think my grandfather was the little lad your great-grandmother sang to sleep."

Peggy's mouth opened wide at the unbelievable coincidence. "Maggie wrote a lot about a woman named Caroline, who was her childhood friend and Liam's mother," she said with anticipation.

"Well, that cinches it," Liam grinned. "My great-grandmother's name was Caroline and she was from Ireland."

They both smiled at each other. It was kismet.

"When we go to my apartment, maybe my grandfather will be up and you can ask him yourself. Sounds to me like we're family," Liam said.

"Well, not exactly family, but familiar," Peggy said as they dropped off the horse and strode toward the imposing edifice across the street.

The Dakota, located at 1 W 72nd Street, Central Park West, was one of the most celebrated buildings in New York. It was a haven for celebrities and the elite, including captains of industry and Judy Garland, Lauren Bacall, Leonard Bernstein, and Rosemary Clooney.

Peggy raised her eyes up and down in awe, gaping at every nook and cranny, and noticing the detail of the ledges, balconies, columns, archways, decorative iron railings, planters, and urns. The slate and copper roof was punctuated with gables and turrets, and finial-topped peaks reminded her of some of the older buildings in downtown Chicago. Peggy loved architecture and gaped at the marvel that was the building.

Peggy got a warm sensation again as they entered, as if she were walking in Maggie's footsteps. She remembered Maggie's glowing description of The Dakota as the biggest and most beautiful building she had ever seen. Since Peggy had read Maggie's letters over and over again when she was growing up, she recognized key features of The Dakota, from the shiny white marble floors to the grand wooden paneling. Strolling through the lobby to the elevator, she scanned every square inch.

When they entered through the door of the apartment, Peggy felt a rush of feelings overwhelm her, nearly knocking her off her feet. It was exactly as Maggie had illustrated in her letters.

Carved wooden fireplace mantels adorned the walls, and sparkling gas Baccarat crystal chandeliers glistening above an enormous Queen Anne mahogany table fit for a king. Twenty blue damask wooden chairs perched against the long table, against the floor-to-ceiling windows with matching draperies.

Remembering Laurie's dinner party etiquette, she wondered what kind of dinner parties were served in that mammoth room.

As she passed into the main salon, she stared up in awe at the soaring ceilings and the surrounding walls covered with squared wooden wainscoting. The equally towering windows, cased with wide carved trim, streamed great beams of sunlight on the inlaid wood floors.

She dizzyingly swirled around a little bit and Liam put his arm on her back to brace her.

"Piggy, are you falling for me?" he smiled.

"Hardly," Peggy said pridefully, straightening herself. "I just feel like I've been here before. I can't explain it."

"Far out. Well, I firmly believe sometimes shadows from long-past lives visit us where we least expect," he said earnestly. "If you feel a connection, it's probably true. Let me go see if my grandfather is up, and then I have something to show you. Stay right here."

Peggy slowly turned around and around, excited that she was somewhere Maggie had been before. It was a similar feeling to being in the attic, a closeness that she couldn't express, and didn't try to. She just wanted to embrace it.

All her life, Maggie had been her hero and now she felt closer than ever.

Liam entered pushing a wheelchair carrying an older gentleman with wrinkles and partially balding with gray hair that covered the clearly handsome man he once was.

"Piggy, this is my grandfather, William Donegal. He's a little hard of hearing, so you need to talk loudly," Liam said.

Peggy puckered her face with a curious look for a moment and then released it.

"Oh , Liam is short for William."

"Yes," he laughed. "Actually, I think Maggie came up with that nickname. I'd love to thank her. William is so formal. He never used it either."

Liam leaned over and shouted in his grandfather's ear.

"Granda, this is my new friend Peggy. We think her great-grandmother Maggie used to take care of you when you were little."

Peggy smiled at him as he stared squinting at her for a long time as she tried to see a glimpse in his eyes of the little boy with cherub cheeks Maggie wrote about.

"I was born in this house. You saved me, Maggie. Remember?" he grinned brightly and gently touched her hand.

"Granda, you're confused. This is Peggy; Maggie was her great-grandmother," Liam said kindly.

Granda continued staring at Peggy. "No, Liam, this is Maggie. I would know that face with those green eyes and red hair anywhere."

"Sir, I've been told I look a lot like my great-grandmother. Can you tell me a little about her?" Peggy asked sweetly.

"She told me stories and sang to me, holding me every night. She called me her wee bern," he smiled.

The old man didn't veer his gaze from Peggy's face and began softly singing a lullaby. Peggy immediately recognized it as one Red sang to her when she was little.

"Too-ra-loo-ra-loo-ral. That's an Irish lullaby." Peggy smiled and joined him singing.

Then he reached up, shook her hand, and placed something in it. "I remember your voice. I hear it in my dreams every night. I'm glad to hear it again when I'm awake. Welcome back, Maggie. I kept this with me always, just like you said."

Peggy looked down at her hand. It was an aged piece of satin tattered at the edges and yellowed with time, but its embroidered message was still clear:

Wish, wish, shining star, make us be who we are, and if ye take us far from ours, keep us forever Anam Cara.

She stared at it, closed her eyes, and held it to her heart. Tears streamed down her face. It was the same saying on the pillow her father gave her from Maggie. She would know Maggie's embroidery anywhere; stitching is like a fingerprint. No one is the same.

Granda smiled at her and she returned his grin. They both knew.

"We'll be back—I want to show Peggy something," Liam said and Peggy followed him.

Liam led her out of the salon into a study covered in four wall-to-wall bookcases full of different colors of green, black, brown and red leather-bound books. He opened a drawer at the bottom of one bookcase and took out an aged white box.

"Wow, this is an unbelievable coincidence. Who would think that a girl I nearly ran over in the park was connected to my family?" Liam said and unfastened the lid of the box to reveal its contents. "This is what I wanted to show you."

Peggy eagerly peered inside and gasped. There were Irish linens and Irish lace-lined handkerchiefs with the initials CSD. She smiled as she reached in and touched the handkerchief.

"Maggie did these," she said.

"Yes, they belonged to my great-grandmother Caroline. I believe they were a wedding gift from a childhood friend—that must've been your great-grandmother. What a small world," he said.

As Peggy studied the intricate embroidery, she looked up at Liam and they both smiled at each other, knowing they had established a link.

"Let's get you down to the Village, Piggy," he said and grabbed his keys.

As they traversed the back stairway, Peggy told him she remembered Caroline mentioned in some of Maggie's letters and a newspaper article in Maggie's scrapbook about a viscountess dying.

"So you're a viscount?" Peggy asked.

"No, I'm Liam," he chuckled. "My grandfather is the viscount. Only one at a time, that's how it works."

As they meandered through The Dakota courtyard to the garage, Peggy imagined his car would probably be a Porsche or some kind of sizzling sports car. When they reached the garage, she noticed any number of vehicles that would be suitable for a Donegal heir.

With each car they passed, she thought that would be the one. But he kept walking until he reached the end of the garage and stood in front of a VW bus. It was painted in every color of the rainbow in spectacular waving ribbons, with colors and shapes intricately drawn together to become one.

Peggy looked in amazement walking around the van. "This is far out."

She couldn't believe his words came from her mouth, but they felt right and nothing else could aptly describe the miraculous kaleidoscope canvas of the van.

Liam proudly smiled standing next to it like a new father. "Do you like it? I call it the Psychedelic Slug Bug or Psybug for short. I painted it. I see it as a warp through time and space."

"It's definitely groovy, but don't you think we've experienced enough time and space warps through the past today?" She laughed.

"Yes, I guess you're right. Jump in and let's go," he said.

Peggy handed him her suitcase and guitar to load into the slug bug.

"Can you play the guitar?" Liam innocently asked.

"No, I just like to carry it around so it balances out my suitcase." Peggy laughed, returning his prior zinger.

"You got me on that one, Piggy. What's your last name, anyway?" he asked.

"McIntyre," she said, as they both sat in the front seats.

"Ok Piggy Mac. What kind of music do you like?" he asked with genuine interest.

She still wasn't sure if she liked the idea of his nickname, but decided not to correct him, as now they were like family.

"I like all kinds of music. It was always part of my family. My mother was a big band singer in the 40s and taught me how to sing and play piano. And my father showed me how to play guitar. Blues and jazz were his favorites, so I grew up on a blend of both, but I like folk music the best."

"I unfortunately don't have any talent as a musician, but to express myself, I like to write poetry and paint," he said.

"I can see you're a gifted artist. I love poetry too, but mostly I write song lyrics. It's my dream to be a folk singer. That's why I'm out here to absorb everything and try it out," she explained.

"Yeah, you got to let your freak flag fly, man. I turned my back on the man and his uptight soul-sucking money grub to pursue my dreams. My father wanted me to go into the railroad business. It's been in our family for generations, but it's just not my scene. Too many stiff collars and neckties. A suit is definitely not in my wardrobe," he said.

 Peggy chuckled out loud. She meant to laugh internally, but she felt so comfortable with him. It just came out.

"Hey, what's so funny?" He smiled.

"Nothing, I just feel the exact same way about suits. Last week I was in secretarial school wearing pantyhose, tight skirts, and heels. What a drag. Everything about that life suffocated me. That's why I left," she confided.

"I wish I could leave, but for right now I just escape every once in a while to commune with natural people," he quipped.

"What do you mean by natural people?" she asked.

"If you don't mind a detour, I'll show you."

Peggy nodded curiously. Within a few minutes, through the windshield of the bug, she saw an archway that reminded her of the Arc de Triomphe get larger in her perspective. She smiled and immediately took a cleansing breath. Something told her she was in the right place. It was a sign.

"What's that doing there? It looks like the one in Paris."

"Yes, it does," he said sitting up straight and sticking his chin up jauntily and said in a posh stuffy voice.

"That's the Washington Square Arch. It's all marble and was designed by architect Stanford White in 1891 to commemorate the centennial of George Washington's 1789 inauguration as the first President of the United States," Liam stated, aping a tour guide.

"Thanks for the lesson, professor," Peggy kidded.

"Sorry, sometimes all my education slips out of my mouth. I was an architecture major for a while in college after business... before accounting and... two after finance. Or one? I forget." He chuckles.

"That's a lot of education," Peggy said, surprised.

"Yeah, that's what my father thinks. If it weren't for Granda, he would've thrown me out on my keister for flunking out of college. I did manage to learn a few things here and there, but nothing ever stuck. It just seemed too regimented for me, but that's not why I brought you here. Look past the arch and tell me what you see." He smiled wryly, waiting for her reaction.

Peggy leaned forward and looked closely through the windshield as the picture came into view. She saw people—hundreds of people—gathered on a bright Sunday afternoon. It was more people than she'd ever seen in one place in her life. At first they were like little ants or dots in some kind of painting. Then as they got closer, she was amazed at the assemblage.

"Welcome to Washington Square on a Sunday afternoon." He smiled and parked the Psybug, motioning her to get out, repeating his fake posh tour docent voice. "Historians say that they used to have duels and hangings in the square, but now it's full of life. They even turn the fountain off on Sunday so nobody gets sprayed."

As they walked toward the arch, Peggy began to hear music—wonderful, joyous folk music—with people singing in unison. She closed her eyes, breathing deeply.

"This is where I come every Sunday. Everyone gathers and spontaneously plays music, taking turns, and others simply enjoy. And there are artists who put their work around for other people to view and sometimes buy. It's completely unorganized chaos, yet it's peaceful and often transcendent," he said. "Give me your hand so we don't get separated. It gets kind of crowded."

With so much in her scope, Peggy's head darted back and forth like a ping pong ball as Liam pulled her through the crowd to the center fountain area.

There were people in costumes doing unusual performance art and musicians singing and playing. Artists lined the edges with paints and easels, displaying their work or painting somebody's portrait or just painting anything.

Scanning the crowd, Peggy saw the happy looks on their faces and experienced a serenity in the air like she'd never felt before.

There was a man dressed like a clown with bars painted on his face miming all the animals in the zoo. And a woman dressed like a ballerina and covered in silver paint wearing ice skates standing like a still statue atop a melting block of ice.

She spun around so many times, trying to see everything, she began to get dizzy and swooned, bumping into a girl with black curly hair.

"Careful, girl, are you having a bad trip?" the girl asked, concerned.

Liam braced Peggy again and laughed.

"Piggy, you have to stop falling for me or people will think that we're a couple."

From her compromised view looking up, Peggy saw a short girl with big round glasses dressed in loose layers of tie-dye clothing.

"Your name is Piggy?" the girl laughed.

"Hey, Maxi. I haven't seen you in a while," Liam said and hugged her.

"I've been protesting a lot lately. Seems like the man keeps crossing lines, so we need to stand on them," she said.

"Maxi, meet Peggy, budding folk musician. She just arrived from Chicago. Peggy, meet Maxi, the little lady with the big voice and giant personality. General agitator and tough as nails armor with a gooey mushy inside center," Liam smiled.

"He's being kind about the mushy part, but he's right about the general part. We are warriors against oppression and injustice. And since you're a musician, you've come to the right place. Every day you can hear all kinds of music and discover anything you want. It's like a smorgasbord."

"What do you know about smorgasbords? They're not kosher." Liam laughed.

"What my mother never knows, never hurts her. I'll catch up with you later. I need to see someone about a protest." She rushed off and disappeared into the crowd.

Peggy laughed and shook her head. It was all mesmerizing.

"Don't mind her; she's dedicated to the cause," Liam said.

"What cause?" Peggy asked.

"All of them. Civil rights, the war, equality, fairness, it's all up in the air now. Maxi organizes a lot of protests so our voices are heard." Liam smiled and pulled her arm again. "Hey, I want to introduce you to some artist friends of mine—come on!"

He ushered her through the sea of people near the edge of the pavement, where the painters were showing their work.

Peggy was astonished at the various levels of artistry. She was particularly taken by the more abstract paintings and sculptures that were free and undefined.

"I've never seen anything like this before," she said to Liam, gaping in awe at the eclectic artwork. "In the Art Institute in Chicago, they have all different kinds of paintings, landscapes, cityscapes, and portraits, but nothing like this."

"Isn't it wonderful? It's free expression. Nothing like you'll see in an old stodgy museum. Kandinsky, Miro, Pollock, they've been doing it for decades, but it's really taken off. I think the trend now leans toward surrealism but with an expressive and avant-garde edge, anything goes.

That's what I love about painting. There are no rules anymore," Liam said passionately, pointing at the artwork in front of them. Peggy stared at him as he spoke of art in admiration of his passion.

"That's exactly how I feel about music," Peggy said. "It doesn't matter what other people think, it only matters what's in your heart."

"Right on. That's one cool chick," the painter said.

"Peggy from Chicago, meet Dogger from everywhere," Liam said, and Dogger nodded at Peggy in response.

"Art is all about taking what's on your insides and making it on the outside," he said, barely looking up from his painting.

"So what do you think?" Liam said. "Is this enough natural people for you?"

Peggy smiled brightly. "It's outta sight. I've come to the right place."

After a few hours, the music stopped and the crowd thinned as the golden hues of the sun began descending into the sky.

"We better go to the East Village to see my aunt before it gets too late," Peggy said. She and Liam walked back to the Psybug.

She looked down, realizing they were still holding hands, but she didn't mind it. She found a connection to Maggie, a new friend, and a new home with people who understood how she felt, all in one day.

She knew her rash decision was right. New York was the place to be. And now so was she.

The short ride to Jane's house in the East Village was filled with random discussions of art and music.

"I've always thought my poetry would make good song lyrics. Maybe we can collaborate on something?" Liam asked as he pulled in front of Jane's row home.

"I'd love that," Peggy said. She gathered her suitcase and guitar and got out of the slug bug. "Will I see you soon?"

"Yes, who else is going to be your guide to enlightenment here? I'll be in touch." Liam smiled and pulled away.

The minute Peggy knocked on the door, Jane threw it open, laughing and hugging her.

Suzy's friend Jane was like a godmother to Peggy. Since she was a child, Peggy loved Jane's fairylike spirit of adventure and fun and soft whimsical air about her.

"I'm so glad to see you!" Jane said, without letting go. "Your mother's been frantic, calling every few hours. They all think you've lost your mind."

"Actually, I think I've never been more clearheaded in my whole life. I hope it's ok to show up on your doorstep, but I knew you'd understand," Peggy said, kissing her on the cheek.

Jane laughed. "Oh, I don't understand… yet. I want to and you'll tell me, but it doesn't matter. I'll always be here for you."

Peggy put her things down and sat with Jane over some tea.

"It was horrible, Auntie. I saw my whole life flash before my eyes and I hated what I saw. I couldn't sell my soul for marriage to be completely bound to someone else. I know my parents mean well, but they're forgetting what it was like to be young and to find your own path in this world. I had to leave," Peggy explained.

"Sometimes parents want the best for their children so much, they can't see what's in front of their own face. If you were unhappy, I don't blame you for leaving. Your mother may have forgotten the anticipation and hope when we came to New York. We had stars in our eyes and were full of dreams. It wasn't easy, but a lot of them came true. I think her heart and love for you have clouded her memory," Jane said, looking at Peggy with love in her eyes. "But you need to call her and make sure she knows you're all right."

"I know, you're right. I'll call. But first, let me tell you about the thrilling things that happened today," she said.

Full of excitement and wonder, Peggy described her experience in Washington Square and her encounter with Liam—and his connection to Maggie.

"This all sounds like more than a coincidence to me. It's a sign," Jane nodded. "Now go call your parents. I'm sure Red will love that you found a bond to Maggie."

Peggy went into the hall and dialed. Her parents were upset at first, then just sad. They didn't yell or anything. And after Peggy explained her feelings and reasons, she felt they understood as much as they could. She promised to write to them and hung up the phone feeling a little resolution. That chapter of her life was closed and a new one awaited.

Settling into the room Jane gave her, she couldn't wait to tell Maggie what happened.

Dear Maggie,

I took the biggest leap of my life and yet somehow I landed on soft ground. New York has been one surprise after another, but I feel more connected to myself and to you and my family than ever.

I walked into Central Park and felt my parents and you with me every step of the way. When I entered your home, I knew you were with me. I met your wee bern Liam, but he's an old man now. He dearly remembered you and even thought I was you. That was a huge compliment. In this new chapter of my life, I feel like you—strong, determined, and boldly ready for what life brings, unafraid.

I even met your friend Caroline's great-grandson. And we made an instant connection. I think he'll be my best friend. We already have shared history and so much in common. Isn't that ironic that your great-granddaughter and her great-grandson would become best friends, just like you were?

He showed me such wondrous things and yet I know I've only scratched the surface. I can't wait to see what's yet to come.

Chapter Seven

The Village

Waking up for the first time in New York, Peggy deeply breathed in and out, ready to jump into a new adventure.

Jane planned to show her the East Village. It was made up of a diverse blend of traditional storefront businesses with an inexplicable mixture of Old World values and bohemian sensibilities; Peggy saw quirky contradictions everywhere. An American hardware store stuck between a Polish bakery and Ukrainian restaurant. Busy city buses going up and down the street passed old men in suits, hats, and ties playing chess in the park. Then, as if on cue, a multicolored painted car like Liam's drove by with "love" written on the windshield and peace signs amid the sedans and station wagons. And a woman with a plain everyday dress and cardigan walking down the street with no shoes and flowers in her hair. It was a gas.

Signs in funky and artistic illustrated letters were the calling card for more progressive venues like The Other newspaper, the free clothing store Diggers, and a big yellow and red sign saying "Something They Ate" and

"The Leather Bag." And a blue building with the dome and a marquee painted in a rainbow of colors exhibited ultimate free expression with no constraint. It was as if two planes of existence converged and lived harmoniously.

Peggy couldn't help peering through the window of some of the nightclubs. During the day, they were different, just empty boxes that looked a little grungy and rundown. But she wasn't disappointed, as she could imagine how wonderful they would be when filled with people and music.

Ambling down St. Mark's Place, the aromas from the mix of Eastern European delicacies filled her senses.

Jane took her to a Ukrainian diner and introduced her to Kolaches and Perogies with flavors that danced in her mouth. As much as she loved the luncheonettes and Automat in Chicago, they would pale in comparison to this delightful feast.

"This is a remarkable place," Peggy smiled as she toggled her head from side to side, noticing everything in sight.

"Yes. It was very different when we first moved here, but I like seeing the young people on the streets doing their thing. In my day, the older people thought boogie-woogie music was going to be the end of everything. Of course, it wasn't, and since then we've had many different kinds of music that people labeled as doomsday. I think music is music. I like their freedom of being. To quote from their vernacular, I dig it. It's groovy," Jane said.

Jane led Peggy toward to a dark storefront with a picture of a hand on the shingle. The sign read "Madame Fortua."

"I've always wanted to go in here and never had anyone to do it with. Let's go—this could be fun." Jane grabbed her hand as they crossed the threshold into a dark room with red lighting, filled with eerie music and the aroma of strong sage incense.

Sitting at a red velvet cloth-covered table trimmed with gold tassels, a young woman told them to sit down, without ever looking up at them. She had long black hair tied with multicolored silk kerchiefs, a crocheted poncho, and small round amethyst-colored glasses.

Jane started to talk, but the woman interrupted. "No need to speak. I know why you are here. Madame Fortua sees into the abyss to shine the light on your future."

Madame closely gazed into the foggy crystal ball in the middle of the table and then peeked up at Jane with a searing glance. Then she stared at her open palm.

"I see a grand opportunity walking through your door soon," she said in a mysterious Slavic voice. She let go of Jane's hand and returned her eyes to the crystal ball.

She took Peggy's palm, put it down, and then peered into the ball again.

"Now you... have an interesting light ahead. For you I see a long road with many pathways to choose. BUT... I see a connection... a calming warmth wrapped around you on your journey. That is good."

As they left, Peggy couldn't help thinking about her enigmatic fortune, wondering where the pathways would take her and what choices she would have to make. She was especially fascinated about the warmth the fortuneteller mentioned.

"That was out of this world, but I really dug it," Peggy said.

Jane grinned and nodded. "It was fun. I doubt there's any truth in it, but I like to keep an open mind."

Strolling down the street, Peggy noticed some of the more hip people around them and thought about Madame's den and how cool she looked with her freaky out of this world style. She compared her plain collared tops and capri pants and realized how square they were. She asked Jane where she could get some cooler threads.

They looked through a few stores, but the best place was Diggers. People donated clothes they weren't using and others could get what they needed and couldn't afford. Peggy roamed around the store, picking different clothes at random, everything flowy and loose with tons of colors. She found some multicolored long skirts and macrame halter and sundress that would pair well with Maggie's vintage vest, and she made a donation. She loved the Bohemian ideals of sharing and caring. No more uptight heels, hose, and binding skirts or suits. Everything from her toes to her red hair could be mellow and completely free.

At the next store, The Leather Bag, Jane found a perfect braided fringed headband for her.

"Here, this will complete your look," she said.

Peggy donned the headband as if it were the crown of her new kingdom. She was home.

When they returned to Jane's house, there was a message on the pad from Jane's husband. It said Liam will pick you up at 9 o'clock.

As promised, Liam would be her guide and introduce her to the folk music scene. Peggy was thrilled to launch her new essence at the mecca of the new music movement, Greenwich Village.

When Liam picked her up that night, he gasped when he saw her new hippie chic look.

"You look… way far out." He smiled and touched her hair, amazed at its length and curliness now that it was freed from its ponytail.

"It's only Monday, are you sure that the clubs will be busy? Isn't it a work night?" she innocently asked.

Liam laughed and shook his head. "OK, Alice, let's find your wonderland."

Greenwich Village was the nexus of the beatnik and hippie counterculture of performing arts. The basket clubs had hoot nights where people would get up and show off whatever skills they wanted—poetry, music, performance art, dramatic readings, or mime—and pass a basket for coins or dollars to show appreciation. Others had planned sets with more popular paid artists.

Liam decided to give her the experience from top to bottom.

They started in a club called The Bitter End. As they hit the door, Peggy became Alice stepping through the looking glass and came out in her own fairy tale.

Her mouth opened wide and her jaw dropped in astonishment.

Peggy remembered the emptiness of the daytime Village clubs juxtaposed with the current state, filled with all the life and color of the people and artists. Just like the East Village clubs she saw in the daytime, the decor was a little rundown, with black chipping paint and broken stucco on some walls, revealing the brick underneath. But it didn't matter. In the darkness of night with a packed house of people wearing dark sunglasses, the mood was electric, magically transforming the place to somewhere dreams are made of.

Amid the hanging cigarette smoke, the stage lights shadowed it swirls while spotlighting the performers. On the stage, the lone beat of a bongo played by a man dressed all in black with a beret while two women with long straight jet black hair in red leotards bent into unusual combined shapes shouting "war, crime and death" at the audience.

"Close your mouth, Alice, there are flies in here and you don't want to taste them. That's Ravyn—she's not a wild animal, just a friend. Let's find a seat." Liam chuckled and put his finger on her chin to close her gaping lips.

Peggy was so lost in amazement, she didn't even catch his wry remark.

Aptly, just like Alice, Peggy was in a foreign land full of wonderment. Her bright green eyes popped as big as saucers as she watched an array of people take the stage. There was a young man with long dark hair, wearing a red bandanna around his head, playing a guitar with two sisters in long mismatched dresses and cascading blonde hair, one playing the autoharp, singing about oppression, all singing in high soprano voices.

After that, a balding older man with a long gray ponytail wearing faded, tattered jeans and sandals, with color round glasses in front of his pale skin played the banjo and sang old folk songs.

With each and every performer, she noticed differences that made the old songs their own. Like a student at Juilliard, she studied the increase or decrease in tempo or change in the inflection of their voices to go high and low. Some added the syncopated rhythm of bongo drums or the exotic sounds of a mandolin or sitar. And one featured a solo trumpet blaring while dancers gyrated freely and then stood still in statuesque poses. But it all worked together to communicate a greater message. It was strange, weird, and fantastic at the same time.

At another club, Cafe Wha?, they drank espresso. Peggy loved the whooshing sound of the machine, so loud and distinct it almost added another instrument to each performance.

All night it seemed like a caravan of people crawled around every square inch of space converging at different clubs, like nomads separating and then meeting again on the trail, staying for minutes or hours visiting with friends and listening to poets, music, and performers of all kinds. For hours they drifted from club to club, each with one surprise after another.

In Cafe Figaro, a very serious poet in a black knit cap had everyone stand in two lines facing each other and gave everyone white cards; each contained black lettering and one word that they couldn't see. One at a time, each line chanted the words from the other side with the rehearsed precision of a marching band, yet it was completely extemporaneous and electric.

Four cappuccinos and a few drinks into the night, Peggy felt a little dizzy and swerved against the wall as they descended two stories below into the top dog of all the clubs, The Village Gaslight, which ironically hid in the basement under the street.

"Are you falling for me again? Piggy, don't crash on me now; this is the big Magilla. You never know who will be here. It's a happening place." Liam held her tight to his body.

Located on Macdougal Street, the Village Gaslight, according to Liam, was a common haunt for well-known groups and singers. It had a mix of scheduled sets and spontaneous performances when someone would jump up on stage.

Liam and Peggy could see the glow of multicolored lights as they descended the stairs. The small dark club had a big red stage lined with posters and notices precariously pasted on the back wall.

"Last time I was here, Bob Dylan debuted a song. He was in the audience and the spirit moved him, so he decided to sing," Liam explained.

The venue was like a shoebox, with a ceiling barely above six feet, just enough so taller people didn't have to crouch but did have to watch their heads on the leaky pipes, which

streamed water down the walls and sometimes through the ceiling. But it all added to the brooding charm and trippy vibe.

After they sat down and listened to a few artists, the woman with the long black hair he called Ravyn approached them with Maxi, Liam's friend from Washington Square.

"Can we sit with you? This place is packed." Maxi said. "There's a rumor that Peter, Paul and Mary are going to perform for the first time. They've been rehearsing nearby."

Liam smiled and the two women crammed into the small table and shared the lone empty seat. As they were both very petite, it wasn't a problem.

"Peggy McIntyre, this is Ravyn," Liam said.

Peggy extended her hand, but Ravyn only nodded and swung her long mane to sit down.

Like her namesake Poe object in Nevermore, Ravyn was imposing and mysterious.

"Maybe Peggy would like to sit on her boyfriend's lap," Ravyn said in a low, monotone voice with a distinctly Russian accent.

"Oh, we're just friends," Peggy quickly interjected.

Suddenly there was a calming hush over the loud ambling crowd as two bearded men with guitars and a blonde-haired woman seemingly floated through the tables onto the stage.

The whole audience was agog with anticipation.

"That's them," Maxi excitedly pointed and whispered.

Their anticipated arrival was met with very satisfied faces and ears, as they melodically harmonized to a beautiful song written by Bob Dylan.

The lyrics posed many questions about war, suffering, and freedom that Peggy had rarely contemplated, but she focused on the synchronicity of their voices, weaving together perfectly to sound as one.

When they were done, the audience was aghast with deafening silence until one person stood and began to snap their fingers. They were followed by a wave of others, until everyone was on their feet. Peggy closed her eyes; it sounded like a summer rainstorm.

"That song is everything." Maxi snapped as fast as her fingers could meet.

"It's transcendent," Ravyn said in her aloof voice.

Liam was transported, too, as evidenced by his enthusiasm.

Gazing at the audience it was clear that not only were people amazed at this new sound, but also they were astounded by the poetic and prophetic lyrics.

Peggy mostly appreciated the musicianship. Most singers longed for the intricate combination of voices that they displayed, but even though the message in the song was lost on her, it deeply affected everyone else in the room.

"That song will change the world," Maxi said as everyone sat down.

"It should open some eyes," Ravyn added, flinging her hair again, nearly hitting the people at the table next to them.

"I am captivated," Liam said looking at Peggy. "What did you think?"

Peggy felt on the spot; she didn't understand the song the same way they did.

"Great harmonies," she blurted out and met the blank stares of the other two women.

"Don't you understand the effect this is going to have on the movement?" Maxi asked, confused.

"It is a rally cry," Ravyn added.

All Peggy could do was smile and nod, yet the women's stares did not ebb. They glared at her as if she were an alien.

"Come—we go," Ravyn said with mild disgust.

Peggy was embarrassed and quickly put her head down and sipped her drink.

"Don't worry, Piggy, those guys are deep thinkers. Everything's about the movement to them. You're a musician—it's understandable that you liked the music more," Liam sympathized.

Peggy thought about it for a minute and began to feel cross.

"You know, I think it was kind of mean of them to judge me. They don't know me and I don't know their movement," she said, her green eyes gleaming.

"Now, Piggy, don't get your Irish up. There's a lot to be upset about these days. We're getting into a war in Vietnam and black folks are being oppressed, and in some cases slaughtered. And individual and women's rights are being suppressed," Liam said.

"Well, how was I supposed to know?" Peggy said, embarrassed again.

"You will now, Piggy Mac. But don't worry about them. They'll calm down. Maxi is an agitator and Ravyn is a socialist. They love to argue with people. Wait till they get to know your sparkling personality. They'll love you as fast as I did. Right, buddy?" He gently tapped her on the arm with his fist.

Peggy's head was whirling from caffeine and beer overload. She wasn't sure if he was making a cheeky joke at her expense with his unusual fist tap or if it was a retaliatory put down, since she told everyone they were only friends.

She hoped he didn't expect more than friendship. They had an instant connection and she liked him as a friend, but after her last near-miss experience with a man, she wasn't ready to couple herself to anyone, anytime soon. There was too much in this new world to explore. She finally found freedom and wasn't giving up. She found the missing piece to her puzzle of life. And it fit.

Chapter Eight

An Irish Lad

A few weeks went by and the fantastical seal had been broken. Peggy and Liam frequented the clubs so much she felt like a fixture, but her excitement never waned.

She even won over Maxi and Ravyn by allowing them to enlighten her on the perils of society. This education motivated her with hope that change could bridge the continental generational divide and heal the wounds of strife.

Like a kid on Christmas morning, each night she looked forward to every performance, absorbing and appreciating the abundant artistry. She longed for a time when she could trod the boards with her guitar. But that day obscured in the distance, as she couldn't conceive of being ready. Infused by her fellow musicians, she used them as a muse for her own creativity.

Liam shared some of his poetry and she desperately tried to combine it with the musical passages she wrote in her notebook, but nothing struck a chord.

"I think you're expecting too much. Isn't music just an expression of your feelings? It doesn't have to be perfect, just real," Liam counseled.

Peggy remembered her writing session earlier in the day, surrounded by heaps of wadded-up paper, adding more to the pile in frustration.

"I'm not looking for perfect. I'm searching for me. Who am I? What sound do I want to sing? I feel ideas swirling around my head, then almost grasping something, but can't get hold and it escapes me once again," she told him, exasperated.

Every evening she came back from the clubs, enthusiastic with ideas filling her head, but later when her fingers plucked her guitar or struck pen to paper, she lost them.

"I hear the music in my head, but why won't it come out of my mouth?" She sighed.

Without giving up, Peggy hoped immersing herself in the Greenwich Village club scene, would make it all click.

To earn her keep, Peggy put her newly minted typing skills to work at The Other, an underground newspaper for the progressive beat generation. Maxi was one of their shining stars, writing scathing articles on oppression and injustice.

Peggy liked the energetic vibe there. Everyone was angry about something, but they believe in empowerment to change it.

Every day brought a new adventure through the door. Today it was Maxi, who dragged a young Irish man with red hair into The Other office.

"Peggy McIntyre, meet Kieran O'Connor from Belfast, Ireland," Maxi said.

As soon as she saw him, she gasped and nearly dropped the paper she was carrying.

Kieran was tall with a square jaw and rugged handsome looks. He had dark orange-red hair and green eyes, just like her.

"Hiya. You have a grand Scottish name," he said, extending his hand to shake Peggy's.

His hand was coarse with many calluses, but his handshake was gentle and kind.

Looking at the two standing next to each other, Maxi laughed. "Hey, you two look like identical peas in a pod."

Still holding Peggy's hand, Kieran lingered, gazing into her eyes, and smiled with a sideways grin. "How dare ya now compare my freckled mug to this bonny lass with her mysterious emerald eyes?"

Peggy lowered her head and giggled a little, almost embarrassed.

"I'm Irish too. My great-grandmother was from Ireland, County Donegal." She returned his smile and he kissed her hand.

"I'd know a fair darling of Isle anywhere," he said.

Peggy sighed as she slowly retracted her hand. Watching the interaction with some impatience, Maxi grabbed Kieran's arm in haste.

"Look, Romeo and Juliet, you can have a staring contest later. Right now, we have a story to write."

"Please pardon my impertinence, but would you allow me to sit and have a pint with you at the pub later?" Kieran asked, grinning.

Maxi dragged him to her desk before she could answer. Peggy just grinned and waved, completely entranced by him.

For the next few hours, Peggy went about her duties, but couldn't take her eyes off him. As he worked with Maxi, Peggy studied everything about him, fantasizing about running through rolling green fields together. She knew it was a silly schoolgirl crush, but there was just something that drew her attention and her breath.

Just as she was focused on typing up a story, he came up from behind, surprising her.

"You'll pardon me, lass, but Miss Maxi asked me to give this to ya for typing." As he handed her the pages, their hands touched again and Peggy jolted in her chair, as if a charge of static electricity leapt into her.

As they froze like statues, locked in each other's eyes, Maxi impatiently broke the trance.

"OK, Irish, let's go to the pub—I mean club." Maxi sheepishly grinned. "Peggy will be along soon."

Watching them walk out the door, Peggy took the news copy and furiously typed as fast as her fingers could go. She moved with lightning speed; wondering in her mind if there would be sparks flying off the keys. She needed to get to that club.

Soon after, Peggy gleefully joined Maxi and Kieran at The Bitter End for a drink. Maxi and Peggy hung on every word as Kieran spoke expressively of his love for Ireland and pain in his city.

"I love me home. There's nothing like it. The vast green hills and fields go as far as the eye can see in every direction and the deep seeping dew in the morning so thick you could almost wear it on your person like a jumper. Do you know the Irish flag is one and the same with the soil and its people?

The green of the land of our Emerald Isle, the white skin and our orange hair." He chuckled a bit, but then sipped his beer and looked broodingly serious.

"But the trouble sometimes makes everything seem black and white. Bullets fly to and fro at any hour. Gangs of men trudge down the streets throwing bricks and stones at will, shattering windows without a thought or care to what they hit? Neither the old nor the wee bern are safe to walk the streets. It's a dark time, it is."

His face sunk in sorrow as he told tales of the riots and gun-filled gang warfare from different factions, aligned by religious affiliation. They fought with each other for and against freedom and unification for Northern Ireland with the rest of the Emerald Isle from British rule.

As he spoke, Maxi burned with anger at the injustices while Peggy sat watching him, spellbound. Lost in his endless green eyes, she could almost see the Emerald Isle itself in their reflection. Although she paid little attention to what he said, transported by his charmingly thick Irish brogue she was captivated by every word and lilt in his voice. It filled her with a soothing and comforting feeling of warmth, as if she was hearing Maggie speak.

"The ruling English class is dominated over Ireland for far too long, siphoning their resources and leaving them desolate while they sit pretty on their island, not caring if their Irish subjects are embroiled in a battle of brother versus brother. It's sickening," Maxi proclaimed.

Kieran looked at her and chuckled. "My my, me lass, ya speak as if you yourself were on the front lines. Maybe I need to take you back to Belfast so you can solve this for us."

Out of nowhere, Liam sat down at the table, startling Peggy from her swooning trance. "You're not getting our Maxi until she fixes the problems in America," he said.

"I can be outraged about both," Maxi objected with a sly grin on her face and jokingly bowed to introduce Liam. "Kieran O'Connor, meet Viscount Liam Donegal, conveyed from Ireland via Manhattan."

"Don't listen to her. My family is from County Donegal, so is Peggy's. Our great-grandmothers came over together. And I'm not the viscount, my grandfather is. This is America—we don't have that here," Liam said, dismissing her comments.

"Aye, laddie, you don't have aristocracy in America, but there are still aristocrats. It's a birthright from generations past," Kieran kindly corrected him.

Liam waved him off and chuckled. "Nah, it doesn't mean anything here. My grandfather was born in America. It's just a meaningless title that some people used to gain entry into elitist circles. That'll never be my bag."

"That's what I love about America. Everyone thinks they're the same," Kieran said wryly in response.

"Then you should stay here!" Peggy said abruptly, smiling with hope in her eyes.

Kieran laughed and put his hand on hers. "Now that's a fine welcome lass, but I'm only here for a wee bit to tell our tale."

When he touched her, a greater rush of electricity shot through her body with 1,000 volts of power, increasing its intensity from the former jolt before.

Liam immediately noticed Peggy's reaction to Kieran, as if he felt the electricity himself with a punch in the gut.

Turning toward the stage, Liam saw Ravyn come forward. "It's time for the hootenanny; Ravyn's on first," he said.

"Your friend is an owl's nanny?" Kieran asked curiously.

"No, silly," Peggy giggled. "Hootenanny is when anybody can go up and perform."

Clad in her signature black from head to toe, Ravyn danced in time with a goatee shouted a dissertation about war while slamming a plain bucket on the floor with rhythmic precision. Ravyn commanded everyone's attention, slowly moving her body into seemingly impossible positions to demonstrate the words while flicking red scarves to accent and portray the needless death.

"That was powerful," Kieran said afterward. He looked down at the ground with big puppy-dog eyes. "Reminds me of home."

"The world is lousy all over," Maxi added with a gruff gloom, gulping her beer.

"It's like me mother used to say when times had our faces dragging to the ground," Kieran started singing, "Oh, Danny Boy…"

Both his way of twirling words and the passion in his soulful face made Peggy immediately spark.

She recognized the song as one her father sang to her and Maggie sang to him when he was little. Without realizing it, she began singing along with him, her beautiful voice like calming sea waves bringing in the tide.

Their voices entwined like a grapevine, weaving in and out to become one.

When they were done, everybody within earshot clapped enthusiastically and they both flushed with embarrassment.

"Peggy, you have a great voice. Why don't you go up there?" Maxi asked.

"I want to, but I just haven't found my sound yet," Peggy replied.

"You sing with the grace of a hummingbird. And I could almost hear a little Irish in your voice. No doubt your ancestry does you proud," Kieran smiled.

Liam jumped in his chair with excitement, as if a lightbulb had gone off in his head. "Right on! What if you sang some old Irish folk songs? You could play them on your guitar too. Nobody's doing that."

Peggy looked at him curiously as she contemplated the idea.

"Aye, the lad's got a notion. Many of the old Irish folk songs speak to today's problems. I'd be happy to teach you a few," Kieran said and clasped her hand.

"Far out!" Peggy eagerly smiled ear to ear and squeezed Kieran's hand in appreciation. It was a good idea and she'd have a wonderful reason to spend more time with Kieran.

Liam flinched and looked down, regretting his suggestion as he watched them hold hands with emptiness in the pit of his stomach. Peggy was smitten with Kieran and it appeared mutual. He hadn't thought he had feelings for Peggy, except for friendship, until now.

When the evening ended, Kieran walked Peggy to Jane's front door and kissed her hand. Again, the electrical wave move up her spine inch by inch, leaving her whole body tingling at the same time.

She went in and quickly darted up the stairs to tell Maggie everything.

Dear Maggie,

I met the most wonderful son of the Emerald Isle today. Kieran. Everything about him makes me feel things I've never felt before. I keep picturing him running hand in hand through emerald fields of flowers with me. Every time he touches me, I feel it in all the nerves in my body, like I've been electrocuted—but I experience no pain, just a rush of benevolent electricity that makes me feel alive.

His accent is darling and alluring. Each word draws me in further, although I admit I'm so entranced I barely hear what he says. I only hear beautiful music playing.

I never felt this attraction with Michael. It's like a magnetic field, drawing me closer to him. I don't know what it is, but I can't wait to find out.

The next week, Peggy and Kieran spent every available hour together learning songs. He was funny, gentle, and kind. Peggy fell more under his spell, grateful he opened up his heritage to her.

Picnicking at lunch in the park, he held her in front of him as they sat on a wool blanket, teaching her the chords and words to each song. Of course, she'd been playing guitar for years, but learning the chords this way was more fun.

She introduced American delicacies to him like peanut butter and jelly, bologna sandwiches, and hot dogs.

"I like this bologna and mustard. It tastes like a banger back home, but we never thought to put it between slices of bread," he chuckled.

"Back in Chicago, we have all kinds of sausages—Polish and Italian—that are smothered with peppers and sauces and eaten on a nice roll. It's very popular," Peggy explained.

"I love all the words you Americans use for things. What do you call these crisps again?" he asked playfully.

"Chips, potato chips," Peggy giggled. "Although it makes perfect sense to call them crisps, since they are crispy."

"Our chips are fried strips of potatoes; I think you call them French fries, but they're not French," he laughed.

"Why do you think there are different names for the same food?" Peggy asked.

"I don't know, but I'd love to make you a traditional Guinness stew and soda bread; you'll never eat anything else again," he said.

"I'd love that." She smiled, realizing she was so hypnotised by him, she'd agree to anything he said.

The next Sunday, Peggy and Kieran found themselves shopping for ingredients so he could make his stew with meat, potatoes, onions, carrots, and Guinness beer.

Peggy invited Liam, Maxi, and Ravyn for their impromptu Irish feast. All day she and Kieran cooked in Jane's kitchen together, as Jane and Tony went downtown to see a friend's show. Peggy never really liked cooking, but she knew her way around the kitchen. So did Kieran. They laughed and sang while he showed her how to cut things properly, draping his big arms around her.

Cutting some carrots with his head nestled next to hers, she laughed and turned her head abruptly so they were face to face. Staring into each other's eyes, the attraction could no longer be denied. They moved toward each other and kissed deeply.

Peggy whisked into a dream world. Her head swirled like a merry-go-round from the passion of their lips and bodies pressed together.

As they'd been sampling all the ingredients, including the beer, the taste of his kiss was sweet and savory all at once, but more intoxicating than a pub full of Guinness.

She didn't even know how long it lasted. Like she was frozen in a blissful eternity, enjoying every moment of their embrace until it ended too quickly.

Kieran pulled away when he heard the boiling stew pop. "That was a right good snog, but if we don't stop, we'll be covered in stew before we know it." He beamed with a satisfied smile, his hand still touching her face. And then the doorbell rang, interrupting them with her friends' arrival.

As they feasted on the delicious Irish stew, soda bread, and Guinness, Peggy was sure their tryst showed on her face like a beacon. She and Kieran sat next to each other, holding hands and stealing quick glances at one another.

The discussion was lively and raucous, as usual; they talked about music and politics with impassioned regularity. But there was a not-so-secret truth hanging over the table. It was obvious.

Maxi mischievously smiled when she saw Peggy and Kieran with their less than subtle canoodling, certain of their connection. Ravyn was oblivious as usual, with her impervious Russian shell. Her world did not extend beyond her own aura.

Liam retreated slightly. He knew what was going on, and even though he and Peggy pledged to be best friends, he knew in his heart he had feelings for her. But he said nothing and acted his part as a best friend. Kieran was only going to be in New York for a little while.

SUMMER OF LOVE

In advance of the next Tuesday hootenanny, Peggy learned two Irish folk songs to perform. Ravyn told her everything she needed to know about hoot nights.

"Don't let the audience distract you—you are there to perform and you want all eyes on you," she instructed in her deadpan manner. "Don't worry if they do not like you. You perform for you."

The daunting prospect hung in the air. What if they didn't like her? But forearmed with the wisdom of her group and ready or not, she was as prepared as she could be.

As she got ready to take the stage, Kieran gave her a strong kiss of Irish luck that she hung onto like a life ring.

Liam helped her put on her guitar and saw the nervousness in her eyes.

"Ravyn is right, in a way. Sing for yourself. Sing to Maggie. Sing to me. You're sharing your gift with all of us, Piggy Mac."

Peggy smiled at the boost of confidence and made her way up to the stage. She took short breaths walking toward the red brick backdrop of the stage like it was the last mile—anxious, nervous, and terrified. But perpetual motion moved her forward. This was her time.

When she got up on the stool and looked out into the crowd of dark sunglasses, she held her breath, telling herself... these were her people. She momentarily closed her eyes and heard Liam's voice in her head... sing for yourself.

She meekly whispered her name into the microphone.

"Louder!" someone in the crowd shouted.

Scared but determined, she loudly said "Peggy Mac" and the microphone squeaked. Everybody, including Peggy, laughed. It was the relief she needed to relax.

Seeing out into the sea of smoky blackness ahead of her, she sang with abandon. Her voice lifted up and down melodically as she skillfully strummed and picked the strings, exuding sweet sounds.

The audience was captivated by the lovely old tunes they never heard before, and when she struck the last chord, applause filled the room.

In a fit of adrenaline, she quickly bounded off the stage and sat right down at the table with her friends, chugging her beer in relief.

Kieran rose and kissed her. "Your gran would have been prouder than a new mother at baptismal."

"Yes, Maggie would have loved it." Liam interjected, defiantly shooting a satisfied grin at Kieran. "I see you kept the name Peggy Mac."

"It seemed to fit." Peggy smiled, not noticing the subtle exchange between the two men. But the sideways glance drew Maxi's attention like a lightning rod. She squinted her eyes and quickly toggled her head from Liam to Kieran, but decided not to say anything for now.

Just in time to break the tension, Ravyn joined them at the table and handed a basket full of money to Peggy.

"What's this for?" she asked, confused.

"They like you. They give you money. That's how you know," Ravyn said succinctly. "Last lesson, always try to play first—there's more money in everyone's pockets and the audience is fresh, wanting to be entertained."

"Yeah, remember when John Sebastian played and the crowd really dug him, but when the basket came back, it was empty because Richie Havens played before and cleaned everyone out?" Liam laughed.

While she saw the basket passed before, Peggy didn't expect money on her first time out. She stared at the basket flabbergasted and laughed. "Well then, the drinks are on me."

At the end of the night, the group went their separate ways.

Riding the high from her performance and a few too many basket beers, as she called them, Peggy giddily danced and strolled through the park with Kieran.

She kicked her shoes off and waded into the fountain at Washington Square. "I'm on top of the world," she said, raising her hands in the air.

"I'm glad you're glad, at that." Kieran laughed and kissed her. She kissed him back hard, jumping off the fountain ledge throwing her arms and legs around him.

With the darkness of night pierced only by the dim streetlight glow, they passionately kissed and embraced, slowly tumbling to the grass as if they were one person.

Breathless, they laid side by side under the faint light, staring into each other's eyes.

"I know you're leaving soon, so let's make this a night we will both remember," she said coyly.

Kieran grinned and scooped her up in his arms, carrying her to a dark spot by a tree. With clothing hastily soaring up to the tree's branches, their bodies slowly intertwined, divinely making love.

They were in tune to the rhythm of beautiful music in her head. As they took turns caressing and kissing every inch of each other, they rolled back and forth on the grass like a symphony that ebbed and flowed with both intensity and soft sweetness.

Afterward, they lay together, giggling and laughing, humming the Irish folk songs that made up the soundtrack of their passion.

"Don't worry," she said. "I don't expect anything. I'm just grateful to have one night with you."

He gazed at her with dumbfounded surprise. "Peggy McIntyre, you're a hell of a bonny lass, you are." He slowly stroked her hair and then nuzzled her neck with warm wet kisses.

"Careful, we'll have to do that again."

With a spark in his eye, he enveloped her with a strong embrace and made love to her again with such intensity; she gripped the blades of grass for strength.

After they caught their breath, they playfully kissed and petted each other for a little while longer before putting on their clothes and happily strolling hand-in-hand to her house.

When she walked through the door of the still house, Peggy floated on air right up the stairs and pulled out her journal to tell Maggie everything.

Dear Maggie,

Tonight was out of this world. I performed for the first time in front of people. It was terrifying, thrilling, and intoxicating. I absolutely have to do that again and again. And it meant so much more to me singing the songs of your youth. I know they were important to you.

And to make the evening a complete success, Kieran and I made love... twice. I know in your day that would've been scandalous, but it felt right to me. For my first real sexual encounter, I couldn't have asked for a sweeter lover.

I know he's going back to Ireland and I have no illusions of a relationship. I just wanted him. That's what's so great about what's happening right now.

SUMMER OF LOVE

Maxi tells me that women can do anything. That we are empowered by our own spirit to love or not love whomever we want—there are no restrictions. Men have been doing this for centuries. Why not us?

Both of my firsts tonight gave me an unbelievable feeling of utopia. I think I can do anything I want now on my terms. I feel alive and I definitely intend to enjoy every minute.

It's such a shock to think only six months ago I was shuttered and locked in a world where I had no power over anything. Now I feel relief, and a freedom to express everything I want. It's brilliant!

For the next few days, Peggy and Kieran enjoyed every minute together, sharing every bit of each other while they could. On his last night, they all gathered at The Village Gaslight to bid him goodbye.

It was their hoot night, so once again, Peggy got on the stage, but this time her nerves were lessened and she was more comfortable. For her song, she planned a special goodbye.

"This one is for our Irish friend Kieran who sails home tomorrow," she said. "Will everyone raise their glasses? Slán abhaile. We wish you good health and good travels. May the road meet your feet till we meet again."

Then she soulfully sang "When Irish Eyes Are Smiling" directly to him in a slow folk rhythm, gently picking the high strings on the fret of her guitar with keen exactness like an angel with a harp. Sweet tones lifted her voice up and down about how he stole her heart away in a haunting but joyful cadence, conveying her love and gratitude.

Kieran fixed his unwavering gaze at Peggy, displaying a wide grin while she sang to him. But Maxi watched Liam staring at Kieran. It was the elephant in the room. Liam was jealous and Maxi knew, but once again, she slyly grinned and said nothing, tucking that information away in her brain's file cabinet. She knew his secret.

The next day, they all took Kieran to the dock together. He said goodbye to Maxi and Ravyn, hugging them, and shook Liam's hand. Then he swept Peggy up in his arms tightly and kissed her deeply until they were both breathless.

"Goodbye, me lass. You made America a wonderful place I will always remember." He blew a kiss to her as he walked toward the gangplank. "Come and visit me soon. I'll show you a right good time."

Peggy joined arms with the rest of them waving goodbye. But she wasn't sad at all. She connected with herself and her Irish roots in a way she could never have predicted. Emboldened with the strength of her soul and spirit of her heart, she could now go forward to live her new life just as it came, one day at a time.

Chapter Nine

Exploration

A few days later, Jane bounded through the door with exciting news, interrupting Peggy making dinner in the kitchen. Since Jane refused to take any rent money she offered, Peggy helped out by cleaning and cooking when she could.

"An old friend contacted me at the theatre today. Tony and I have been asked to direct and choreograph a show in Los Angeles for the next six months to a year. It's a great opportunity," Jane told her.

She was happy for her aunt and uncle and feigned excitement when Jane filled in all the details of the show, but with the sudden prospect of homelessness, Peggy couldn't help but question where she would live.

"I bet you're wondering about the house," Jane said. Peggy shook her head as if her mind was just inexplicably read. "No, it's a logical question. We don't know how long we're going to be gone, exactly, so we'd like to keep the house and we were thinking you could still live here and take care of it for us?" she asked, hopeful.

Instantly relieved, in the next moment Peggy pondered a frightful thought. Would she be able to take care of this house on her own? And did she want to live by herself?

"Of course, this means you'd have to call your mother or drop her a line once in a while, as I can't keep filling her your life," Jane chuckled.

"I'd like to stay, but you'd have to take some rent from me and I can pay the utilities," Peggy asserted.

Jane stared at her, hesitating, and then smiled. "Well, thank you, that would help, but you need to pay only what you can afford."

Her last sentence rang through Peggy's head over and over with the question looming on her mind. How much could she afford?

She couldn't really rely on any basket money from the clubs, so her job at the paper was her only income. Peggy worried it was not going to be enough to contribute to their mortgage and cover utilities.

Jane said she'd be doing her a favor by staying and taking care of the house. And if they instead got a more permanent renter and needed to come back in six months, they wouldn't have a place to go. It all made sense, but Peggy didn't want to take advantage. And she still didn't know if she wanted to live alone.

That night they met at Cafe Wha?, a basement coffeehouse famous for poetry readings, with revolving musicians and comedians launching careers. With its contradicting black walls and white marble tile, low ceiling, and poor lighting, performers and patrons alike affectionately dubbed it "the cave."

Among the low chatter in the small cafe, Peggy shared her concerns with Liam and Maxi about taking care of the house alone.

"Would you be open to a couple roommates?" Maxi asked. "That house is much nicer than the room Ravyn and I share over the Ukrainian restaurant. It's a little cramped, and the aromas wafting up through the window make me wanna eat more and more. I think I spend twice my rent money eating in that restaurant."

Peggy lit up with enthusiastic relief. "That would be great. We could split the cost and you can each have your own room. It will be fun to have roommates."

They were interrupted by the unmistakable sound of a sole drum beat that often preceded Ravyn's performances, this time with a man pounding an upside down steel washbin.

The lights turned down, and the lone chugging sound and steam-filled release of the cappuccino machines hauntingly accompanied the echoing drum. It almost sounded like a steam train coming into a station.

That was the vibe of the heavy but creative outlet for the deeply thoughtful poets reciting their hearts for all to hear at Cafe Wha'? Anytime they went there, Peggy always knew she would come out feeling like a small fish in a massive world pond, larger than herself.

Slinking onto the platform in her camouflaged black leotard, Ravyn's long black hair was unusually concealed in a white beret and white boots.

She stared straight at the audience and spoke in the echo of the hushed room with syncopated repetitive beats punctuating her sentences.

"Black... and white... From top to bottom, we see the starkness in the dark of night...Some cloaked with only the moon as a guide, some revealed, accompanied by false pride... Since the beginning of time divided, one on each side...But in the light of day, they are one, all bathed equally by the sun's rays... The brightness shows souls peacefully intertwined beyond the sickness of the discriminative mind... They shop... They eat... They love... They live... under an umbrella sky of humanity... Never again to be separated under a veil of harmful insanity."

Then a tall, strapping black man wearing all white with black shoes approached Ravyn on the stage and dipped her, kissing her in a passionate embrace. And as choreographed, they mechanically straightened up, standing close to each other and entangled their arms together like a pretzel.

"Forever one yin and yang, fulfilling the creator's master plan..."

Finger snaps of admiration rang throughout the room in return for the enlightenment of their adoring audience with Liam whistling his approval.

"I love her poetry, but somehow, when she stares through your soul like that with that accent, you feel scolded and about to face a firing squad." Liam chuckled with a bit of nervousness in his voice. "Piggy, could you borrow that guy's guitar and help me out? It's my turn now," he gulped.

Caught off guard, Peggy didn't know what was going on, but as best friends do, she immediately complied without knowing what came next.

She borrowed a guitar from the neighboring table and curiously followed Liam up to the stage. She sat on the side of the stage on a stool, while he stood in front of the microphone.

Peggy braced herself for anything while waiting for instruction.

"I can't believe I have to follow that," Liam said with a little crack in his voice, but the crowd's soft laughter seemed to ignite him.

He nodded to Peggy and she began delicately picking and strumming the strings freestyle as he spoke.

Peggy noticed writers often liked to have soothing music during their performances to help accent and showcase their words—a resonance to imbue meaning.

She saw the hesitant look in Liam's eyes as he uttered his private words. She didn't know what prompted him to finally present his poetry, but was glad she was there to support his endeavor.

"I am awake, so I can see, no one will pull the wool over me… My eyes are open, both ears are piqued… I hear exactly what some people speak."

Peggy felt blindfolded. She didn't know where he was going, but she closed her eyes and tried to feel the inflection of his voice and match the pace and tone of the music accordingly.

"My vision is clear, whether far or near, sometimes the world is what it appears… My mind never sleeps, for it can't escape the worst of us who will not abate…My heart aches for those who suffer oppressed, rhetoric cannot put them asunder or make us regress."

Starting off with another crack of his voice, she saw the immediate difference as his words flowed through him like a trickling creek, meeting the open sea.

"My head is not obscured in the sand. I smell the stench of hypocrisy in man. My body rejects the lies I am fed. It will never put me to bed…"

She was swept away by his words, so poignant and powerful. She had read many of his poems before—a best friend's privilege—but none as targeted as this. She wondered about his inspiration.

"My voice is loud, I say it proud… I am awake. I see everything. And I hear all sound."

When he was done, there was a moment of stunned silence, and then cascading waves of snaps starting softly and then roaring, obscuring every other sound, even the cappuccino machines.

They both returned to the table and Peggy gratefully deposited the loaned guitar with its owner.

"Welcome to the movement, Liam," Maxi smiled with wonder. "That should be a rally cry for the masses."

"The delivery was a bit simple, but I like," Ravyn said with rare approval.

"Well, that's a five-star review if I ever heard one," Liam laughed. He looked at Peggy with wanting anticipation. "Thanks for playing on the fly. It really helped calm me down. Did you like it?"

Peggy gazed at him and grinned, clasping his hand in hers. "I think it's the best thing you've ever written."

He smiled and squeezed her hand without letting go all night.

A few hours later, Ravyn and Maxi went to another club with Ravyn's new lover—the man dressed in white from her performance named Tusk.

Still reeling from the performance high, Liam asked Peggy if he could walk home with her.

The further away they walked from the clubs, the quiet village streets became solemn and stolid, like a swaddled sleeping giant, recuperating and ready to awaken for the new day.

Amid the soft glow of the remaining gas lanterns, the walk was peaceful, clearing the mind from the heavy thoughts at the club.

"I'm just curious—what made you decide to read your poetry after all this time?" Peggy asked.

Liam chuckled, smiling. "You did, Piggy."

Peggy squinted her eyes at him in blank confusion. "What do you mean I did?"

He grabbed her hand and swung it back and forth as they strolled.

"You gave me both the inspiration and the strength. Even though you were unsure, you were brave enough to try, so how could I do any less?"

Peggy smiled at him and nodded. She understood.

The rest of the way home, they giggled and laughed, pretending to play hopscotch on the sidewalk. Liam jumped on a light pole, mimicking Gene Kelly and Singin' in the Rain.

It was an easy relationship. Peggy felt more comfortable with Liam than with anybody before. He was her confidant and her North Star on all uncertain matters; her friend till the end.

When they reached the door, he surprised her.

"Hey, what would you think if I moved in with you three?" he said in a half-teasing, half-serious voice.

"Silly, you already have a home?" Peggy giggled at his joke, while fumbling for her keys.

"No, really, I've been looking for a way to get out of the old Central Park West barn. I'm in this area all the time. It would be helpful to be closer," he asserted.

Peggy still wasn't sure if he was serious or not.

"What would your parents and grandfather say if you were living with three women?" she laughed, dismissing his obvious gag.

"I'm 21. I'm old enough to leave the nest and make up my own mind. Didn't you hear Ravyn tonight? Black and white can mean women and men too."

Peggy stared at him a minute to take his temperature. "Are you being serious?"

"Yes," he said, earnestly. "This makes tons of sense. We're all just friends, right?"

She nodded, still dumbfounded with surprise.

"I need to check with the girls to be sure first, but ok," she said, tentative by his impulse, but kissed him goodbye on the cheek and went into the house.

Before she knew it, another month went by. As her uncle and aunt winged their way toward the West Coast, her trio of friends moved in a parade of beanbag chairs, a lava lamp, beads, and funky furnishings to make the ordinary house an eclectic den of alternative personality befitting each of its residents.

Exhausted, the new housemates sat on the floor around a coffee table littered with Chinese takeout boxes and a jug of wine, toasting their new relationship as housemates.

"I'm sure none of you thought of this, so I took the liberty of drafting a few house rules for us all," Maxi said, handing a paper to Liam.

They all paused a moment, muted, while reading and passing around the typed sheet of rules.

"Bathroom schedule? Cooking schedule? Cleaning schedule? This is like the Army. What do you think we're going to do, suddenly act like zoo animals?" Liam scoffed, handing the paper to Peggy.

"Zoo animals are caged. We are free," Ravyn corrected, ignoring the paper and passing back to Maxi.

"Come on, Max, do you really think we need this? Rules of engagement? What does that even mean? We're all friends here," Peggy said.

"That's exactly why we need it. We are friends and we want to stay that way. Living together is entirely different than working together and going out to clubs at night. This is all day, every day in your underwear, toothbrush in your mouth, fighting over shower schedules and who's going to wash the dishes," Maxi stated.

"I know, I'll settle this right now. I volunteer to wash the dishes all the time and I don't need to shower," Liam kidded.

"You may do dishes, but you must shower or you move out now," Ravyn ordered and pointed toward the front door. "Do svidaniya."

"No, really, you guys," Maxi insisted. "This is real life. Having some rules and parameters is just a good idea."

"I thought you didn't believe in rules," Peggy grinned slyly.

"Only when I live with someone. Out there beyond that door, there are no rules," Maxi said definitively, with her fist on the table, placing the list in front of Liam again.

"OK, OK, I'll sign, we'll all sign," Liam laughs, writing his name on the paper and handing it to Peggy who quickly signed and gave the paper to Ravyn.

"Nyet, Ravyn signs nothing," she said and affixed an X to the parchment.

"Now with that settled, let's have a real toast," Liam said, raising his glass. "To the crazy lad and the three bonny lasses."

"To the four musketeers and a brand-new adventure," Peggy added. They all clinked their glasses and emptied them together.

With that settled, they retreated to tidy their rooms and Peggy helped Liam bring some of his boxes down to the basement. He gallantly offered to crash in the basement, so each of the girls could still each have their own room.

"Are you sure this is OK? It's awfully dark and dank down here," she asked, squishing her nose with guilt.

Liam looked at her seriously with one of his deadpan faces.

"I love sleeping with the washer and dryer. The rhythm of the cycles keeps time with my poetry like a metronome. Besides, if I'm going to be an artist, I need a studio and a place to brood like a starving artist. I've been living the wrong life. I'm not gonna starve. I have a trust fund. But this way, at least I can pretend," he laughed.

Peggy always appreciated his witty and quirky sense of humor, but was concerned. "You never told me. How did your family take the news of your moving out?"

"To be honest, I chickened out. I told my parents I was moving into a swanky Manhattan apartment building. They were fine with living among the elite and potential heiress wives. They didn't even ask for the address. They wouldn't care as long as they think I'm living the highlife. But I told Granda—he understood, and I quote… 'Drink all the life you can, my lad. It goes fast and one day you'll be sitting in a chair, looking out the windows of your memory.'"

"Wow, that's so sad," Peggy said. "We'll need to visit him at least once a week. Maybe then he'll realize I'm Peggy and not Maggie."

"Oh, he knows who you are. He's not off his daft rocker. He says you remind him of Maggie and after all, your name is Margaret," Liam assured.

"OK, then it's a date. I'm going to turn in. I'm wiped," she said.

"Sure, go ahead and leave the hunchback in his gloomy cell," he said. He started walking in a circle, hunched over and grunting.

"Alas, kind sir, I must leave you, but I'll see you tomorrow morning bright and early. I think it's your turn to make breakfast. Oh, and do the dishes—remember, you promised." Peggy giggled and threw a pillow at him.

Thanks to Maxi's rules, the four musketeers' household ran like a well-oiled machine and despite their constant partnership, they worked, lived, and played together in surprising harmony.

Ravyn's revolving door of lovers made their brief appearances, coming in and out of the shadow of the doorway, under the cover of darkness and in the ebbing hue of the sunrise, never lingering—at her direction.

"Men are like candy. I want a different flavor every day and if they stay too long, they'll melt," she said when Peggy invited one of her man friends to join them for breakfast.

While Peggy didn't believe in treating men like candy, her experience with Kieran had awakened her to a new possible existence.

She also didn't want or need to keep one man for life. She decided to open herself up to the exploration of men, intimacy, and her own sexuality and taste a variety of candy.

One night when playing for her favorite hootenanny audience at The Bitter End, from the stage, she saw a man with a large nest of mousy brown hair held back by a red bandanna. His face looked a little rugged, but his eyes were obscured in silhouette by the colored stage lights in her face. But she did notice his carved muscular arms and full neatly-combed chest hair with a tan leather vest between them.

She'd never seen him before, but was intrigued when he sat straight in front of her with an innocent knowing grin, as if he'd always known her.

At the end of her song, she looked down again and he was gone. As she exited the platform, though, there he was with his guitar, reaching out his hand to help her down.

"Your voice is as beautiful as you are. I feel like I've heard it all my life." He kissed her hand and went up on the stage.

Peggy felt that electric feeling again, with tingles of current surging through her body. There was something about that guy.

She returned to her table to find reporter Maxi ready for the scoop of the day.

"Who is that and why was he kissing your hand?" she said, intrigued.

"I don't know, but I'm willing to find out." Peggy smiled and intently watched him sing.

He played the guitar sporadically, strumming in strong irregular intervals. She was enticed by his power and conviction as he played a dominant rock beat.

His voice was gruff and unpolished, matching his coarse exterior, rendering Peggy breathless by his commanding presence. She unconsciously leaned forward, nearly lifting off her seat as he played.

"I like this one," Ravyn said. "He reminds me of Russian bear."

With that imagery in her head, Peggy was even more enthralled. She watched him as he bounded down from the stage stairs and shot her a smile.

"Let's all hear it for Chuck," the announcer said.

Even his name was strong, Peggy thought.

"What are you waiting for? Go sit with him," Maxi said, reading her mind, urging her innermost thoughts.

Peggy looked at her friends, almost asking permission. Then she excitedly but demurely walked over to his table.

"I could feel the raw emotion in your song," Peggy said, staring at him with her best come-hither look.

Penetrating her shield with another crooked smile, he lured her with his cavernous brown chocolate eyes. He grabbed her hand and kissed it again, inviting her to sit, and she melted right into the seat.

"I prefer your way of singing. You take me on a journey with your delicate little fingers picking and sweet, sultry voice. I'm putty in your hands," he said, squeezing her hand.

Her body fluttered with excitement and anticipation. Her mouth went dry and she could barely utter a word.

"Sweet and strong. Sounds like we could make beautiful music together," she said and then gasped inside when she heard the cheesy words come out of her mouth. She had no thought in her head—it was pure animal instinct. She felt it in every fiber of her being. She wanted him.

"Well, that's an enticing offer, but I did promise to sing one more song. Wait for me?" he said, kissing the inside of her palm, so she could feel the scratch of his shadow whiskers against her hand.

Peggy nodded, unable to speak, frozen to the warm seat with her lips pressed together.

He walked up to the stage, leaving her with burning embers, ready to flame out. Peggy looked up and saw him staring straight at her, as if he were singing the song just to her. She found it hard to sit still as she felt the fire of desire.

She stared at him from top to bottom over and over, picturing herself running her fingers across his bare chest through his coarse hair down to his belly button and a small streak of wispy hair to his tight jeans. It was intoxicating, as if he had poured kerosene on her seat.

When he was done, he left his guitar at the table and with an enticing stare, led her to the back door.

In one fell swoop, he pushed open the door with his foot and lifted her onto a nearby crate in the alley, cradling her between his strong arms and the red brick wall.

His eyes still focused on hers, he leaned in and kissed her with the strength that she thought would gladly suck the living being out of her body. It was everything he was; the strong Russian bear taking her with an all-encompassing force that made her feel like gelatin and steel at the same time as she returned his passion, with all her might, pressing against him and grabbing his long hair to ensure his lips were glued to hers until they simultaneously shrieked in satisfaction.

When they were done, both sweaty and breathless, he looked at her and they both laughed.

"Wow, that was something. You're obviously more than you appear. A sweet and delicate dove on stage who morphs into a passionate tiger when it counts," he said.

Feeling the power within her, she flipped him so he was pinned against the wall and wrapped her legs around him. "You ain't seen nothing yet."

At some point, it was so intense; she felt like she was having an out-of-body experience. Channeling her rock and roll urges, she ravenously grabbed him again, roared, and kissed him hard, throwing herself at him twice more until he begged to stop.

"Little girl, I'm not gonna have enough energy to walk back into the room. Can I take a raincheck?"

"Of course, and thank you," Peggy said, smiling.

As they walked back into the club, she felt like the queen of England, with power swelling through her entire body. For the first time in her life, she felt like an individual, not a woman, but a person who could lead her own life the way she felt, at any time she wanted, without thought of convention or restriction.

When she returned to her table, Maxi and Raven bugged their eyes at her impatiently curious to know what happened.

She smiled and sipped her drink casually, drawing out their curiosity, and smiled. "You're right, Ravyn. He is like a Russian bear."

Chapter Ten

FRIENDS AND LOVERS

Summer 1965

Dear Maggie,

I am loving life. Since I came to New York, I'm really coming into myself. Among all these artists and great thinkers, I see the world in a whole new light. Women can be anything they want. We don't have to be shackled by some arcane notion that we're the weaker sex. After all, if it weren't for us, there would be no more people. But more than that, our limitations need only be what we put on ourselves, no one else.

I know you didn't have that kind of right in your day, but McIntyre women have always been strong. I don't know why it took so long for women to rise up. I'm glad I'm here for it. I'm sorry you're not. I think you would have liked this a lot.

Exploring my music, my body, and my mind has given me an inner strength and calmed my wandering mind. This is what I've always wanted.

SUMMER OF LOVE

It was late summer and Washington Square was alive on a Sunday afternoon. She dropped a postcard of the Washington Square arch in the mailbox for her parents. Since Jane left, she made good on her promise to keep them informed with a veil of separation between her real life, so they wouldn't worry.

Every couple weeks, she sent them a postcard of New York monuments telling her about places she ate or things she saw. She told them she had two girl roommates and her friend Liam, omitting him as a roommate, and singing in the clubs and the square, but made it sound as harmless as possible.

The scalding weather prompted the Good Humor carts to line the perimeter, and the crowds were as lively as the heart of the flickering summer sun.

Peggy was sitting by the dormant fountain singing with a group of pickers from the clubs playing guitars. She loved these fun, impromptu sing-alongs, as it gave people an opportunity to collaborate and mindlessly jam, merging their individual gifts into one glorious voice.

Out of the corner of her eye, she saw a tall man looking at her. At first she dismissed it, but then realized he was staring at her from many different angles, blending into other parts of the crowd. She was curious.

He had cascading curls of light brown hair falling under his multicolored knit cap. Rather unusually, he was wearing a wool knitted scarf wrapped several times around his neck in the near 90-degree heat.

Then suddenly he popped up from nowhere, sitting right next to her as the jam session broke up.

"Are you a figment of my imagination?" she said to him.

"I am real, but are you? I've never seen such beautiful hair that is as deep as the burgeoning horizon and eyes that sparkle like the Emerald City of Oz," he said.

Peggy smiled and blushed at his complimentary poetic words. She decided to flirt with him a little.

"Perhaps if you draw a picture, you won't have to stare at me this long," she kidded.

Despite her joke, his gaze never faltered. "That is exactly my plan. If you will, my name is Gene and I am an artist. I search everywhere for inspiration and I only paint things that move me to my very core. Your beauty is a force of nature that fills me with unbridled passion and washes over me with the warmth of a thousand sunbeams. I need to capture that feeling on canvas. Will you pose for me or doom me to ache with a hunger never satisfied?"

She was taken by surprise. His wonderful words lifted her into another dimension of being. The idea that someone was so fascinated by her was alluring.

"How can I refuse that? I can't be responsible for someone starving."

Gene's eyes lit up. They were somehow mysterious, a blending of color between many hues. And she looked into them, gleefully not knowing what would happen next. He held out his hand to help her off the fountain's edge.

"Come now, the inspiration is overwhelming me," he said with curious urgency.

He led her to an area on the perimeter of the park, where all the artists set up their canvases, and sat her down in front of him.

Peggy relished the idea of being the subject of someone's fantasy and relinquished to become a muse of art. He arranged her in different poses, stepping back each time to frame her just right. Each time he began, he abruptly ceased only minutes later sparking frustration.

"No, this isn't right. None of this is right. Your goddess-like beauty needs a backdrop befitting the ethereal plane. This just won't do."

He grabbed her hand and a paintbrush, canvas, and easel and sat her down beneath a nearby tree.

He gazed up at the sun for a moment, and then at her under the tree, and grinned.

"Nature with nature," he said and silently continued his work.

Peggy dwelled on him scanning up and down, wondering. She was intrigued by his intensity, devoting body and mind to his work, and the dichotomy between his whimsical wardrobe of multicolored knitwear and his obvious intense immersion in his art.

She was so captivated by him, she didn't see Liam approach her.

"Hey, Piggy, I finally found you. What are you doing?" Liam asked.

"Liam, shh," she said, trying not to move her face. "I'm being painted."

Turning around, he noticed Gene intently staring at Peggy and toggling back to his canvas. Liam puckered his face in disapproval.

"I thought you were gonna let me paint you. When did this happen?" he asked as if wounded.

"Enough!" Gene shouted. "I'm sorry, my beauty, there are too many distractions here for me to focus. My studio is right over there. We can have complete serenity."

Liam immediately looked alarmed. "Now look, friend. She's not going anywhere with you."

Peggy rose from the ground to object. "Liam, I appreciate your big brother protectiveness, but it's fine."

She shot a tempting smile at Gene and he returned with an appealing glance, raising his chin in agreement.

Liam noted the exchange with concern and then falsely switched his demeanor to curiosity.

"Of course. You're right. But I would love to see your studio," he falsely claimed. "I'm a painter too and I really enjoy the processes of fellow artists. Let's go, Peggy." He took her hand and smirked, pretending interest.

Gene made no response, gathering his tools and leading them to his loft.

Across the street, catty-corner from the park, they walked to the stairway at the side of the building above the corner bakery.

"Wow, this place smells great. It's gotta be murder living above a bakery. I'd be hungry all the time," Liam quipped.

Gene glanced at him with ambivalence. "It doesn't affect me. I'm a naturalist and I don't eat anything that didn't come directly from the ground."

"Sugar and wheat come from the ground, friend," Liam crooked his smile, correcting him.

"I would eat sugarcane if it grew in this vicinity, but the sugar that comes out of that mill is processed," Gene said definitively.

"Really—that's so interesting," Peggy said, masked to the obvious male bravado on display.

A walk up the stairs revealed an enormous open room with tall ceilings and giant windows on every wall, streaming sunlight in every direction.

The space was a gallery of works in progress. Fabric canvases with wet paint on the floor, drawings on parchment tacked to the walls, and a few large pieces of wood, some with painting, some with none, leaned up against the wall. Peggy was immediately drawn to one in particular, standing between two windows overlooking the park.

The painting on what looked to be a piece of wooden crate was of the fountain and small indiscernible colored dots of people.

"You have an amazing view of the park," Peggy said with enthusiasm. "Is this one of the Sunday afternoons?"

"Yes," Gene said, barely smiling underneath the cloak of his serious artist face.

"Sometimes I watch the park from up here. It gives me a different perspective. You see there are lines and different shapes and sizes and colors of dots for the different people. I sometimes see dashes, sometimes solid, all making up the landscape of the assembly," he explained with introspection.

"Outta this world," Peggy admired. "Will you paint me like that?"

He nodded stonefaced in agreement, placing her on a seat in front of the window, where the sunlight would hit her orange-red hair.

"No. Your beauty would outshine any other backdrop. You must only be shown with nature to complement it." He touched her face as he looked longingly into her eyes. Peggy swooned and smiled.

"Hold that look," he said and ran to his easel and began furiously drawing.

Liam watched their exchange with slight disappointment. While he was curious about a fellow artist, Gene's interest in Peggy was his only concern. But it was clear, they had forgotten his existence.

He wandered around the loft, silently pondering Gene's art and motives. The work was so sporadic, almost schizophrenic, but Liam recognized the vision was good and the talent was exceptional.

Although he would never usurp another artist's work, he quickly glanced at Gene's preliminary sketches of Peggy. It was a drawing of her in a field of flowers with a natural, ethereal movement. He paused and gasped inside as he viewed her through Gene's eyes, seeing her in a new light.

Then he looked at Peggy posing without pretension and glowing from the attention, realizing the inherent connection between the two of them. He recognized the invisible tether between an artist and his subject, and his objection diminished.

He feared whatever he felt for her, Peggy would always consider him a best friend or a brother, nothing else.

Two hours later, they went back to the house and Peggy's head was in the stars.

"Isn't Gene's art interesting? I've never seen anyone so versatile. I'm can't wait to go back and finish the painting tomorrow," she said.

Liam was silently, reticently, nodding in solemn agreement.

The next day after work, Peggy went back to the loft alone. Gene was anxious to continue painting while the muse was upon him. He asked her to wear something that looked natural, so she wore a white macrame flowy cotton sundress she got at Diggers under her denim jacket. It had been growing colder as the sunny September summer bonus traded in for an autumn breeze.

When she entered the open door, she stopped as she saw him standing in front of the window, completely nude. She was startled, but her heart jolted and skipped a beat. She was immediately attracted to the descending sunlight accenting his golden skin and light hair on his chest.

As soon as he saw her, he ran over smiling and swept her into the room with his arm over her back, making her whole body tingle.

"My beautiful emerald, you pale goddesses." He grinned and escorted her to the chair in front of the window.

"Is this dress OK?" she asked, removing her jacket.

He stopped and gasped.

"It's perfect. You're perfect. I must begin." He scrambled over to his easel and picked up his paints.

Bathing in the warm rays that beamed through the window, Peggy watched Gene work, fantasizing about him.

She watched his sandy curls fall across his face as his head tilted up and down, looking over the canvas.

Studying the contours of his chest, legs, and arms with the hair precisely combed into light patterns made her feel a fire burning in her chair.

It was that electric feeling she had had before, a magnetic prurient urge that left her longing. And when he stared at her for long periods of time, she pictured herself jumping into his arms. The longer she sat there, the geyser inside her began to make her bubble up as though she would burst.

"When can I see it?" Peggy asked, flirting.

He was in the zone of his work and barely acknowledged her question. "Not done."

She began to feel antsy, constantly shifting in her chair and bewitchingly making faces. At first he ignored them, but as she continued, it made him smile.

"All right, you win. We'll take a break," he said. "I have wine, cheese, and grapes." He walked over to a small table with adjacent refrigerator and hot plate.

Peggy took a few grapes and seductively put them in her mouth, one at a time.

Sipping her wine slowly, Peggy slinked around the room, luring him to follow her. Softly touching his artwork, following the sleek edges of the canvas with her hands, she asked him questions.

"I love your sense of passion in your work. In this one, I can see every emotion pouring through." She licked the wine from her lips and took another sip.

Gene followed her like a puppy dog on a leash, pressing up against her back each time she stopped to see his work.

She was pushing every button at once. She wanted him and was not going to relinquish her hold until her thirst was quenched.

"I was wondering, would the painting be more natural like… this?" she asked, untying her shoulder straps. Her dress fell to the floor, exposing her body with an aura of golden sunset rays shining around her.

Unbridled, in one move, he lifted her up into his arms and gently laid her on the floor under him, kissing her shoulders and caressing her body.

With her throbbing fully released, she pulled him atop her milky skin, grabbing his long sandy hair and kissed him passionately.

As he e rolled over so she was straddling his body, their lips remained locked.

Heaving and breathless, they spun around the loft floor trading positions until they rolled onto his wet canvases lying on the ground.

Still captivated in their embrace, they ignored the wet greasy paint, making love over and over again until the singular glow of a street lamp shone through the window on their limp exhausted bodies.

After catching their breath, Peggy laughed at their nakedness, completely covered from head to toe in multicolored paint.

"Look, we're a human portrait in living color."

"That's an incredible idea," he said, jumping to his feet and pulling her up to stand in front of his easel.

He put the canvas he was working on down, replacing it with a loose fresh canvas, tacked to the top of his easel.

"Don't move," he said.

With globs of wet and drying paint all over her skin, face, and hair, she felt like an abstract painting come alive. But she didn't move.

Slowly he directed her to shift her leg one way or her arm another way until he molded her in the exact position of his inspiration.

As the paint dried like concrete, the zeal in her body dwindled and reality began to set in.

Suddenly, instead of the warm pools of hazel eyes, she saw a manic genius totally devoted to his work. Even with his formerly light brown locks dripping paint onto his face, arms, and chest, he was wholly entranced in his art, without regard for anything.

Her fatigue increased to a pinnacle and she slowly slumped into a rainbow pool on the floor. Despite the intoxicating physical connection, the thrill receded.

"I'm really tired. Can we continue this another time?" she asked in desperation.

His confused look at her sealed her thoughts. Even unbridled passion can't make up for obsession in the light of day. She knew it was the end of the road.

Borrowing a paint-covered kaftan to cover her body, she threw on her jacket and with her white dress in a bag, slunk out of the loft without looking back.

She returned home, thankfully, without encountering her roommates. After a long shower, she was able to remove most of the paint from her pale skin. She wrapped herself in a towel and plopped on her bed, taking out her journal.

Dear Maggie,

Men continue to be a mystery to me, but I'm having a wonderful time exploring and searching for an answer.

I've given into lust and passion, reaching into the recesses of my sexuality with gratifying success physically, but emotionally, my needle hasn't moved.

Freely giving your carnal self to another has been enlightening, but I'm starting to wonder if that's all there is. Each time I feel satisfied, yet once the reverberation of the experience finishes, I'm empty and drained like someone who glutted a feast and wants no more food until the hunger aches again.

I love the freedom, but am beginning to suspect lust is a fleeting façade. Maybe what's left is what I still hunger for. Do I want love? A relationship? I don't know what that is or where to find it.

SUMMER OF LOVE

At the paper a few days later, Peggy was helping Maxi research a series of articles about black voting rights protests in the South after trials of voter suppression from unpassable literacy tests, scare tactics, and death threats. Five months earlier the famous march from Selma to Montgomery where 2,000 black and white people marched for four days and nights to the capitol building in Alabama to demand voting rights legislation gained notoriety and some change. But as the fight continued, The Other editor wanted to explore the aftermath and coming battle by bringing an outside activist to shed light on the problem and solutions.

"Peggy, Maxi, this is Tara, she's a reporter from Alabama and is here to give us some testimony from what she experienced during the marches in the South," Ken, the editor said.

Tara was a beautiful, tall, and thin black woman with creamy chocolate-colored skin and a towering Afro.

Peggy couldn't help but look at her determined, chiseled face and stolid dark brown eyes as she listened to her harrowing journey.

"On the first day, Sunday, we all gathered at the church in Selma with one purpose in mind, to demand our God-given right to vote. But it quickly degraded. I was stunned as the police surrounded us, dressed in army helmets and gas masks that made them look like aliens, brandishing nightsticks and wielding them with complete disregard. They moved their horses into the crowd, aiming to trample people in the way. I saw one person after another fall to the ground, having no way to defend themselves. Then the teargas billowed in the air, choking me and blinding my eyes. I felt my legs fall out from below me and I tumbled to the ground. I heard a gunshot, and that's the last thing I remember."

Maxi, Peggy, and everyone else in the newspaper office listened without making a sound, riveted to what she was saying.

"When I woke up, I heard that young Johnny had been shot for trying to protect his mother from a horse, and several of the others were taken to the hospital because of beatings. Dr. King told us that we must not be assuaged from our mission or deterred, for we were on the side of right. Then he gathered every able person in front of the church and we marched for four days until we reach Montgomery. There, he spoke on the steps of the capitol, demanding that the state legislature codify what God has already provided—that all are created equal in his eyes. He stared out at the crowd and proudly said it was the greatest witness of freedom ever seen on the steps of the capital in Montgomery."

Peggy was stunned writing her words in shorthand to ensure she captured every syllable.

When Tara was finished, the entire room went silent for a few moments until Maxi stood up and clapped slowly at first, then others joined her until it reached a crescendo.

"You are an amazing person, Tara, and I really appreciate your telling your story," Maxi said. She offered Tara their couch at the house and their hospitality.

Rejuvenated, the others went back to work while Maxi and Tara sifted through her photographs to illustrate and outline their article together.

Peggy quickly went to her typewriter, typing all Tara's words as if they were the gospel. Tears gathered in her eyes, and she felt every expression flow through her fingers right up to her heart. Tara's account was horrifying and sad.

At the dinner table that night, Tara was engaging. She was a natural storyteller able to spin a yarn of homemade folktales about growing up in the South, as well as with the intricacies of her encounters and resistance for change.

"This is just like communism," Ravyn said. "I left Russia so my life would not be dictated by the men in power. Everyone has a right to live their own life as they see fit, without anyone saying or doing otherwise."

Peggy watched in amazement as Maxi, Ravyn, and Tara discussed all manners of oppression and revolution.

They spoke with such conviction, with certainty that their cause was true and right. Peggy appreciated and envied them for their complete passion and commitment without restriction or reservation. In contrast with her friends in Chicago, who were equally committed to their own personal happiness, her New York friends seemed to be on the right path for making a change for everyone, not just satisfying themselves.

But Peggy also noted Liam's complete attraction to Tara. His eyes were glued on her with an attentiveness she'd never seen from him.

He sat for nearly an hour without his typical glib comment or joke, entranced by her strong aura.

She watched, amused by his crush. Although Liam got along well with a lot of women and was a complete flirt, he rarely went home with anyone and she never saw him so intensely bewitched before. And he continued gazing at her all night, speechless.

After everyone cleaned up, they sat on the floor. Peggy played guitar, singing marches and folk songs, until the candles ran low and the wine jug was empty.

Everyone went to bed and Peggy lay awake, thinking about Tara, juxtaposing her experience and devotion to her cause with her own life. She wondered if her pursuits of the flesh had interfered with her music and chastised herself for not concentrating on her work. Maybe Gene was right—you have to devote everything to your muse.

She decided to swear a vow of chastity until she wrote and performed more poignant songs to express her feelings about the world around her.

For the next weeks, she spent the hours each day between work and the clubs with her nose to the grindstone, even staying home some nights while everyone else went to listen to new performers.

Late one night she lay in her room, picking her guitar and humming lyrics, until her grumbling stomach interrupted her. She was so focused on her work she had forgotten to eat. Thinking she was alone in the house, she went downstairs to get some food for her roaring stomach, when suddenly she heard sounds and voices coming from below.

Curiously, she listened at the closed door to the basement and heard some laughter amid groans and soft voices. She recognized Liam and Tara were in the basement making love.

She smiled and quietly giggled, immediately moving from the door to respect their privacy, and took some food back up to her room.

Between munching and writing, thoughts of what she had overheard kept recurring in her brain. She wasn't surprised, given Liam's obvious desire for Tara and their inept covert attempts to hide their flirting. Peggy saw a few glances and touches here and there that eventually grew into handholding and quick pecks on the cheek. But she didn't know their relationship had progressed.

At first the feelings of gladness that her friend had found someone warmed her heart, but overnight, a feeling of loss and loneliness entered her subconscious.

What did this mean for her friendship with Liam? He'd always been her right-hand man. If he was in a devoted relationship, would she take a backseat? Could they still be close friends? She was upset at herself for her selfishness, but equally saddened.

Sitting at the breakfast table the next morning, Peggy now saw the little hints were now bullhorns as the two openly embraced in the kitchen and kissed at the table in front of everyone. It was no longer a secret; they were a couple.

Peggy watched, uncomfortable at both her feelings of emptiness and ashamed for her thoughts of jealousy of Tara.

All day at the paper, she found herself glaring at Tara and then admonishing herself for her behavior. But she kept it inside. No one knew.

That night, when she was home alone, she wrote of her confusion to Maggie.

Dear Maggie,

I am embarrassed by my own thoughts. How could I listen and type the words of this woman whom I consider a champion and hero and then secretly scorn her for occupying my best friend? What's wrong with me?

Am I someone who is never to be satisfied? Do I always want what I don't have and then get rid of it? Since coming to New York, I've gone through men like a revolving door, but the constant in my life has been Liam. He has been my friend, my confidant, and the first person I want to tell anything to.

I don't know where I'm going or what I want. I need to focus.

The next day it was time to visit Granda Liam. Peggy, Liam, and Tara took the subway to Central Park West. Since Liam moved in with Peggy, they kept their word to visit Granda every week.

Peggy enjoyed getting to know Granda and his delicious sense of humor. She knew now that he didn't think she was Maggie. He was sweet and quick with wit, but he also was giving of his life wisdom, never scolding or dictating, but freely sharing his thoughts.

When they arrived, Liam introduced Tara to his grandfather, and then they left the room to tour the apartment, leaving Peggy and Granda alone.

"Don't worry, my lass. She is just a steppingstone on his path and soon you will both find yourself walking the road together."

"No, Granda, Liam and I are best friends; we're not interested in each other. I'm happy for him," Peggy assured.

He smirked at her with glowing eyes. "Trust me, you'll find yourself on that road together, and my mother and Maggie will be looking down on both of you with pride. Mark my words, we'll see emerald blood combine with a new babe in that nursery."

Peggy kissed him on the forehead, shaking her head no, but he smiled at her with a knowing grin.

When they were done with that visit, Liam wanted to take Tara horseback riding in Central Park. It was a beautiful day, but Peggy opted to sit in the grass with her notebook and wait alone.

As she sat in her favorite place, she ignored all around her as Granda's words echoed in her mind. She considered him a wise man with a lifetime of experience, but she couldn't understand why he mistook their friendship for something else.

Then her confusion turned to stubborn opposition, thinking maybe in his time women and men couldn't be friends. She treasured her friendship with Liam. And from the moment they met, she knew there was something about him, and that grew to a lasting friendship.

When she heard her name and saw Liam and Tara riding their horses on the path waving to her, she looked up and waved back. Liam looked so happy and content, leaving a sinking feeling that hit her in the gut and ran up her spine. What if Granda was right? What if they were supposed to be more than friends?

Chapter Eleven

Peace

Tara's few weeks on their couch turned into a more permanent residency with Liam in the basement, leaving a miserable Peggy in a constant state of confusion, embarrassment, and jealousy, all at the same time. But she never let anyone know of her inner turmoil.

Day after day, she watched Liam with Tara, wondering if Granda was right and then immediately dismissing his opinion. She was determined that she and Liam would remain as friends.

Luckily, she was busy at the paper, helping Maxi, Ravyn, and Tara plan a demonstration to mark the six-month anniversary of the Selma march, to raise visibility of the plight of voter suppression in the South.

As they planned the protest, Peggy's nerves and excitement peaked for the huge demonstration. Maxi and Ravyn had opened her eyes to a world of activism for ongoing societal problems that plagued everyday existence. But as involved she was in planning every aspect, she was still unsure of what to expect.

In the biggest city in the country, it was fairly difficult at any given time to stage an organized march, so they opted to take a stand in Central Park, where many could assemble in peace. On the day, Peggy could hardly believe it as she scanned the vast audience of people filling the grassy park area shoulder-to-shoulder.

Tara spoke first and eloquently stated the institutional peril for black people in the South. Providing personal anecdotes, she painted a clear picture of what was really going on, and she both enlightened and appalled those in attendance.

After a few other activists took their turn, some popular Greenwich Village musicians and the people in the crowd huddled in the crisp October air on a sunny Saturday and chanted, sang, and played harmonious sounds of freedom and righteous change.

Peggy's thoughts surged from excitement and thrill to communion and satisfaction as she listened to the speakers and experienced a truly transformational human moment that she helped occur.

As the last speaker of the day climbed up on the top of a fountain, he began sculpting an exciting narrative with his words, centering on freedom and change and each individual's personal responsibility to be a mechanism for the future.

Peggy was frozen, captivated by his forceful oration and enticed by his radiant vibes.

Jesse was a writer for a large New York underground newspaper. As he spoke, Peggy began to fantasize, watching his mouth craft a beautiful word salad, so smooth they were like icing on a cake.

She began to feel familiar tingles and started rethinking her sexual sabbatical. Given her mixed emotions about her friendship with Liam, she even reasoned that she needed another encounter to clarify her feelings. And her undeniable attraction to the intelligent and expressive Jesse was the perfect remedy.

He had gorgeous long black hair tied in two ponytails wrapped in colorful beaded braids. His manicured beard was not too long, but just enough to be a respectable hippie. The beard was an attractive lure. She wondered what it would be like to kiss a man with a mustache and beard. Would it tickle?

At a certain point, his words faded to the background as she daydreamed. Without warning, she was awakened from her trance by loud whistles. She looked around and saw the police were attempting to disperse the crowd with their horses, shouting as the chaotic assembly ran in all directions.

Remembering in horror Tara's stories about the horses trampling protesters in Selma, Peggy urgently hunted for Liam. She saw him and Tara running over the green to the other side of the park. Then she noticed Jesse, still shouting for peace and calm standing on the ledge of the fountain. Without a thought, she ran to him, grabbed his arm, and fled as fast as she could with him in tow to the safety of the bridge where she and Liam had first met.

In a hidden area under the bridge, they huddled together out of sight.

"Thank you for helping me. I'm Jesse," he whispered. Their faces were so close that barely any air passed between them.

"I'm Peggy Mac," she said without thinking.

Their glance lingered as they tucked further into a large cubbyhole on the underside of the bridge, squeezing closer together to keep out of sight.

Eventually, hearing no sound, they emerged to see the sun setting peacefully on the horizon.

"Wow, isn't it incredible that it only takes a beautiful sunset to restore peace and balance in the world," Jesse remarked in wonderment.

Staring up at the gorgeous colors combining together, Peggy paused. "Wouldn't it be nice if people of all colors could exist in harmony and create a stunning picture like that?"

"Wow, that's really profound. Are you a writer, Peggy Mac?" he asked.

"No. I'm a musician and I write some songs," she answered.

"With lyrics like that, I have no doubt your words will be on everyone's lips in no time," he smiled at her. "Can I walk you home? Since you saved me from a jail cell today, that's the least I can do."

"I'm all the way in the East Village," Peggy said, pointing in the direction of home.

"I love the East Village," he said. He gently took her hand and walked forward alongside her, which elevated her already tingling body.

They talked about music, poetry, art, and trouble in the world. Just like his speech at the protest, she was drawn to his intellect and devotion relieving the pain of others.

He was a good listener; she told him about her music and ambitions for the future.

Jumping on the subway in the late evening, the train was still crammed with people, and they found themselves face to face and body against body once again. Hypnotized by his intense brown eyes and long black eyelashes, she faltered once, when they went over a bumpy track, and he put his arm around her to steady her. Peggy felt her tingles overdrive into flaming sparks.

To see if he felt the same way, she deliberately pressed against him. He moved his arm over the subway pole and around her, so they were instantly locked in an embrace.

By the time they reached her stop, the familiar static electricity surged through her whole body.

"Can I show you something?" she asked his nodding head as she took his hand and led him to the solitude of nighttime Washington Square.

As they walked in the dense darkness, they saw fewer and fewer people as they reached the archway entrance.

Standing at the foot of the arch, she pulled him close to her so their bodies were pushed together and sweetly whispered in his ear. "This is my favorite place in the park. It marks the past, present, and future standing the test of what has been, and what can be. To me it's a monument to hope and an entrance to a new tomorrow."

Enthralled by her words and enticed by her wanting lips, Jesse leaned down and kissed her.

Thrilled, Peggy kissed him back in response and locked her arms behind him, leaning back against the arch.

His kiss was strong yet gentle and his arms were warm and soothing, just like his words.

As their kiss began to intensify, a sprinkle began and shortly escalated, becoming a steady gentle rain.

Briefly releasing their kiss, they once again squeezed together arm in arm under the protection of the archway.

In the coolness of the late October night air, he wrapped his coat around her and she pressed him against the pillar. Their bodies softly entangled interlacing into one. Their heaving breath blew puffs into the air above them as they grasped each other, clinging in unbridled passion.

By the end they were soaked to the skin and gleefully ran hand in hand to her home for shelter.

But when she came through the door, the reception was much colder than the outside weather.

"Where have you been? We were worried sick about you!" Liam shouted with ire.

"Peggy, we didn't know if you were in jail or hurt in the hospital. You can't just disappear like that," Maxi scolded.

Peggy was in shock. She went from the heights of amorous satisfaction to shame in only a few minutes.

"Sorry, I didn't think about it. We huddled under the bridge in Central Park to stay away from the police and when we came out, everyone was gone, so we came home and got caught in the rain," she said innocently with a smile that hinted a note of afterglow.

"Da. Get out of wet things and I will make coffee," Ravyn said, walking into the kitchen.

"Liam, can Jesse borrow something dry?" Peggy asked.

"Sure," Liam said, annoyed. He stomped down the basement stairs and soon emerged with some pants and a shirt. He handed them to Jesse, frowning at Peggy.

"You can stay here tonight," she told Jesse, glaring at Liam. "Your things will be dry in the morning."

"I better call my paper and let them know they don't need to bail me out," Jesse said. Maxi showed him to the hallway phone.

When he was gone, Ravyn made curious eye contact with Peggy, as if telepathically asking her what had happened on with the handsome rebel.

For the next hour, they all ate sandwiches, drank coffee, and exchanged stories about fleeing the police.

Based on Maxi's information, no one was badly hurt. The few people who were arrested were immediately released with an intervention by Jesse's newspaper. The crowd dispersed easily and the police were satisfied with just scaring a few people.

Peggy increasingly noticed that throughout the last hour, Liam's dissatisfied glances never abated.

She was fine. She didn't understand why he was upset.

As they adjourned to the living room, Jesse sat on the floor, openly placing his head in Peggy's lap. Then Liam abruptly grabbed Tara's hand and pulled her toward the basement door.

"Let's go to bed; it's been a long day." He glanced at Peggy, with a little disdain still in his voice.

Maxi and Ravyn stood stunned and puzzled by the tension hanging in the room.

"Good idea. Come on, Jesse." Peggy lifted his head and got up in one motion, pulling his arm. "See you all in the morning," she said in defiance, leading Jesse up the stairs.

As they lounged in her bed exhausted from the day's events, Jesse fell fast asleep, but Peggy could not get Liam's attitude out of her head. She grabbed her journal.

Dear Maggie,

I am so upset. I understand maybe I should've come right back from the protest and I appreciate his concern for me, but what's Liam's problem? I'm fine. I came back. It couldn't be Jesse. He's with Tara, after all.

Could he be jealous? Maybe Granda knew something. Did Liam confide in him that he has feelings for me? I don't understand. Can best friends become more? Should we?

Finally fatigue took her over and she was able to fall asleep, despite the burgeoning questions in her mind.

The next morning, after only a few hours of sleep, she woke from an early morning kiss from Jesse, who was already dressed and ready to leave.

"Sorry, kid, but I've got work to do and a story to write. Thanks for the night and the save. Can I see you soon?" he asked.

Peggy looked at him with gentle eyes. "The evening was great, Jesse, but I have a few things to work out. Let's just call it a magical encounter."

He shrugged, held up a peace sign, and quietly left.

She fell back to sleep, awakening a few hours later. It was Sunday, but soon the dry morning turned into a rainy day, postponing any hootenanny in the park that week.

Hours later, Peggy went downstairs and passed the basement door, where she overheard an argument between Tara and Liam.

"I must go to Chicago. They're planning more protests there and I can join Dr. King's disciples. We can get the word out," Tara earnestly explained.

"This is New York—there's no better place to do that," he debated.

"You know I must continue my work," she said solemnly.

Hearing Tara begin to walk up the basement stairs, Peggy quickly hurried into the kitchen to get out of sight. Soon after, she heard the front door open and close. Tara was gone.

Liam entered the kitchen and looked surprised to see Peggy.

Not letting on that she knew about Tara, Peggy handed him a cup of coffee with a caring glance.

"Are we good?"

Liam returned her look with kind eyes, took the cup of coffee, and nodded.

The next couple of weeks, everything was back to normal. The group frequented clubs where Ravyn, Peggy, and Liam all performed.

Peggy became more comfortable and relaxed on stage. She debuted new music she pieced together, merging Irish folk melodies with her lyrics about love and life, addressing many of the questions she expressed to Maggie in her journal. The club crowd called her the Irish songbird.

Liam was growing more confident in his own art—painting more, writing more poetry, and performing with Peggy in accompaniment. The four musketeers were simpatico once again.

Chapter Twelve

Blackout

On one Tuesday afternoon, Peggy came home early from work carrying pints of vanilla and chocolate ice cream to a house filled with the smell of Guinness stew. She found Liam in the kitchen listening to music.

"Happy birthday, Piggy," he said and kissed her on the cheek. "I'm making your favorite, Guinness stew."

She smiled at him with appreciation and quickly opened the freezer to put the ice cream in.

"Oh, no, there's so much ice in here, there's no space. It looks like we need to defrost." She sighed and closed the door.

"Why don't you put it out the back door? November brought Jack Frost early. It's cold enough to keep it nice and cool," he said.

"Good idea. Maxi's bringing the cake and Ravyn's getting the candles, so looks like we've got everything taken care of." She opened the door, put the ice cream outside and quickly closed it.

"Brrr, it's horribly cold. I guess winter is here to stay." She returned to the kitchen, inhaling the savory aroma.

"You're really getting good at that stew," she said, taking a piece of bread and dipping into the pot.

"Hey, no sneak peeks," Liam laughed, gently coaxing her away from the pot. "I hate to admit it, but Kieran's recipe is the best. Don't tell my mother's cook that though."

Suddenly, the song on the radio began to slow down, making a sound like a drunk singer.

"Is the record player broken or on the wrong speed?" Peggy asked.

Liam looked at her curiously and walked toward the Hi-Fi cabinet. "No, it's the radio. What could be wrong with that?" he questioned.

As the song got slower and slower, they both stared at the radio. Then the lights flickered and a few minutes later, everything went off at the same time.

"Oh, it must be a fuse. I'll go down to the basement and fix it," Liam said, feeling his way in the dark along the wall to the door.

Peggy looked out the window. "Everything's dark—the neighbors, the street, nothing's on."

"Typical New York blackout." He laughed. "This is your first one, right?"

"What do you mean first? This happens a lot here?" Peggy asked with a touch of concern in her voice.

"Not a lot, but it does happen. No problem—you're with a native New Yorker. First thing we need to do is find the candles and flashlights. Then we'll build a fire in the fireplace, so we don't freeze to death," Liam said calmly, taking candles out of the drawer.

"But what about the girls? How are they going to get home?" Peggy said, concerned, fumbling around for matches in another drawer. "The phones should still work. Should I call the paper?"

"Don't be concerned, Piggy. They're New Yorkers. They know what to do. You stay wherever you are with whomever you're with. None of the buses, trains, or subways run in the pitch dark and without electricity. And it's not very safe to walk, unless you're close to home. It'll be fine—I'll just get everything comfy and cozy and they'll make their way back when they can."

Liam placed candles around the kitchen and living room while Peggy trailed him, lighting them.

Liam continued. "We can't open the refrigerator or we may lose everything in it, but we're lucky we have a pot of stew, loaf of bread, jug of wine, and ice cream on the back porch. We're set." He lit a fire in the fireplace.

Peggy sat down where she was, still taken aback by Liam's ease of moving in the dark. He took the bowls from the already set table and filled them with stew. Then he skillfully brought the full bowls back to the table, without spilling a drop.

"Come on, Piggy—luckily everything's at the table already. Let's eat while it's hot. There's nothing else we can do but hunker down and wait."

They ate the stew and broke the bread with their hands, both hesitant to use a knife in the dark, and drank several glasses of wine, toasting her 20th birthday.

"It's hard to believe I've been here for more than a year. It seems like so much has happened to change my life and it's all because of you," she said, raising her glass to Liam.

He clinked his glass with hers. "I may have started you on the road, Piggy, but you took off from there. I've watched you grow with pleasure, but I'll take a little credit."

"You made enough stew for an army. Should we put it in the oven? It may stay hot or at least it won't spoil."

"Good thinking," he complimented her and worked his way over to the pot, putting it inside the stove, and then gracefully walked back to the table.

"How are you so comfortable in the dark?" she asked.

Liam laughed. "When you live with your parents and grandfather, you learn to move stealthily in obscurity without making a sound. If I didn't sneak out, I would've never had any life as a teenager. I came up the servants' stairs in the back and sneaked in through the kitchen. My mother's housekeeper and cook, Mrs. Moynihan, was a deep sleeper and she snored like a freight train. But the trick was getting past everyone's rooms to my room. Granda is a light sleeper. Sometimes I'd sleep in the library and slip into through the kitchen early, pretending to be an early bird. I even stowed some pajamas, a robe, and slippers in a chest in the library under some old blankets. They were none the wiser."

"Great, you can lead me. I'm not as good moving around in the dark, even with candlelight. And if you can get to the back door, we can have ice cream."

"Consider it done, milady." He bowed and moved through the hallway into the shadow less night by the back door.

Hearing a dull thud, Peggy yelled out concerned. "Liam, are you OK?"

"Yes," he said from the darkness. "I bet I'll get a big bruise from knocking into the door. I guess I'm just out of practice."

Shortly he returned with the ice cream. "We'll have to eat out of the containers. Can you grab the stew spoons from the table?" Liam asked.

"Ok. I guess we can lick the stew off to get them clean," she said, carefully walking to the table to get the spoons and then back into the living room.

Sitting side by side on the couch, they playfully dipped their spoons, eating out of each other's container.

"Better eat it all. I'm not going back out to the back door," he laughed.

"If we don't, it'll melt," she agreed.

Once their stomachs were full and the ice cream containers were empty, they sat bloated, lying on the couch.

Peggy looked at her watch. "It's already 8 o'clock. Shouldn't they be home by now? Maybe I should call."

"Go ahead and take a candle," he advised.

Piggy slowly made her way to the hallway via her lone candle, groping her way along the wall to reach the hallway phone and dial the newspaper office.

"Hello, this is Peggy. Are Maxi and Ravyn still there? Oh, OK, thank you. Stay safe!" she said and hung up the phone. Then she made another quick call to her parents and retraced her steps into the living room.

"Liam, they both left early. Maxi was supposed to pick up my cake and Ravyn was headed to pick up candles. They could've been safe at the paper if it weren't for me," she said, worried.

He put his arm around her and pulled her close to him. "You didn't cause the blackout, besides, they know what to do. Don't worry about them. Everyone's safe; I'm sure of it," he said, comforting her as she held onto him and started to shiver a bit.

"Are you cold? We can go by the fire and huddle under a blanket," he said.

Peggy sighed and moved to the fireplace. Liam grabbed the wine and glasses and sat next to her, draping an old wool Indian blanket around them both. "We might as well drink the rest of the wine. No one else will." He filled up their glasses.

To put her at ease, Liam started to softly sing one of her Irish folk tunes.

As soon as he began, she laughed a little, distracted and relieved by the clumsy and sour tone of his voice.

"Please don't sing," she joked. "We don't wanna attract any wild animals."

"Then you sing," he laughed.

"I don't have my guitar. It's upstairs," she objected.

"Piggy Mac. You make beautiful music with or without a guitar."

Peggy sang one tune after another, her voice matching the beat in her mind. As she sang, Liam stared at her adoringly, unconsciously pulling her closer to him.

Sparked by the firelight reflecting in his sapphire eyes with his heaving chest pressing against hers, she suddenly felt something unexpected. She saw him in a different way than she ever had before.

"By the way, who else did you call?" he asked.

"I called my parents in Chicago to let them know I was ok. They may have heard about the blackout on the news and I didn't want them to lose sleep," she explained.

"Didn't you tell me they fell in love in New York during the war?" Liam asked.

She smiled and sighed, thinking of the stories they told her of their whirlwind wartime romance.

"The whole thing was like an old movie. Boy's and girl's eyes meet serendipitously in a USO club. They fall in love. He goes to war. Then just when you think all is lost, he sweeps her off her feet, marries her, and they have a baby. The end," she said fondly.

"That sounds sweet, but I think you missed a lot of the good stuff in between," he laughed.

"Yes, but it's always been the grand love affair that no one could ever live up to," she sighed.

He gazed into her eyes and said, "Call me a hopeless romantic, but I believe in all-consuming, all-encompassing, everlasting love."

She gently moved his wispy blond hair out of his eyes. At that moment, he slowly leaned in and kissed her.

Although the kiss surprised her, she instantly found herself fading into it. Their mouths fit together so well and his kiss was gentle and warm.

She felt a tingle and then just as she started to get lost in the sensation; he pulled away.

"That was a surprise." She smiled.

He looked at her, uncertain. "Was it a good surprise?" he asked, waiting for her response.

She smiled back at him, held her hands on either side of his face and hard-pressed her lips against his. The tingles instantly changed to rockets until he gasped for air and she released him.

"Peggy, you've been dating too many insatiable artists. Let's try this slow and easy. I want to enjoy every taste," he grinned.

From that moment, she let him take the lead. He slowly kissed her neck, whispered in her ear, and gave her lingering kisses down to her chest, igniting a burning fire that consumed her all over.

She sighed heavily, holding her breath with each touch.

He moved his hands all around, gradually kissing and caressing each part of her body, while she gripped his leg in anticipation. As the fire within her began to rage, she could take no more.

She threw off the blanket and ripped open his shirt, pushing him to the floor. When she was on top of him, she whisked off her dress and unbuttoned his trousers. He smiled.

"OK, I'm putty in your hands," he said and gently touched her from her navel to her lips, pulling himself closer, deliciously covering her mouth with deep wet kisses. She wrapped her legs around him until they were completely entangled like a rope with every part of each of their bodies touching the other.

It was like nothing she had ever felt before. Instead of a quick jolt of lightning that surged throughout her body and then left, she felt as if every nerve ending had been plugged in at the same time, lighting up everything in her body at once.

Their bodies were moving as one, flowing into each other with slow burning warmth and fulfilling comfort, giving her an ease of ecstasy she had never thought possible.

He then gently turned her body against the floor, pressing against her, making pure and true love to her again.

By the warm firelight, they made love over and over again all night, until at dawn they fell asleep in each other's arms.

SUMMER OF LOVE

Hours later, Ravyn and Maxi unknowingly walked into the front door and saw Peggy and Liam lying next to the fireplace asleep under the Indian blanket and glanced at each other, smiling.

"What's going on here?" Maxi asked with a shocked sly grin.

"I knew they would," Ravyn said, barely paying attention. "What food do we have?"

Standing over them, Maxi shook them awake.

Slowly opening their eyes, Liam and Peggy looked at each other, smiled, and kissed. They were happy and there was nothing to be ashamed of.

"Hi girls. Glad you made it back. If the stove is working now, you can heat up the stew, I guess. It may still be good from last night," Liam said and started to get up.

"DON'T get up. I'm still full, anyway. I ate a whole cake. No, a half of a cake... with the baker's son. We took turns." Maxi grinned with a Cheshire smile, hinting at her amorous activities.

"I'm starving. I worked up an appetite. I spent the night in a car with two wonderfully inventive men I met. Sorry—we used up all your birthday candles," Ravyn said, ravenously eating the cold stew right from the pot.

"That was lucky you had them for light," Liam said.

"Not for light. The bright full moon lit up the sky. Used them for sex. I still have some on me. I could scrape off," she said unapologetically.

Maxi, Liam, and Peggy just looked at her without surprise. How else would Ravyn spend a blackout?

"Sounds like we all had a good night," Peggy said, putting her dress over her head. She headed upstairs and took out her journal.

Dear Maggie,

This was the greatest night of my life. Liam and I finally consummated our friendship. I don't think I've ever been so happy. I've had men before and thoroughly enjoyed the experience, but this was transcendent. I never felt more spiritually or physically connected to another human being. We were like one person.

Maybe best friends make the best lovers—we know so much about each other, and it's so natural. It's like our friendship was the groundwork for building an amazing relationship and making love was the sweet icing on the cake.

I didn't think this kind of love could ever happen to me, but it did. Until now, I wasn't even sure I wanted that type of permanent relationship. But now I'm finally truly and completely in love with the most wonderful man in the world. I'm born anew and my life with him starts today.

It took nearly a full day for New Yorkers to get back to normal with full buses and trains resetting everyone to their destinations all day, resuming normal existence. Since Maxi and Peggy could walk to the paper, they arrived early with some sandwiches for the others who were there together all night. They joined them hard at work compiling news from the wire services.

SUMMER OF LOVE

The Associated Press wire explained that the blackout, which left 30 million people over 80,000 square miles without electricity, was caused by a faulty relay in the Adam Beck Station of Ontario, Canada.

"United Press estimates 800,000 people were stuck in subways. And the NYPD reports only five lootings," one editor said.

"Yeah, because they had blinding antiaircraft search lights and human walls of National Guard everywhere. I was on a bus when the blackout occurred and finally made it downtown late in the night and saw it myself," another explained.

The rest of the newspaper staff came in sporadically, all regaling each other with tales of interesting encounters over the 14 hours in darkness, many involving shared bodily warmth on the cool November day.

Besides comforting each other, some wires reported the many deeds of kindness some New Yorkers offered.

An AP account told of one man said he was stuck on the road and eventually ran out of gas with many others. But amazingly—people actually went around sharing food, water, blankets, coats, whatever they had with each other. "Quite frankly, I was surprised, but proud to be a New Yorker," the man said.

"This tops, that," Maxi said and read a United Press wire from another survivor. "I was lucky enough to get off the subway before it shut down, but I had a long way to walk. So this cab driver pulls up and offers free rides to me, and few other people pile in after. He doesn't know how long it's gonna take, but he wouldn't take any money. Can you imagine that?" A woman told the UP.

"This says the New York Times used a press in Newark last night to put out a special edition. They talked to people stuck in elevators, and a bunch of tourists lying in hotel lobbies. It was definitely a night to remember," another person in the office remarked.

"Good thing we still do everything manually. Hey, what if we put out a special edition called What did you do in the blackout? Everybody call everybody they know and get stories," the city editor Tom said.

Peggy and Maxi looked at each other and giggled. They weren't about to tell their blackout stories in the newspaper.

The next day, a poster was placed in the New York City subway...

Thanks, riders, for staying on your best behavior during the blackout. When the lights went out, you were at your brightest.

Chapter Thirteen

Family Roots

After the newspaper staff all pulled together to put the special issue to bed, Peggy and Maxi went home, beat.

The events of the last few days swirled around like a whirlwind, scrambling Peggy's brain. In the wake of another daylight, she began to doubt, unsure that her rendezvous with Liam was just a time and place thing or a forever event.

She walked in the door, not knowing what to expect on the other side and found Liam cooking up a storm.

"Welcome home, tired workers; I have sustenance and merriment for you," he said, pointing to the table set with bread, wine, meatloaf and chocolate cake. "We'll forgo the candles this time."

"He's getting to be a good wife," Maxi kidded, elbowing Peggy. "You'd better snap him up before somebody else does."

Liam smiled and overtly kissed Peggy on the cheek. "So, what's the verdict? Are you snapping me up?"

"What do you think?" Peggy grabbed and dipped Liam, kissing him like in a movie.

"I'm glad you finally got it, Piggy. I was waiting for you to see what was right under your nose." He laughed.

Peggy and Liam were a couple. While it could've been awkward, the friends and roommates pledged to seamlessly transition from four individuals to two women and a couple, without friction or drama.

Liam would keep his studio in the basement, but moved his clothing into Peggy's room, and they tried to keep their romantic exercises in the bedroom. Ravyn and Maxi had their own separate behind-closed-door activities too, so everyone respected each other's space.

A few days after the blackout, on their way to visit Granda, they saw their first glimpse of Manhattan. To their surprise, there was no damage at all. Central Park West and 5th Avenue were none the worse for wear from the blackout; everything was bustling and trudging along at its usual hectic pace.

As they exited the elevator into the hallway, Liam stopped Peggy short of the front door.

"If it's OK with you, I'd like to tell him about us," he said. Peggy smiled and nodded in agreement.

But when they arrived at the grand apartment, Mrs. Moynihan met them with a somber look.

"The viscount has been ill," Mrs. Moynihan told them, shaking her head. "Your parents are in Europe and during the blackout, it was just him and me. I thought he was asleep and since there was no power, I just stayed in my room. But the next morning when I brought him his breakfast tray, he didn't look right. The old dear groused a little and said there was nothing wrong, but I called the doctor," Mrs. Moynihan explained.

"What did the doctor say?" Liam anxiously asked.

Mrs. Moynihan lowered her eyes and shook her head again. "The doctor said he had a stroke the night of the blackout. It wasn't major, but the doctor said he was afraid there may have been long-term damage."

Liam dropped his head and sighed. "When are my parents expected back?"

"You know the mister and the missus—when they go to Europe visiting their fancy folk, they're gone for an unspecified amount of time, but they did say to expect them home for Christmas," she said in disapproving sarcasm and escorted Peggy and Liam into the library.

Opening the double Tiffany glass French doors, they saw Granda sitting in his chair with his favorite tartan blanket over him blankly drifting into space. Peggy and Liam immediately glanced at each with stunned white faces.

Granda appeared withdrawn and tired, as if the life were drained out of him. But he perked up when he saw Liam and Peggy, as a little spark lit in his eyes.

Although concerned, they pasted on happy faces, clasped hands, and approached him.

"Hi, Granda," Peggy said, planting a little kiss on his pale cheek.

"Granda, we have some excellent news," Liam said.

The old man cracked a smile on the side of his face and chuckled a little, laced with coughs. "I know, you're finally together. I'm glad, but it took you long enough. I didn't think I'd live to see it." He coughed out a few more chuckles and held Peggy's hands, smiling at her.

Peggy and Liam sat with Granda for a while, laughing and singing until some color and life returned in his face.

Cementing a happy grin on his concerned face, Liam interrupted, "May I borrow me beauty for a second, Granda?" he joked with a fake Irish brogue and grabbed her hand, pulling her into the main salon.

"That poor dear man. We must visit him much more to help him," she offered.

"Actually... I know this is ungodly bad timing, as we just got together, but I'm afraid to leave him while my parents aren't here. He needs family around him," Liam told Peggy with uncertainty, awaiting her response.

Peggy instinctively grasped his hand and kissed him. "Of course. I wouldn't love you as much if you didn't think of him," she said and then recoiled realizing... she had just told him she loved him for the first time.

Liam stared at her for a second, but to Peggy it seemed like forever. It was out there and she couldn't take it back. She said she loved him, but it was very soon and she didn't know if he felt the same way.

He smiled and heartily embraced her. "That's wonderful! I love you too. And I don't want to leave you, so would you come here and live with me?"

Peggy squeezed him harder. "Of course, I can't be apart from you."

Liam kissed her with full lips. "Thank you for understanding—we can get our things and move in right away."

"It's time for tea," Mrs. Moynihan interrupted, bringing in a tray with a teapot, cups, and a plate tower filled with scones and jelly sandwiches.

Liam and Peggy followed her into the library and announced they'd be moving in.

"Bless you, me boy." Granda's grateful dough-eyes and the relief on Mrs. Moynihan's face told them in an instant, they made the right decision.

As they had tea, Peggy was distracted. She was glad that he loved her—that was a big hurdle—but couldn't help contemplating what this big change meant for their lives.

It would be harder to go down to the Village and play in the clubs. And she still had her job at the newspaper. She would have to commute every day. And what about Jane's house? Should she just leave Maxi and Ravyn to live in her aunt's house alone? Jane trusted her to look after the house. Maybe she could switch off living in both places, but then could Liam leave his grandfather for some days or could she live without him for a couple days a week? Or she could just go by there and make sure the house was taken care of. There were too many questions… plus they had to break the news to Maxi and Ravyn.

As soon as they entered the door of Jane's row house, there was a telegram lying by the phone for Peggy. She looked down at it, turning ghostly for fear of what lay within. Telegrams were rarely ever good news. She learned that from her mother, when she told Peggy about her first few months of pregnancy waiting for a doomed telegram, when her father was missing. Finally three months before she was born, Red came back into the New York Harbour with his ragtag crew and half-sunken ship.

She decided to rip off the Band-Aid quickly and tear the telegram open. It was from Jane. Their show closed and they were coming home in one week.

Handing Liam the telegram, she was unsettled, but he grinned brightly. "This is great. Now we don't have to worry about maintaining two houses."

"But what about Maxi and Ravyn?" Peggy looked at him, confused.

"They can come with us or maybe Jane will let them rent rooms from her," he said.

After dinner, Liam and Peggy sat Ravyn and Maxi down and explained everything about Granda's condition and Jane's telegram.

"Wonderful house or grand mansion apartment in Manhattan? This is not a problem," Ravyn said bluntly. "We had twelve people in one small room in Russia."

"I'm sure Jane would let you stay for a little while until you found something, but we would only be at The Dakota until Liam's parents come back," Peggy said.

"Yes, there's no way we could survive, living with my parents. They're so square, the two make a rectangle." Liam laughed to relieve the heaviness in the air.

"To be honest, Ravyn, I think we need to leave family with family and start looking for another place. How would it look to my fellow anarchists if I lived in a swanky apartment in Manhattan?" Maxi awkwardly chuckled.

The four hugged together in a huddle, each realizing it was the end of an era.

A few days later, Liam and Peggy moved into The Dakota.

Peggy walked around the opulent apartment, as if she were a visitor in a time and place she didn't recognize.

All around her were fancy wood paneling, crystal chandeliers, oriental rugs, and damask draperies. To Peggy, it resembled a stuffy museum more than a home. And she would never get used to having servants, but Mrs. Moynihan kept shooing her out of the kitchen.

But an important silver lining outweighed her discomfort with her lavish surroundings. Everywhere she stepped she felt an ethereal warm presence, echoes of Maggie's spirit connecting with hers. Combined with a great feeling of love emanating from Liam and Granda, it gave her a peace she never experienced before.

Peggy remembered the fortuneteller's prediction of the welcoming and calming bond that would journey on her path with her. She thought the fortune was about Maggie, who was her spiritual guide on a vision quest of sorts, but now, she knew the fortuneteller meant it was Liam who would be along for the ride with her every step of the way.

In the next few weeks, Liam and Peggy spent many hours with Granda. They walked with him through the park. And Liam played chess with him daily. They even tried to teach Peggy to play by letting her assist each of them, like teaching a child to ride a bike with training wheels.

Mrs. Moynihan told Peggy, their company made all the difference.

"It's a miracle, it is. The viscount's demeanor has changed overnight with you two around. He has a twinkle I haven't seen in years. It's like you breathed life into his very soul."

Each day at tea, they listened intently as Granda told stories his mother had shared with him about Maggie and Caroline growing up in Ireland.

Peggy didn't know much about Caroline before, only what she had pieced together from Maggie's letters and the few newspaper clippings about her death. But the stories he told painted a picture in her mind's eye of the two as little moppets and girls prancing through the emerald fields playing together.

Listening about the friendship their great-grandmothers shared, Liam and Peggy held hands under the table and gazed at each other. Knowing how much their great-grandmothers had loved one another cemented a special bond no one could ever duplicate. To Peggy, it reinforced the fortuneteller's prediction. They were meant to be together.

"My mother said she and Maggie grew up like sisters. She always said it was the great regret of her life that she let Maggie go. She talked about her constantly and missed her until her dying day. In fact, on her deathbed, the last thing she said before she closed her eyes the final time was 'Maggie,'" Granda said with a heavy voice.

Tears streamed down Peggy's face and Liam kissed her cheek. They were family... not of the blood, but of the heart.

One day when she came home from her long commute, Peggy secretly watched Liam with Granda. He was so gentle and kind. She sighed, mooning over him. Every day he made her love him more.

"Hello to my favorite men," she sprang into the room, kissing Liam and giving Granda a peck on the cheek.

"Piggy, we have a wonderful surprise for you," Liam beamed.

He took her hand and brought her over to a table with a big wooden box, tarnished in varying hues of yellow and brown.

"We found this in an old trunk in storage, when we were looking for an old chessboard Granda's father brought over from Ireland," Liam said with enthusiastic anticipation.

He pulled off the top and revealed a vintage black and gold sewing machine.

He didn't even have to tell her. She knew immediately, it was Maggie's.

"Mother told me she bought this for Maggie as a reward for coming to America with her. Maggie loved it, as it saved her poor fingertips from turning purple from handsewing. When Maggie left without it, Mother said it would break her heart to let the sewing machine go," Granda explained.

Peggy ran her fingers along the curved top, admiring its elegance. Although it was ancient in comparison to modern sewing machines, it was a charming reminder of yesterday and Maggie that made it more valuable.

She kissed Granda on the cheek and gave him a hug, then ran into the bedroom. She couldn't wait to tell Maggie about it.

Dear Maggie,

I feel you all around me here at The Dakota. It gives me a sense of belonging in this strange place. Everything I touch, I feel your fingertips, and everywhere I walk, I feel your aura surrounding me like a favorite blanket. Liam tells me his room, our room, was once the nursery. I feel you the strongest there. Every night it's like you're tucking me in, just as you did with Granda.

With Liam, everywhere feels like home to me. I never expected to feel so completely loved. Now I know what my parents have been talking about for so many years.

And today Liam found your sewing machine. I'm so excited. I know how much this meant to you and I will treasure it always. I may even try to learn how to make Irish lace.

Time went by quickly and before they knew it, Christmas arrived.

Living in an Irish-American household with two Irish parents and Irish servants, Granda grew up with all Irish holiday traditions.

Peggy was excited to experience her first Irish Christmas and wanted to shower Granda with all the trimmings.

Although Red cherished his dual Irish and Scottish ancestry, Peggy's Christmases were usually American in nature, so she pestered Mrs. Moynihan to teach her every tradition.

"The mister and missus haven't done Christmas at home in years. They usually drag the poor viscount to some fancy socialite dinner party where he's miserable. It would be my pleasure to put on a right proper Irish Christmas for him," Mrs. Moynihan said with pride.

The week before Christmas, Liam's parents cabled to let them know they would be staying in Paris for Christmas. Peggy was anxious to meet them, but after Liam and Mrs. Moynihan described their fancy Christmas tendencies, she was glad it would be a small and meaningful family gathering.

Liam and Peggy gleefully went together to pick out a Christmas tree and dragged it from a nearby lot up the servants' stairs to the apartment.

They searched through the family's storage for heirloom tree trimmings and ornaments and decorated the tree with Granda looking on, laughing and singing carols.

And for the first time, Mrs. Moynihan let Peggy into the kitchen to help prepare a traditional Irish Christmas feast.

They made roast turkey with roasted potatoes and vegetables and an Irish Christmas cake—a whiskey-soaked dark fruitcake with white frosting all around it. And of course, little mince pie tarts filled with candied fruit and spices.

"In Ireland, they leave a pint of Guinness and a pie for Santy, but since there are no wee ones, if you don't mind, I'll take the Guinness and we'll all eat the mince pies." Mrs. Moynihan joked and unusually cackled out a laugh.

Peggy set the table with all the Irish lace linens Caroline brought over from Ireland, which were made by Maggie and her mother, Katherine, for Caroline's wedding trousseau.

"They are well preserved because the missus never pays mind to them, in favor of her linens from those fancy Fifth Avenue places," Mrs. Moynihan grimaced when she showed Peggy the beautiful intricate old linens.

Finally, the feast was ready and Liam rolled Granda into the dining room to surprise him.

Overcome with emotion, he gasped at the beautiful table and feast and smiled with a single tear falling from his eye.

"This is the most wonderful Christmas ever with my loved ones around me."

Liam wheeled him to the table and chivalrously pulled out the chair next to him for Peggy. Mrs. Moynihan started out of the room and Liam stopped her.

"There are four places, Mrs. Moynihan—please join us," Liam said and pulled out a chair. She looked around in both directions, then sparked a smile and sat down.

Picking up the Christmas crackers, she and Liam had made, Peggy could hardly contain her excitement.

"This is my first Christmas cracker," she giggled. "Let's all do it together."

The foursome broke open the wrapped trinket, donned the traditional colored paper crowns, and took out the jokes that were inside.

"Granda should go first," Peggy said.

Granda unfolded his joke and said, "Who hides in the bakery at Christmas? A mince spy."

They all laughed. Peggy sat anxiously bouncing in her seat like a child at their first Christmas.

"Now it's my turn. Why was the turkey in the pop group? Because he was the only one with drumsticks! Now you, Mrs. Moynihan," she laughed and goaded.

"Oh, no, not before Master Liam," she blushed.

"Go ahead." Liam waved her on.

"All right. What athlete is warmest during winter? A long jumper!" she laughed giddily. "Now you, Master Liam."

"Ok. What's green, covered in tinsel, and goes ribbit ribbit? A mistle-toad." He laughed and pulled a sprig of mistletoe out from under his chair, popped to his feet and held it over Mrs. Moynihan's head.

"Fancy a bit of a peck, old girl?" Liam joked in his Irish brogue.

Mrs. Moynihan flushed and spun her face to the side as he gave her a kiss on the cheek.

Then he turned to Peggy and held the sprig over her head with one hand and put his arm around her back, dipping her back in her chair with the other.

"And now for me love," he continued in his brogue, kissing her.

Liam carved the turkey and Peggy poured the Irish Christmas punch, made of warm spiced Irish whisky, and raised her glass for a toast.

"Nollaig shona dhuit! Happy Christmas and Merry Christmas!" she proudly shouted, and the four clinked glasses.

After the meal, the foursome retired into the salon for coffee and presents.

Using Maggie's sewing machine, Peggy embroidered and laced some handkerchiefs for everyone, including Mrs. Moynihan.

"They're not great; I'm just a beginner," she warned as she handed out the identical boxes wrapped in gold foil and a green ribbon.

Mrs. Moynihan opened the box and was so touched by the gift, she nearly cried.

And when Granda opened his, he teared up, rubbed the handkerchief against his face, and motioned Peggy to come to him.

"You are the sweetest lass that ever lived. Maggie would've been so proud of you," he said, bringing Peggy to tears.

"Now my turn," Liam said and placed a very large box wrapped in red foil with a giant gold bow across Peggy's lap.

Puzzled, Peggy slowly opened the box and gasped. With big saucer eyes, she delicately lifted a beige antique satin dress with intricate Irish lace from the box. She looked at Liam and smiled in surprise.

"Granda says this was his mother's wedding dress and Maggie made it," Liam said. He got down on one knee in front of her, brandishing a small aged and faded green velvet box.

Inside was a traditional Claddagh engagement ring with two hands holding a crowned heart. It was adorned with a large emerald inside the heart flanked by shimmering emeralds and diamonds in the crown and around the burnished gold band.

"This was Caroline's wedding ring. I thought this would be a wonderful way for both our great-grandmothers to walk down the aisle with you at our wedding and bless us. Will you marry me, Piggy?"

Peggy excitedly jumped to Liam and embraced him, nearly crushing the wedding dress box.

"I will! I will!" Peggy gleefully shouted and kissed him.

"I'll never be a happier man than to see my two darlings waltz down the aisle together and be wed," Granda said with tears in his eyes. When the two were done kissing, they leapt up and kissed him on either cheek, then Peggy ran out into the library.

"I just have to call my parents. They'll be so happy! What a great Christmas gift for us all."

Chapter Fourteen

BEGINNINGS

With a wonderful beginning to a brand-new year, Peggy eagerly tried an old Irish New Year's tradition Mrs. Moynihan taught her.

"You open the back door of the house just before midnight to let the old year out and open the front door to let the new year in, and then you shout 'Happy New Year' to your neighbors," she explained.

Peggy didn't know her neighbors, since many of them were celebrities or the wealthy New York elite and valued privacy. She rarely saw anyone in the building's corridors or elevators more than once and no one spoke to each other.

But at midnight on New Year's Eve, she threw open the front door and screamed, "Happy New Year to all me neighbors!"

Suddenly a middle-aged blonde woman passed her in the hall and without stopping commented in a droll sexy alto voice, "Darling, all your neighbors know it's New Year's. You don't have to shout to remind them."

Embarrassed, Peggy quickly shut the door then giggled. She recognized the woman as Lauren Bacall and ran to tell Liam of her first celebrity sighting.

They decided to get married on Valentine's Day in a free-spirited Central Park wedding, right on the bridge where they'd first met.

Peggy busily used her sewing skills and Maggie's sewing machine to slightly alter Caroline's wedding dress. Remarkably, they were similar in size.

The wedding would be a quiet, intimate gathering of their close friends, Jane and her husband, her Aunt Kate, and Suzy and Red, who were coming in from Chicago.

Peggy fervently urged Liam to cable his parents and advise them of the wedding date and ensure they're home for the wedding, but he earnestly resisted.

"We want to do this our way, not theirs," he insisted. "They're coming back on the 10th—that means they'll be here, but won't have enough time to try and change it into a fake society extravaganza."

She didn't understand his relationship with his parents, but nodded in agreement.

The week before the wedding, Peggy was trying on the wedding dress when Granda rolled by in his chair and stopped at the doorway, secretly admiring her.

"Maggie, you are the most beautiful bride that ever lived," he said, startling her.

She smiled and kissed him on the cheek. "Thank you, Granda, but it's Peggy, remember?"

He gazed at her and placed his hand on her cheek.

"Maggie, I missed you. Mother says that you went away but it wasn't my fault. I'm so glad you're back." He giggled and rolled down the hallway with a big grin on his face.

Worried that he was losing his grip on reality again, Peggy quickly took off the wedding dress and found Liam to tell him what happened.

"I think we should call the doctor. He's confusing me with Maggie again... and he giggled. It's as if he's regressed to childhood," she warned.

The doctor came in the late afternoon and examined Granda. By then, he was back to his old self, but some recent color that had returned to his face began to wane.

"How is he, doctor?" Liam asked, concerned.

"Well, right now, he says he's tired, but he does recognize reality. His vitals are stable, but given your indications of his moving in and out of reality, it sounds like the stroke may have affected more parts of his brain than earlier diagnosed. We'll have to keep an eye on him," the doctor explained.

Peggy and Liam braced each other, saddened by the news. Given Granda's renewed sunny disposition since they moved in, they hoped he was improving, but an unfortunate decline seemed imminent.

"Should we try to move up the wedding?" Peggy asked, as wet tears glazed her green eyes. "He can't miss this. We need to have him there."

Liam held her tight and whispered to her. "Don't worry, he'll be there. He wouldn't miss this for the world."

Suddenly they heard Granda yelling from the library. "Teatime, Mrs. Moynihan!"

They both smiled at each other and went to have tea. He was fine now. They would hold onto that.

On the 10th of February as promised, Liam's parents, Madeline and Bryne, rolled into The Dakota like a tornado, leveling everything in their wake.

Liam kept them abreast of Granda's condition through cables, remaining mum about the pending nuptials. But within an hour of crossing The Dakota's threshold, both parents cornered Liam in a closed-door meeting in the library, while Peggy, Mrs. Moynihan, and Granda listened from the main salon, hearing everything.

"It's bad enough you're marrying someone we don't even know, but you can't even have a normal wedding in a church with a proper reception and, of course, a picture in the society page? It's expected!" Liam's mother, Madeline, said.

"Don't take offense lass, they'd say that about anyone who doesn't have dollar signs before and after their name," Mrs. Moynihan whispered and Peggy touched her hand with gratitude. Peggy knew her new in-laws would not approve of her.

"This bohemian lifestyle is past its expiration date, William. You need to take responsibility as a member of this family. We have a position in New York and you have a job waiting for you at the railroad. It's time you grew up and left all this flower child nonsense behind you," Liam's father, Bryne, said.

"I'm glad you're both back to see me get married, but Peggy and I are doing this our way. We live our lives according to our terms and no one else's. I'm sorry if you can't accept that, but it is my final decision. You are free to come to the wedding or not. That's your choice." Liam definitely opened the door entered the mail salon, still brandishing his kind eyes of blue steel, standing strong like the Rock of Gibraltar.

"I'm sure you heard everything; you're busybodies," he laughed, shaking his head at them.

"You'll not them take your spirit, son. It's your life, after all, and one thing I've learned in all my years is… only you can live your life, no one else," Granda assured.

Still a little shaken from his parental row, Liam sweetly smiled at Granda and tipped his hat to him as Mrs. Moynihan wheeled him away. Peggy stepped toward Liam and tightly embraced him. Without words, each knew nothing anyone says could upset their bond.

The next few days were tense when Liam's parents were around, but like a secret club, Liam, Peggy, Granda, and Mrs. Moynihan joyously reveled in the preparations for the wedding.

With their jaws out of joint, Liam's parents Madeline and Bryne sulked around the apartment, turning up their noses in the air to everything. But since the apartment and the inheritance belonged to Granda, as head of the family, they could do very little to stop or even alter the wedding.

Peggy lamented her instantly acrimonious relationship with her future in-laws, but based on Liam's description, she expected no more. Instead she focused on the happy occasion and her parents' arrival. There would be plenty of people in attendance who loved her and Liam and wished them well on their special day, so a few sourpusses couldn't dampen her glee.

Needless to say, when Suzy and Red came into town, she spared them a prior meet and greet with Liam's parents, but instead met a Jane's the night before to present Liam.

Liam extended his hand to shake Red's when Peggy introduced him, but Red stood stolidly, glaring at him.

"You didn't ask for my daughter's hand," he said with a somber face and then broke up chuckling and gladly shook Liam's hand. "Sorry, I had to try to make you nervous, it's a father's job, but I just couldn't hold it."

Liam laughed and patted Red on the back for his brief deception.

"We're thrilled for you." Suzy kissed Liam on the cheek.

"Between's Jane's reports and Peggy's cards, we were all hoping you two would get together. And it's finally happened."

Peggy looked slyly at Jane and grinned. "You knew?"

Jane smiled and nodded. "I suspected on day one, but then it became more obvious."

Kissing Jane on the cheek, Peggy chuckled. "Well, I wish you would have told me and saved time."

Jane hugged her. "You weren't ready to see it yet. Everything happens in its own time."

Valentine's Day came on a bright and sunny winter day in New York with a rare warm snap offering up a 55° afternoon with no wind, rain, or snow in sight.

Before the ceremony, Suzy and Red stood on one side of the Central Park bridge with Peggy.

She wore Maggie's lace gloves, Caroline's wedding dress, and Maggie's broach for good luck. From a crown of flowers in her hair dangled long green and yellow ribbons that fluttered in the breeze.

"We're so happy for you, honey," Suzy said as she and Red held Peggy's hands.

It was a joyous occasion. And their family and assortment of their Village friends gathered lining each side of the bridge to watch them journey together across the bridge.

Accompanied by the rushing of the babbling brook below, their musician friends played guitars and flutes sweetly humming a traditional Irish wedding song. Red and Suzy strolled partway along the bridge with Liam on the other side walking to meet Peggy in the middle. As Liam and Peggy walked to meet the other, everyone along the bridge gently tossed flower petals, showering them with love.

Ravyn unusually dressed in a yellow muslin dress to and Maxi in pale green, with baby's breath tucked in their hair, shaped a garden of rose petals into a circle in the middle of the bridge for the impending nuptials.

When Liam and Peggy reached the middle, a friend they called Preacher pushed Granda's chair next to Liam. Dressed in his finest tuxedo tails, Granda gladly sat next to Liam as his best man.

Preacher addressed the couple and those in attendance to officiate the ceremony. "Beginnings are a groovy part of the circle of life. As Liam and Peggy speak their love truth to each other, we can all dig their spirits joining together. Let's listen."

Peggy's eyes sparkled and beamed into Liam's adoring gaze.

"Sweet Liam. I waited my whole life for you and yet somehow I always knew you were there. Our embers began with friendship and grew strong and steady into a bright flame of warm love that binds and consumes us. Within its fire, it'll keep us bound together, always burning, always joined, never extinguishing, never to ash."

Liam took Peggy's hands in his and smiled, pledging his love in verse.

"My darling Piggy. From the moment I saw your emerald eyes, I lost my soul within their glow. I knew in an instant, a life without you I could not know. You have my love and its deepest depths forever and ever, until my last breath. I promise to be true and walk with you as a partner, each day anew. Side by side, I will always be your groom and you my bride."

Then Preacher pushed Granda's wheelchair in the middle of Peggy and Liam, per his request, and he held both their hands.

"My darlin' dears, an old Irish blessing. May love and laughter light your days and warm your heart and home. May good and faithful friends be yours, wherever you may roam. May peace and plenty bless your world with joy that long endures. May all life's passing seasons bring the best to you and yours."

Granda joined Peggy and Liam's hands and Liam and Peggy each kissed Granda on the cheek. Then Preacher moved Granda's wheelchair and tied their hands together with a shiny satin ribbon, per Mrs. Moynihan's direction of Irish tradition.

"You are now husband and wife, married for life. Far out," Preacher said amidst the sobs of onlooking happy tears.

Then Liam took Peggy in his arms, dipped her, and kissed her as their friends delivered an approving roar of claps, snaps and cheers.

Red and Suzy gleefully rushed to hug and kiss Peggy and Liam.

"Our little girl is a married woman now, Red," Suzy said.

"I know you'll be happy, my girl," Red said. "I can see sheer bliss in your beautiful eyes."

"I will Dad. I finally know in my heart what I've seen from you and Mom my whole life, everlasting love," Peggy smiled and took Red's hand and guided him to Granda.

"I'm happy to connect you two. Dad, this is Liam. Our Maggie took care of him when he was a babe and sang and told stories to him. You have a lot in common. He loved her too."

Red's green eyes lit up and he gladly shook Granda's hand. Peggy lovingly grinned as she left the two men trading stories about Maggie and joined Liam.

Even Liam's parents were touched by the outpouring of love and happiness showered on the couple and shook both their hands with congratulations.

Until dusk fell, the group sang, danced, ate, drank, and played music in the park in tribute to the union. As the sun peeked its last light on them, Peggy and Liam bid goodbye to their friends and family, who were all luminous in the reflected rainbows of love.

After the merriment ended, Liam and Peggy went back to their room in The Dakota. Madeline and Bryne had left with Granda earlier to put him to bed, and then went out to their club.

Alone again, Peggy lit candles around the room, recreating their first time together and lay down on the bed. Even though they had made love many times since, Liam lay on top of her slightly trembling.

She laughed and kissed him. "What, are you afraid to make love to a married woman?"

He softly fixed his eyes to hers and cradled her face in his hands. "No. But all of a sudden I'm afraid of disappointing you. This is permanent. From now on, I'm the only man you'll have."

She grabbed him and held him close. "No chance of that, you're the only man I want forever."

Into the night they made love until the candles dripped down to their final flames and they both lay next to each other, exhausted.

Basking in the radiance of their love, Peggy beamed at her new husband lovingly, silently sleeping and looking like a cherub, and picked up her journal.

Dear Maggie,

I did it. I got married. Today I wondered how you must have felt when you became a wife. I am washed in an inner peace and glow like sunlight's coming out of my ears.

I'm so happy. Liam is the most wonderful man and my best friend.

I really never thought I'd get married. I considered myself a nomad moving through life, enjoying the company of many people. I always thought marriage would be a prison where I would be stuck in a certain role and couldn't be free, but Liam changed my mind. He doesn't believe in any boundaries or rules and when I'm with him, I'm freer than a butterfly escaping her cocoon.

I know I'm loved and yet there is no ceiling above and no ground below. We can do anything we want together.

I felt you and Caroline with us the whole time. It was my pleasure to wear her dress, that you made and your gloves. I hope you two are pleased. Now you are blood relatives.

I can't wait to see what comes next.

Chapter Fifteen

Endings

The day after the wedding, Granda's strength left him and he was confined to his bed, with a doctor and nurse hovering over him.

He called Bryne, Madeline, Peggy, and Liam to his bedside. Confused by their summoning, they entered the dark and ominous bedchamber and saw a strange man sitting off to one side in the room.

Between coughs and sighs to fill his lungs with air, Granda spoke very slowly and quietly.

"I want there to be no mistake or surprise when I'm gone. Every family has its secrets, but I've been keeping one from all of you. I am not the viscount of Donegal," he firmly stated.

His confession was followed by gasps and stares from Madeline and Bryne.

"But Father!" Bryne interrupted.

"Just hold on now, let me explain. My father, Bryne Donegal, was the viscount and passed his title on to me when he died. A title that would bequeath to my son and grandson after him. You know that, but what you don't know is that my uncle Robert, the count of Donegal, never produced an heir and upon his demise 15 years ago in Ireland, the title of count of Donegal fell to me. That means the title of viscount would've gone to you, Bryne," Granda explained.

"What?" Madeline said, incensed.

Granda ignores Madeline and looks at Bryne, whose eyes are gleaming in anger.

"I'm sorry, my son, but at the time I felt that you and Madeline were too wrapped up in the vapid society folds of the New York elite already. I feared if you were given the titles of your birthright, you would laud them over everyone in this town and fail to give my grandson a loving home. Unfortunately, that happened anyway," Granda said.

"Now, just a minute, Father," Bryne ardently objected.

Granda raised his voice as much as he could muster. "You will let me finish. It's true, maybe it was predestined, as I saddled you with my father's cursed name. You two are unfortunately very much alike. But against all odds, fortunately you produced the most wonderful man who ever walked the face of this earth, my grandson, Liam. You named him right. I know you two don't agree on even the rise and fall of the sun each day, but with my dying breath I'm going to break tradition, as evidenced by my lawyer, sitting over there, by exercising my American rights. When I go, per Irish law and tradition, Bryne and Madeline, the titles of count and countess of Donegal will go to you. And Liam and Peggy, the titles of viscount and viscountess of Donegal will go to you."

Granda gasped a few short breaths and continued. "But as an American-born man, I am dividing my estate, including the lands in

Ireland, between you. Bryne, you will receive all the American real estate and railroad holdings, along with half of my stocks and cash, and The Dakota apartment, with the proviso that it stay in the family for the next generation. And the other half of the stocks and cash and the County Donegal ancestral estate in Ireland, I grant to Liam immediately upon my death, with a separate handsome allowance from my estate to maintain the old castle."

Peggy and Liam looked at each other, shocked, as Bryne and Madeline pursed their faces in anger.

"Father, you can't do that!" Bryne shouted.

Struggling, Granda sat up in defiance. "I can and I will. Bryne, you're a wealthy man and Madeline has blue blood overflowing out of her veins. I knew you would never give anything to Liam and Peggy, so I've ensured that Liam and his heirs will irrevocably pass on the titles and the family homes without interference from you. It's all legal—signed, sealed, and delivered."

Suddenly, Granda slumped down, losing his strength and the doctor leapt to his side.

"Please, you must all go now, so he can rest," the doctor said.

Dumbfounded, the foursome trodded in a single line out of the room in silence.

To avoid a confrontation, at least for the moment, Liam grabbed Peggy's hand and pulled her into their bedroom.

"Piggy, I don't know what to say. I don't want any of this. Their lifestyle is toxic, and money turns people into horrible elitist robots, going through life one dinner party after another, pretending to be more than they are and looking down on everybody who is not. That's not me!" Liam proclaimed, plopping down on the bed in frustration.

Peggy sat down next to him and held him. "I understand, my love—we won't live that lifestyle. As Granda says, only you can live your life as you see fit. But he wanted you to have this and our children too. So we can sock it away for a rainy day and we keep just being us," Peggy assured him.

Liam's face illuminated and he kissed her. "You're a genius. That's exactly what we're going to do. Pack your things."

Peggy looked at him like he was crazy. "But Granda?"

"We'll say goodbye to him before we go, but if you thought my parents were difficult before this, they'll be impossible now. They will build a wall of hate and spite that will be insurmountable and then tumble it right on top of our heads. I won't put you through that," he reasoned.

"But where will we go?" Peggy asked urgently.

Liam laughed. "That's the beauty of it. We'll just go. Get in the Psybug and drive until we stop. We need to find a place to make our home."

They hurriedly gathered their things and planned to leave that evening, while Madeline and Bryne were out at a dinner party.

Peggy dreaded saying goodbye to Granda. She knew his time was short, but also realized Liam was right.

Granda opened up a portal to her, connecting her to Maggie and her Irish roots—all of which she treasured. But he was getting the care he needed and hopefully avoiding more family strife will give him peace.

Carefully entering the dark and grim room, Peggy and Liam quietly stood on either side of the bed and held Granda's hands.

He was worse than the day before. His face was more drawn and pale, lacking life, and he was very weak.

"Granda, it's Liam and Peggy," Liam said softly. "We wanted to say goodbye. I know you'll understand. We need to find our own place to be together."

Granda looked up at Liam, trying to grip his hand. "And that you should, my boy. Your first days as husband and wife should not be filled with family friction. You go find your own life. And live it."

Peggy felt a little squeeze of his hand. She leaned down and kissed him on the cheek, dropping a tear on his face.

"Granda, I'm glad I got to know you. You've given me more than you'll ever know. I'll never forget you."

He looked at her and smiled.

"Ah, lass, don't be sad. It's I who should be thanking you. You two have filled these last months with so much joy. As they say in the old country… family is connected heart to heart. Neither time nor space can keep us apart."

Peggy and Liam waved goodbye, collected their belongings, and marched out of The Dakota for the last time.

After they packed the Psybug, Peggy stopped and glanced longingly in the direction of Central Park.

"Would you mind if we just walked in the park one more time before we go?" she asked.

Liam took her hand and nodded. Together they strolled over to the park in silence with the moon shining on them like a beacon.

He stopped on their bridge and held Peggy in his arms, kissing her under the beams of light. She released and stared at him soulfully, smiling.

"We started here twice already and now this begins our next journey together," she said.

They decided to stop at The Bitter End to say goodbye to everyone. It was hoot night and when they arrived, Ravyn was debuting a new performance about the plight of women in modern society.

In her black leotard, she wielded props and wore accessories to punctuate the differences of life, accompanied by alternating types of music depicting women through the ages. As usual, she never talked, but her performance screamed volumes nonetheless.

The accompanying guitarist's strum sped up and slowed down at planned intervals to show women's past, present and future roles. From pioneer and suffragettes to jazz girls, Rosie the Riveter, 50s housewives, and ladies who lunch, she then looked into the future, appearing as the first woman Supreme Court justice and president.

Peggy watched earnestly, picturing her own evolution and how far she'd come since her days as a secretary-to-be. And who knows what future lay ahead?

After Ravyn was done, she and Maxi coaxed Peggy into going up on stage.

The familiar crowd received her with a warm reception and sang one of her original Irish tunes. She looked into the smiling faces, grateful that she was able to have time to explore her music and sing for people, wondering if this would be her last time in front of an audience or if there were even better things coming.

When she exited the stage, a man approached her and handed her a card.

"Hey, I like your sound; if you're ever looking to record somewhere, I'll soon be opening a studio upstate."

Peggy took the card and thanked him. It was an intriguing offer, but since the studio wasn't ready now, she tucked away the idea and the card in her guitar case and returned to the table.

"You'll say goodbye to everyone at the paper for me, won't you, Maxi?" Peggy asked.

"Yeah, sure. There are so many people coming and going nowadays, I can hardly keep track," Maxi complained. "You know our cartoonist Mary just left with her husband for a commune in the Hudson Valley. They said it's going to be like utopia, living off the land, like on a farm, but it's also supposed to be a creative outlet, like an artists' colony."

"Righteous," Peggy said. "She's very talented. I hope she can do something with her art."

Liam nodded to Peggy. "An artists' colony could be an option for us."

Peggy shrugged and nodded her head as they listened to some other acts. After the night was over, they kissed and hugged everyone goodbye and drove north.

"How about if we drive until we get tired, and then stop somewhere and sleep in the Psybug?" Liam proposed.

"That sounds good. No plan is an interesting idea. I think we'll know when the right place comes. It's a starry night out—they can guide us," Peggy said.

Liam drove as Peggy laid in the bed they had made in the slug bug, huddled in blankets and staring up at the celestial guide. She pulled out her journal.

Dear Maggie,

I'm both anxious and terrified, but strangely I'm not scared. Liam and I are entering into the unknown.

Now I think I understand how you felt leaving The Dakota.

Liam's parents would have made life miserable for us. And Granda wouldn't have been there for long. His spirit is moving to a better plane where he'll be happy and free.

It was inspirational living in that home. I felt your courage and inspiration everywhere. But you knew when to leave and so did we.

Driving on the open road looking at the stars, I'm completely free, unencumbered by any convention. I can breathe in the crisp air. No responsibilities, no rules, no requirements, and no place to be. It's a freedom I haven't sensed since I was a little kid. Everything feels possible.

We don't know where we're going or where we'll end up, but we're doing it together. We can start anew.

Chapter Sixteen

The Farm

Early Spring 1966

They drove north for a week up and down along the Hudson Valley, stopping to experience the vibe of the small farming towns and enjoy the sprawling landscape and then making love and sleeping in the Psybug under the stars. With the moon beaming on them, it felt as if they had their own divine nightlight.

During the day, they saw miles and miles of unfettered and abundant fields. Liam was amazed at the splendor, as he'd rarely gone out of the city into rural New York's small, quaint farm towns.

Everything out the window reminded Peggy of her trip from Chicago to New York, viewing all the farmland, rich amber grain, and rolling green meadows.

In a little hamlet called Farmington, they stopped at a general store to get some peanut butter, jelly, and bread for sandwiches and granola for snacks. Seeing a cute diner next door, they decided to have a warm meal.

Outside, Peggy ran into Mary, the illustrator from The Other and a man, loading bags into a pickup truck.

"Peggy, hi! Small world!" she said.

"Mary! Wow, is this where you live now?" Peggy said, surprised.

"We live in the artists' colony up the road. We just came into town to trade the canned fruits and vegetables we make for some necessities. This is my old man, Jack. What are you doing here?"

Jack held up a peace symbol and nodded his head.

"This is my husband, Liam. We're driving around on a journey of discovery. We just stopped at this diner to for dinner," she replied.

"Forget that—why don't you come back to our house and we can give you a very healthy hot meal?" Mary offered.

Liam and Peggy looked at each other and nodding in agreement.

"Ok, follow us," Mary waved to them and she and Jack got into the truck.

They followed Mary's truck in the Psybug up the winding dirt road and passed a covered bridge. The area was completely undisturbed and remote, and as they got closer, they saw the remnants of dormant farm fields, laced with a thin, clean blanket of snow.

When they reached the colony, they saw a large farm with two barns and a log building with a mill wheel adjacent to a shimmering lake.

Pulling in front of the log building, Peggy saw the inviting timber frame with smoke billowing in the dense air out of the fireplace chimneys and a warm glow of light from within.

Mary and Jack got out of the truck and waved them to come in, stopping them just short of the door.

"Just so you know, they call me Sunshine here. Since I felt reborn, I wanted to change my name to something more earthy," she said.

Peggy smiled at Mary and shrugged at Liam, then entered into a big room covered with furniture and woven rugs, and filled with people.

Peggy and Liam held hands, apprehensively wandering into the group of people.

"Everyone, this is Peggy and Liam. They are friends from The Village on a journey of discovery. I invited them to eat with us," she said.

They were quickly surrounded by a welcoming circle of people extending hands to greet them and a short, round balding man with a kind face put his arms around their shoulders.

"Welcome. I'm called River. We are all on our own individual journeys. I'm glad your path led to us today."

Sunshine and Jack invited them into another room, where they all gathered at a large supper table with about 20 women, men, and children.

Others came in from the kitchen with plates of bread, salad, cheese, pitchers of milk, and a big pot of steaming vegetable stew.

"Everything we eat is from the land and our own hands," Sunshine explained. "And we have chickens, a goat, two cows, and a couple horses."

"In the summer, we plant and harvest our own vegetables, potatoes, oats, corn, and wheat. Our community is fully self-sustaining." Jack added. "We even eat from wood bowls with utensils carved from dead trees we found in the woods."

Looking at the variety of food on the table, Peggy was amazed it was all grown and harvested by the people in the room. And the stew was amazingly flavorful—warm and satisfying, despite the lack of meat.

"Is this an artists' colony?" Liam asked.

"Yes," answered a handsome and ruggedly tan man named Aaron. "I'm a sculptor. There are many who feel the calling of different arts, music, and poetry to express their inner selves."

The dinner conversation touched on many subjects, including music, politics, poetry, art, and life. Peggy found herself riveted. She was astonished that everyone was so open and giving and yet wonderfully intelligent and talented. It was a collection of free spirits with an aura of peace and tranquility.

When dinner was over, everyone picked up their plates and created an assembly line for the cleanup of dishes. It was structured yet natural, and everyone pitched in.

Then the group retired to the main living area and pulled out instruments. Peggy retrieved her guitar from the bug and joined in singing and playing. Hours into the evening, she shot Liam a satisfied smile, sending and receiving a message. They both liked it there.

After singing and playing for a while, Peggy and Liam walked outside with some others to smoke. Some had pipes with tobacco traded from nearby farms. And some were smoking marijuana, which was also grown on the property.

"So what do you think of our little utopia?" River asked.

"I think it's groovy. It's a comforting vibe," Peggy said.

"That's where it's at, man," a woman named Charity said. "Honesty, truth, and community create a good energy that flows in and out of each other and everything around us to fill our souls with peace and harmony."

"We exist in a circle as one with the earth. It feeds us and we nurture and care for it," River added.

Despite the cool temperature, Peggy and Liam wrapped themselves in a warm blanket and relaxed sitting on the big wraparound porch, listening to the beautiful music within, and watching the clear night sky and the stars above.

"I'll say one thing—the city never provided a quiet and calm stillness like this to fully clear your mind," he offered, taking a deep breath to fill his lungs with clean air.

"Why don't you stay the night and see our home tomorrow in the sun's light?" Aaron said and motioned for Peggy and Liam to get up and follow him up the stairs.

On the second floor, he opened the door to a loft. The sloped ceiling was made of cedar timbers to create the open structure of the roof. And the windows beamed in light from the navy midnight sky.

A bed framed with tied logs was draped with a multicolored quilt laden in geometric patterns. Liam smiled at Peggy's contented face and nodded to Aaron. They'd stay the night.

Liam clasped Aaron's hand sideways in a hippie handshake and he gave Peggy a peace sign and left. Peggy threw her arms around Liam and kissed him and he picked her up and carried her to the bed, where they made pure, satisfying love under the glow of the celestial sky with a new energy and vigor they both recognized.

Right after dawn, the rooster crowed, waking them out of a blissful sleep. They glanced at each other covered in the warm sun's light and knew each other's mind. It felt right.

They dressed and Peggy donned Maggie's old straw hat to join the barrage of residents rushing toward the new day's work. Some were in the kitchen making breakfast for the brood, while others were tending to the animals and chopping wood. Men and women worked side by side doing chores, without societal stereotypes or restraint.

In the daytime, the idyllic scene came into view. The dusting of snow from the night before melted with the crisp spring sun and they saw the vast rolling green and amber hillside surrounding the house. The joyous laughter of kids chasing cats, dogs, chickens and goats all around while playing in hammocks and tire swings in the big strong trees filled the air.

Peggy and Liam scanned the picturesque panorama, inhaling the positive vibes with a deep cleaning breath, when Sunshine joined them, arm and arm with Jack.

"It's beautiful, isn't it?" Sunshine said.

"Yes, it's so peaceful and amazing how everyone lives and works together?" Peggy said.

"Yeah. We all dig hanging out together, and farming is cool," she nodded.

"Let's put you two to work," Jack said and put his arm around Liam's back. "Liam, you're with me," Jack grinned. "I bet you're good with your hands. Let's see what the cows think."

Sunshine smiled and handed Peggy an ax. "Want to try your hand?"

Peggy's green eyes grew wide as she eagerly grabbed the ax and followed Sunshine into the woods.

Mimicking Sunshine's every step, Peggy looked around at the trees, huddled under the umbrella of the new day.

"Here's a good spot," Sunshine said. "These trees look as though they're ready to leave us. We only pick trees for firewood that we think are dry and dying, to leave room for the other trees to grow."

"What do I do?" Peggy asked, looking confused.

"It's simple," Sunshine chuckled. "Hold it at a 45° angle and think of every person in your life who has made you angry. Then release that energy with each swing."

Peggy approached the tree with some doubt, but followed directions. She took a deep breath, closed her eyes and swung the ax with all her might, embedding it deeply into the tree.

Sunshine kindly laughed. "That's great, but this time, open your eyes. This is how we rid ourselves of aggression and anger to cleanse our aura and only project peace to those around us. Only take a couple swipes on each side and make sure to avoid the tree falling on you."

Peggy smiled and took another swing, grunting a little. She could feel the negative vibes surge through her arms and hands into the ax. It was liberating. She rotated and repeated around the tree, and soon it came down with a soft thud, sending nearby leaves into the air in a billowing circle.

"I guess this is what they meant by the tree falling in the forest," she grinned, pleased with her work.

They gathered firewood and brought it back to the house, stacking it in nearby piles for eventual use in the fireplaces and ovens, replenishing the older dry wood.

Sunshine laughed. "Let's peek in on the boys in the barn. They should be done grooming and feeding and on to milking. The first cow milking lesson is usually hilarious."

Peeking through the slats in the barn, Peggy and Sunshine watched an uncertain Liam standing next to Jack, who placed a small stool next to the cow and petted her.

"Good morning, Daisy; this is my friend Liam," he said, gently scratching around her ears. "He's new, so be easy on him. Liam, say hi to Daisy and connect with her."

Liam stepped up to the cow with trepidation and looked into her giant brown eyes, petting her head.

"Daisy, please be kind. I am a gentle soul and I'll rely on you to guide me," Liam begged.

Jack chuckled. He picked up a silver pail and set it under Daisy, then sat on the stool.

"It's easy—just pull and squirt," he said, grasping her udder. He squeezed them like hoses until milk squirted into the pail. "Now you try."

Liam looked nervous, but took a deep breath and sat down, slowly gripping his hands and fingers around Daisy's udder and holding still.

Peggy and Sunshine giggled with their hands over their mouths, to avoid being spotted as Jack let out a hearty laugh.

"You have to pull them. Don't worry, it doesn't hurt her. Her job is to make milk. It's like peeing—she's full and you help her get relief."

Liam looked at Jack and then focused on the udder. "OK, Daisy, here we go." He yanked on the udder and a drop of milk came out, as did a moan from Daisy.

"You'll get it. Keep talking to her. If you have the right touch, all is right with the world," Jack said and walked over to the other cow.

"OK, Daisy," Liam said, patting her on the side. "Let's give this another try." He adjusted his fingers around the udder and pulled gently but firmly. A stream of milk shot into the bucket, and Daisy mooed.

Liam was excited. "Far out! We hit the right spot. Let's go, Daisy."

Peggy gleamed with pride watching Liam. His kindness and willingness to try anything shined through.

Sunshine and Peggy walked back to the house, followed by Jack and Liam shortly after. Peggy hugged Liam and they both smiled in satisfaction at what they accomplished, each knowing without speaking. They would stay.

After breakfast, they pitched in wherever they could, from cleaning to mending clothes. By the evening, they collapsed from exhaustion, too tired to make love, falling into a deep happy sleep side by side.

Living off the land, they learned how to make cheese, churn butter, and feed and care for the animals.

In April, they both dug their hands in the dirt and learned how to plant seeds and tend to the garden, vegetables, and crops.

Day in and day out, the group worked together to keep the farm going. They bathed in the lake with natural homemade soap. They all pitched taking care of each other's children. Some mothers even breastfed each other's babies. With their deep knowledge pool, with some educated by life or advanced degrees, each member taught the children what they knew. Chastity, the Rhodes scholar, made sure each child received a well-rounded education right on the farm.

And for a few hours each day, the renaissance of people explored many creative outlets, practicing their crafts, collaborating and improving each other's work.

It truly was a utopia. There were no leaders, no bosses. Everyone did their fair share without complaining or burdening each other. Their days were free from petty bickering and interpersonal strife.

The atmosphere stimulated Peggy with sporadic brainwaves of creativity like she never experienced before. Every nerve ending was electric; waves of music and lyrics buzzed through her head. Everything she saw around her—the landscape, the people, the happiness—was pure inspiration.

She loved to sit next to the lake with her guitar and listen to the swish of the mill bubbling with air as it turned and plunged in and out of the water. The calm, peaceful sound comforted and inspired her to play in time with the shushing sounds of the water, creating new melodies.

Equally motivated with a surge of vision, Liam repainted the slug bug with stars and waves of light like a rainbow Aurora Borealis.

"I think we need to rename the Psybug to the Starry Wanderer," Liam proudly stated.

In their loft, the roof windows bathed them with the sun in the morning and shining moonlight at night. She and Liam happily made love in the nurturing moon's glow and at first light, with the dawn washing them in the warmth of the new day.

Months of spring planting, summer cultivating, and fall harvest were a master class in farming. They both readily labored in the fields with the satisfaction of hard work and the wholesome feeling of contributing to the community welfare.

After their chores, they took long walks, hand in hand, watching the children play and listening to the spontaneous jam session music emanating from the big house. It was a simple yet incredible existence.

Dear Maggie,

We've been on the farm for a while now and are really loving it. I hardly have time to write.

I've learned so much about gardening and working the land. I even have dreams about hoeing the fields. It's almost second nature.

And with your sewing machine, I've been sewing clothes and remaking old garments and teaching others. It's nice to pass on that knowledge.

We share everything with each other for the collective good. There are so many talented artists and interesting educated people—some are former lawyers, teachers, tradesmen, and people with impressive degrees. They all share their wealth of knowledge and we each discover something new every day. I've learned so much.

Everyone has a story of why they dropped out of regular society. Some were sick of the hassles—all the war and hate. And others were looking for an alternative way of living that could create a new world with peace and harmony.

People call us hippies, but it's really just a farm with a bunch of people who have common goals. In the two years I've been a beatnik and now a hippie. I wear those names as a badge of honor.

It's all a dream, living a beautiful existence in a one-on-one relationship with the earth and each other. It's true freedom.

One warm spring day, Peggy sat in the fields posing for Liam as he painted her. She wore flowers in her hair and the braided leather headband from Jane. She strummed her guitar while he painted.

"Someday this will be your album cover," he laughed.

A man with glasses and long gray and brown hair approached them.

"You've really captured the essence of her beauty inside and her spirituality outside," the man said, admiring the painting.

"Thanks, friend," Liam said. "I'm just painting what I see with my eyes and heart." He reached out to shake the man's hand. "I'm Liam."

"They call me Rev. I'm looking for Aaron. He was born of me," he said.

Seeing the exchange, Peggy got up from the field and introduced herself.

"I'm Peggy," she said, shaking his hand.

"You're a rare beauty that's hard to portray in a picture, like lightning in a bottle, but he seems to have brought a pure love to life," he said, staring at her and the picture.

"Well, I hope so! He's my husband, after all," she laughed.

"Oh, are there just the two of you bonded or are there more?" he asked.

Confused, Liam changed the subject. "Did you say you were Aaron's dad?"

"Well, I think we are all children in one family, but yes, he carries my seed," he said.

"Aaron's up at the main house," Peggy said, unsure if he was putting them on.

He raised a peace sign to them and turned to walk toward the house.

"I think it's cool how everyone expresses themselves differently here," Liam remarked.

"It's a mellow way of thinking at life in a new way, not the way you were taught. It's natural," Peggy commented and resumed her pose.

After finishing the painting, Liam and Peggy walked back to the house and saw Rev on the porch, gathered with a group of others.

"Revolution is a change of attitude to make the world better than the one available to us. Society's need for structure can bind you into a box of their making. Order is not good for the human spirit or body. Birds fly free, unconstrained by walls or gravity. They die if their wings are clipped to restrict what comes naturally. They fly because they can," he preached.

Everyone sat mesmerized by his words. The rest of the day, the group listened as he mapped out his philosophy of life.

"You can take your utopia to the next level by experiencing true freedom with no boundaries. Everything you have been taught has limited your journey. Free your mind of all hangups and conventions that are designed by the man to keep you from the true way of the animal kingdom. Embrace a rebirth to make your spirit soar," Rev encouraged.

In the weeks after, Rev became the spiritual guide of the group, introducing dawn yoga, soul awakenings, and nightly marijuana meditation circles where each person would unburden themselves of harmful thoughts and feelings to expel negative chakras and embrace good karma.

Peggy began to see nightly room exchanges; people came out of rooms in the morning that they didn't go into the night before. One morning as she went to gather wood, she saw Sunshine coming out of the tent Rev had erected in the backyard.

When Sunshine joined her in the woods, Peggy couldn't help but ask, "Are you learning a new kind of yoga? I saw you coming out of Rev's tent this morning?" she asked innocently.

"He was advising Jack and me on our new coupling," she said without hesitation.

"New coupling?" Peggy asked with her face scrunched.

"It's been inspirational. Rev explained to Jack and me that marriage is a binary system that restricts your emotional path to only one person. He believes in periodic recouplings with a to share and enjoy each other's energy and essence, filling one another's souls with enlightenment," she said enthusiastically.

Peggy paused for a moment and tried to understand.

"So, you and Jack are going to couple with other people in the house?"

"Yes, I was with Rev last night. It was transcendent. We pleasured each other in ways I couldn't imagine. I never felt more alive. Every fiber of my being was afire with warmth and ecstasy. He's encouraging everyone to uncouple, whenever they wish and then when they've shared enough with each other, you move on to another person or recouple with your original partner. Most people here aren't married, anyway; it's free love," Sunshine explained.

While they continued to gather wood, she detailed the encounter to Peggy and relayed the uplifting out-of-body visions she experienced that left her filled with an ethereal peace.

When they arrived back at the house, Peggy shook her head in confusion and disbelief and went upstairs to clear her mind. Sunshine's descriptions of the lovemaking left her head reeling with images she couldn't erase. She took her journal from under her pillow.

Dear Maggie,

I'm not a prude or anything and I've heard the concept of free love and never judged other people, but I don't feel the need to be fulfilled with anyone other than Liam.

I've had other sexual partners and enjoyed the excitement and electricity of each new experience. It was fun and exhilarating. But with Liam, it's so much more. Our lovemaking gets better and better. It's like we began on this journey blind and have now mapped each other's bodies and know the exact path to take. And our bond and connection renews each time. It's indescribable.

Maybe others don't have that and keep looking for more. I guess I'm lucky. I don't need anyone else to make me happy.

Peggy was lying on their bed when Liam interrupted with concern.

"I heard you came up here—are you ok?" he asked, sitting on the bed.

Without a word, she pushed him down on the bed, sat atop him, took off his shirt, and kissed him. Then she pulled her dress over her head and cuddled up next to him, feeling the sensation of their skin pressed together.

Surprised but willing, Liam enthusiastically removed his pants and kissed her as they aggressively made love, switching positions until they were both completely physically and emotionally drained.

Lying bare on the top of the quilt, Liam panted, trying to catch his breath.

"Not that I'm complaining, but what prompted that?"

Peggy explained the discussion she and Sunshine had had that morning. "I knew that wasn't for us, but when I saw you, I couldn't help myself. I don't know about other couples, maybe we're just different. Every time enhances my love for you beyond space and time."

"I agree. I only want you forever, Piggy," he said, playfully kissing her nose.

They held each other and watched the sunset change from gold and rust, cooling into a darker and darker blue. Then there was a knock on the door.

"Hey, it's Rev. Just making sure you're ok."

Extreme discomfort instantly filled Peggy, as she clutched Liam's arm in panic. She didn't want to talk to Rev about "coupling" and was afraid he heard their vigorous closed-door activities.

Liam smiled and gently removed her grip, put on his pants, and went out the door.

She nervously threw on her dress and sat on the bed trying to overhear their conversation, but they were speaking in hushed tones.

After a few minutes, Liam came back inside and closed the door. Her eyes danced anxiously as she awaited his report.

Liam laughed and put his arm around her. "It's fine. Nothing's going to change. I told him we're happy with our simple binary coupling."

Relieved, she laid her head in his lap and sighed.

While many of the others imbibed Rev's uncoupling and coupling philosophy, Peggy and Liam abstained and were never asked again. But other changes began to unravel the loom of their perfect existence.

In a big group meeting one day, everyone sat in the main room after dinner and Aaron described their financial situation.

"When we began, the first of us bought this building and fixed it up. Rain put up the initial money and never asked for anything back, but now her health is waning and she needs to go to live in the city where she can get the care we can't give her," he explained.

Rev broke in. "What I propose is a collective pool of resources," he said. "Many commune residents offer complete devotion, like monks, and swear allegiance and poverty by unburdening themselves of all worldly possessions."

Everyone else nodded and listened in eager acceptance of the idea. Wide-eyed, Peggy and Liam stared at each other in telepathic concern, but said nothing until they were alone.

That night, they got into bed cloaked in complete darkness and lay side by side in silence for a while, until Peggy spoke.

"This takes sharing to a whole new level. You have ancestral obligations—you can't swear a vow of poverty," she said.

Liam grasped her hand. "You mean WE can't swear a vow of poverty. And I agree. I don't mind pitching in so we can buy the house from Rain, but I don't think the others are in the same boat we're in, financially."

"They probably don't realize it. We've never told anyone about your family. Even Sunshine and Jack don't know you're wealthy," she agreed.

He kissed her hand and whispered, "We're wealthy, viscountess. But we still don't have to tell anyone. I hate to lie, but I don't think anyone's going to audit us. We'll just offer them some cash to buy the house and that will be the end of it. Nothing has to change."

In the next few weeks, the members took up a collection and everyone wished Rain their best. It wasn't a sad goodbye, but rather a grand send-off that included wine traded from a nearby commune that grew grapes and a special feast of quiche, made with vegetables and eggs from the farm and cheese from a nearby colony. Chef, a new resident who had trained as a professional cook, prepared most of the food and taught everyone. And Aneta and Pyter, a Polish brother and sister who arrived a few months earlier, made traditional potato pierogies. The epic celebration continued with joyous music and dancing late into the night.

Chapter Seventeen

Rainbow Studios

Spring 1968

A month later, all hands at the farm prepared the land for the planting season before the spring rains came to nourish the seeds.

But right before dinner one night, River and Aaron came back from the general store in town with solemn faces.

"I have horrible news. Martin Luther King was shot," River said.

Immediately retreating to the main room, Aaron turned on the radio and everyone listened to the news coverage of the shooting. Shortly after, the newscaster delivered tragic news.

"Dr. Martin Luther King, a leading voice in the civil rights movement, has died from a bullet wound to the neck after shots were fired at him on the balcony of his hotel in Memphis, Tennessee. Police have put out an all-points bulletin for a white man seen running from the crime. The governor called 4,000 National Guardsmen to quell the unrest, as many nearby areas have reported youth disturbances. President Johnson has asked every American to join him in mourning the death of the outstanding leader and pray for peace and understanding throughout the land."

Everyone sat by the radio in shock. Some broke into tears, saddened by what it meant for the country. The news stung Peggy and Liam like a knife through the heart.

"I can't believe it," Jack said. "Who would do something like this?"

"There are evil forces of power in this world, children, and they don't like anyone trying to change the paradigm that can reduce their influence and way of life," Rev said gravely.

With little appetite, the group barely ate dinner and went to their rooms for an early night.

Peggy was frozen. Her first thoughts were of Tara, Maxi, and her friends at the newspaper who were committed to the civil rights movement.

Struggling to sleep, she and Liam talked about the devastation their friends in The Village must be feeling and wished they were with them. They quietly hummed the songs they knew their friends would be singing and speculated about the literal performance Ravyn would do about the shooting to evoke and provoke.

Liam finally fell to sleep, but Peggy's mind raced. She thought of Maxi's last letter about demonstrations, protest marches, editorials, and stories in The Other about racial equality. She said despite the passing of the Civil Rights Act, many Southern areas ignored the mandate and opted to punish black people any way they could.

Still unable to rest, she took out her journal.

Dear Maggie,

I can't believe this is happening. How can someone be killed for promoting peace, acceptance, and understanding? We've been living in a shell for so long now on the farm; we've shut out the anger and violence existing right outside our door.

Are we selfish for wanting a perfect existence? Or are we hiding from a reality we should fight to change? I know what Maxi would say. And I definitely know what Ravyn would do. Maybe this has jolted me into the real world again. I guess even utopia spoils eventually from within or from without.

All I know is I'm feeling restless again. But I don't know if Liam feels the same.

Through the window, she stared up at the blackness of the night, mentally singing protest songs encouraging peace and harmony. She thought of Kieran and the troubles of her ancestral country, hoping America didn't fall into the same divided pit. The call was looming louder in her mind with each passing minute.

The next morning as the dawn rose, Peggy gazed adoringly at her husband's angel-like expression, but was anxious for him to wake. All night she argued with herself until she reached a conclusion. They needed to leave the farm. She longed to speak out using her voice and yearned to make a difference beyond the timbered bubble of their utopia.

She tried to will him awake, but soon resorted to more immediate techniques—kissing him, tickling his face and ears, gently poking him, and then finally shaking him awake.

"Liam. I have to talk to you. I didn't sleep all night. I'm really gutted about what's happening. Wake up." She sat on his chest and urgently woke him.

"What's been gutted?" he said, rubbing his eyes and barely awake.

She waited a moment for him to gain consciousness. "I think we need to leave the farm. I want to get back into the folk music scene. They're at the heart of this and all our old friends are doing things to help. I almost feel ashamed that we're hiding." She looked at him with urgency in her eyes.

He took her hand and squeezed it, touching her troubled face. "I feel the same way. I wasn't sure if you did too, but I hoped so. Things are changing here anyway. I think it's time for us to move on."

Abruptly packing up their things, they said goodbye to the people who, for the last two years, made up their family.

"We've loved our time here, but we feel the need to move on," Liam announced to the others at breakfast.

"No hassles, man, that's the best part of our philosophy," Aaron said. "You need to do what your heart feels and go where the wind blows you."

There were no arguments or debates, everyone understood the desire to roam a new trail. And just as they did two years ago, they were back in the Wanderer, nomads with no destination in mind.

"Where to?" Liam said.

"South, toward the city," Peggy said, taking out her guitar and noticing a card stuck in the case. It said Kyle Camden, Rainbow Studios. "I wonder if they ever made that studio. His card says Woodstock, New York—let's check it out. It's on the way to The Village."

"Sounds good," Liam said and they were off again.

By the next sunset, they arrived in Woodstock, a small farming community. As they drove through town, they saw a quaint old downtown area with a few stores and several quiet picket-fenced farmhouses surrounded by acres of newly planted farmland. Finally, they saw a white farmhouse in the middle of nowhere on the edge of town with young people on the porch.

"Look, the sign says Rainbow Studios. This is the place," Peggy said pointing at the hand-painted sign, illustrated with all the colors of the rainbow.

It was a nice early spring day and there were men with long hair and beards sitting on the big porch playing guitars and drinking lemonade.

"Hey, don't we know that guy?" Liam asked as they stepped out of the Starry Wanderer.

Peggy drew nearer, looking at the familiar man more intently. He had long black hair and a mustache, but she immediately recognized his chiseled jaw with the cleft, muscular bare arms, and manicured hairy chest. It was Chuck, the guy she had had a magical and fiery brief encounter with years before in the alley outside the club.

As she approached, he looked at her with a quizzical face and crooked grin. "Well, do my eyes deceive me? Peggy Mac, is that you?"

Peggy gulped and smiled. "Yes, nice to see you, Chuck. I see you've grown your hair."

"Yeah, needed to cover my good looks so women would stop mauling me at the clubs." He shot her a knowing glance.

To quickly change the subject, Peggy grabbed Liam's arm and pulled him toward the porch.

"This is my husband, Liam," Peggy said. She hadn't told Liam about Chuck and she really didn't want him to know about her abrupt onetime get-together.

"Oh, wow. Congratulations to you both. You've got a beautiful woman there inside and out." He extended his hand. Liam shook his hand.

Brandishing the card, Peggy asked about the owner.

"I don't know if this guy is still here, but he gave me this card on my last day in the clubs a couple years ago. We've been off the grid since then. Is he around?" she asked.

Chuck looked at the card and slyly chuckled. "Yep—inside." He pointed to the front door and they went in.

The old farmhouse converted into several studios with living quarters above. They entered a small sitting area; the office door nearby was open and they could hear a man talking on the phone.

"Yeah, yeah, that's out of sight. Well, let me talk to them. OK, gotta split."

As soon as he saw Peggy cross the threshold, he was curious. She looked a little different now. Her red hair had grown very long and displayed its natural frizzy curl. Her cheeks were rosy and bright. The people at the farm always said that was a byproduct of healthy living.

"You look familiar to me," Kyle said.

Peggy smiled and handed him the card. "We met a few years ago and you gave me this card."

"Oh, I remember you—the Irish folk singer. It's been a while," he smiled.

"Yes, my husband and I were on a journey of discovery for a couple of years, but I missed performing. Looks like you made the studio you talked about," she said.

"Yeah, we're small, but we specialize in a lot of the folk singers in The Village. They come out here for clean living, air to breathe, space to grow, and room to make whatever music they want happen. What kind of music do you want to make?"

Peggy took a deep breath and sighed. "To be honest, I have no idea. I'd like to stick to my Irish roots, but I'm very troubled about Dr. King's murder and what's happening. I just want to be a voice of change, if I can make a contribution."

"Well, there's a lot of that going around. Hey, we're starting a session in about an hour. You can sit in with some of the others, sing backup, and get a feel for things. If you're hungry, there's a kitchen in the back. Help yourselves." He pointed to the kitchen at the back of the house.

Peggy smiled excitedly and thanked him, then went back to the porch to find Liam sitting with the guys, sharing a toke, and listening to their music.

"Come inside," she waved to Liam. "Let's get something to eat."

Liam gave Chuck back his joint and followed Peggy.

When she got to the kitchen, she looked through the refrigerator and cupboards and found bread, jelly, and peanut butter.

Standing beside her, Liam laughed. "So I heard you and Chuck got it on in the back alley of the club."

Peggy dropped the packaged loaf of bread on the ground in shock. "He told you?"

"Yeah," he laughed. "Don't sweat it. Before we were together, you had the right to explore your body just as much as I did."

Confused, Peggy reluctantly picked up the bread and began making sandwiches. She felt a soothing energy as always coming from Liam. She wasn't surprised by his laid-back attitude, and maybe not shocked that it came out in the confines of the marijuana truth circle. It made her feel both at ease and on guard. It's not every day your husband meets your former lover or, even worse, a one-night stand. She wasn't embarrassed, just surprised.

After they ate, Peggy nervously went into the session room. Chuck was on guitar with the other guys she met earlier on the porch playing guitar and bass. And there was a drummer, another guy on piano, and two women sitting on stools in front of a microphone.

She felt as if she had entered the middle of a movie. They all knew each other and the group dynamic. She was the interloper.

Not moving a muscle, like she was frozen in quicksand, she darted her eyes back and forth looking around until Kyle's voice boomed overhead.

"This is Peggy, everybody. She's going to sing backup."

The others smiled, waved and said hi, but despite the kind welcome, Peggy tasted the peanut butter over and over again in her throat. As all eyes were locked on her, she slowly slid onto the stool next to the other two women.

As the drummer counted them in and the music began, Peggy noted that there was no music, so she decided to blend in and harmonize with the women next to her as best as she could.

It was a fairly laid-back session for everyone except Peggy. They all contributed something here or there. From Peggy's vantage point, it seemed as if they were making it up as they went along, laying down different takes.

Once in a while, one of the ladies next to her or a gentleman smiled at her when they struck a particularly good sound together. The singing was easy, but Peggy still felt like a fish out of water, but the ice was broken.

After a couple hours, everyone was tired and once again, Kyle's disembodied voice sounded from the booth. "OK, that's a wrap for today, everybody."

The group collected their things and after some casual conversation, they all shuttled out of the room, leaving Peggy sitting on the stool alone, not knowing where to go or what to do. Then Kyle appeared.

"You did fine, Peggy," he said, sitting next to her. "This is our house band. We mostly back up artists who come in to record. I remember your voice—it's sweet and yet very different. If you're interested, you can sing backup with the band and we can spend a couple of weeks working together and see if we can make something happen with your sound."

Peggy blankly agreed and followed him out of the room. She still wasn't sure what was going on or where it would go, but it was a path she was willing to walk into the unknown.

For the next few weeks, she sang with the band and different artists that arrived. She enjoyed the challenge of making up harmonies with the group.

Diverse players and singers came in with folk and both easy and hard driving rock beats. It was a variety pack of the music of the day. Some of it was amazing and some challenged her eardrums.

When in session, she often compared and contrasted her sound with the music they were singing. Kyle worked with her on it a few times a week, while she and Liam wrote poetry and painted, as they lived in the Wanderer in front of Rainbow Studios.

But after a few weeks, she was still not sure where she was going. One late night she sat out under the stars and wrote in her journal.

Dear Maggie,

As much as I love singing Celtic folk music, I'm beginning to think only the people in The Village will appreciate it.

I'm writing music and trying to bridge the gap between the old Irish songs and today's groove and troubles.

Kyle is very patient trying to help me with lyrics and poetry, but I feel like I'm just skimming the surface, not putting a dent anywhere.

I like singing with the group—there's really nothing like when you're in the pocket and you ride along with the others, playing and singing music, but listening to other artists has given me a new perspective on reality. I just don't think I'm good enough to make it on mainstream radio and records.

Maybe that's not important. We're always saying it's all about the experience. How you get there, not where you go. But if I'm honest, I do want to see my face on an album cover and think about people all over the country listening to my records or my music on the radio. I want to say something. I want to make a difference and have an impact.

But nothing's really sticking. I sing and play, but it just doesn't resonate. Maybe I need to settle for helping others accomplish their dreams.

Weeks later, the warm summer colored the abundant fields with landscapes of green and yellow crops were blanketed with wildflowers of all different colors, shapes and sizes.

Liam was entranced, painting the beauty of the rolling hills. Even though the landscape wasn't much different than at the farm, it seemed to get deeper hues.

To help out at the studio, Liam used his skills learned on the farm and started a garden next to the farmhouse, spending his days cultivating the seeds and growing vegetables to cook for the musicians. He was content to help Peggy in any way he could, so she could concentrate on the music.

After one nighttime session, a few of them were smoking weed and watching the turbulent daily news coverage of the escalating Vietnam War and the civil unrest in the country, with clashes between police and anti-war protesters, civil rights groups, and college students.

"Man, it just seems like everybody hates everybody," Chuck said.

"I don't know what's worse, the war here or the one in Vietnam," the drummer, Jimmy, added.

"We're so divided. You have to wonder if people are so stuck listening to their own hearts, they can't hear the beat of anyone else's," Liam sighed.

An idea suddenly occurred to Peggy, and stared at Liam intently with excitement in her eyes. She began to furiously scribble on a newspaper lying on the table next to her.

"I heard two old ladies at the market bickering with each other about something. It wasn't what they said, but the way they looked at each other that frightened me. Why can't everybody just choose peace?" the piano player, Ray, asked.

"You know, I like to think we do our part by helping singers get the word out, but what if we could do more?" Kyle asked, pulling his long curly blond hair off his forehead and thinking.

Out of nowhere, he jumped up with enthusiasm.

"What if we invited everybody in the area over for a little get-together? The house band can play and people can all bring food and we'll just have a good old-fashioned potluck party. Maybe we can make this little town come together in peace and friendship." He smiled.

The small group agreed and joined in his excitement, offering plans and suggestions as Kyle rushed off to his office to make plans.

Meanwhile, Liam noticed Peggy writing and writing, paying no attention to what was going on.

"Isn't this a great idea for a party?" he asked her.

"What?" she looked up, dumbfounded.

He chuckled and smiled. "Never mind—what are you writing?"

She eagerly grinned and grabbed his hand. "Your words stirred something in me. What you said about people only listening to the sound of their own heart. I think it makes a good song." She handed him the bits of scribble paper and he smiled at her.

"This is good."

She smiled and kissed him on the cheek. "Let's go into the Wanderer and work it out?"

In the days that followed, Kyle and everyone at Rainbow Studios worked hard planning the Peace Porch Party.

Liam painted signs to display in all the store windows to promote it, while the others spruced up the yard, practiced the concert set, and made preparations for the tables and food.

Peggy joined in but mostly focused on writing her song. When she thought she had it perfected, she held her breath and played it for Kyle.

When she finished, he didn't say a word. She panicked as he blankly stared at her for what seemed like forever. She liked the song, but she started thinking its greatness was all in her head.

"Crazy! You just blew my mind," he said and grabbed her shoulders. "Peggy Mac, I think I just heard the hit off your first album. I'll see when the band is available and we'll start recording right away. And you're definitely singing that song at the party. I think people will dig it."

Elated, Peggy jumped up and kissed him, then ran out of the room to the backyard to tell Liam. She found him sitting in front of his easel as usual, painting.

"Liam, Kyle liked the song. We're going to make an album!"

"I know," he smiled calmly.

"How could you know?" she asked, puzzled. "He just told me."

"I knew the minute I heard you sing it." He shot her a big grin and picked up the canvas on his easel to show her. It was the picture he painted of her at the commune, but now she was surrounded by the yellow wildflower fields that were around the Rainbow Studios farmhouse.

"Just the plain fields weren't enough to capture your beauty, so I added the flowers. Piggy, meet Peggy Mac's first album cover," he beamed with pride.

Excited, she threw her arms around his neck and sat on his lap, kissing him as if they were stuck together like glue.

Two weeks went by and the tiny town was abuzz about the Peace Porch Party.

Liam, Chuck and Peggy went to the general store to get supplies and overheard several townspeople talking about it.

"Isn't it nice of them to host this party?" An older lady in a blue gingham dress said.

"Yes, what a wonderful way to bring the community together," a man in bib overalls agreed.

"Wow," Chuck whispered to Liam. "I'm surprised they're excited about this. I was sure they wouldn't want to commune with 'young hippies.'"

"No! It's not nice. They're luring us into their den of drugs and debauchery," a lady in a big straw hat with a bird on it said.

Peggy's draw dropped, appalled by the woman's rush to judgment.

"That's right—I've seen them sitting on that porch smoking marijuana and staying up all night performing God knows what demon music rituals," another man butted in.

"And there it is," Chuck laughed. "The straight line from hippies to drugs to the devil."

"They're so wrong. We need to tell them so." Peggy started toward the women and Liam held her back, listening to the other lady speak.

"Now hush, you two, the preacher said everyone is God's children," the lady in gingham scolded.

"If you don't like it, don't go, but you'll be missing out on a community event and you won't be able to gossip about it later. I'm looking forward to it," a lady in a floral dress retorted.

"Personally, I'm looking forward to meeting them. If we don't, we're just falling into this generational divide everyone's talking about," the farmer in overalls defended.

Chuck, Peggy and Liam smiled and chuckled out of earshot.

"Oh, yeah, this is going to be an interesting party," Liam joked.

A few days later, Rainbow Studios was decked out and ready to receive their neighbors.

The band set up on the porch and Liam proudly showed off his garden bounty with an enormous salad, plus sandwiches and coolers of lemonade.

Not knowing the reception their invitation would receive, the group started playing for whoever would show up or just themselves.

"I don't know how this will go, but either way we're gonna have a great party," Kyle said.

Sitting on the porch, singing with the other backup singers, Jasmine and Karla, Peggy tried to have a good time and push her nervousness out of her head. At some point, she would be singing her new song in front of a crowd of people who wouldn't necessarily be her usual audience. At The Village clubs, the people were always receptive and hip. She wasn't sure about the regular farmers and townsfolk.

Slowly, people started to gather and the food tables began to fill with cakes and pies, potato salad, cold casseroles, Jell-O, and more sandwiches.

As the band played, an eclectic mix of people of all ages with varying backgrounds ate and happily listened to the music. The farmers and small merchants of the town mixed with the hippie musicians who lived nearby, several of whom sat in with the porch band for a song or two.

Standing next to the food tables, Liam smiled as a familiar lady in a big straw hat with a bird on it set down a plate of cookies.

He didn't know if she saw the light and was convinced by her neighbors or if she just didn't want to miss her chance to gossip later. Either way, she was there. They were all there.

Finally, it was time for Peggy to play her song. Giving the band a break, she sat alone with her guitar on the porch on a high wooden stool.

She anxiously gazed into the faces of the onlooking crowd and took a deep breath. Then she saw Liam right in the front of the crowd to support her. She let out the breath, sighed in relief, and smiled brightly at his grinning face. All her worries melted away.

Her new song, "Irish Eyes," combined Irish folk music with a hip rock groove. She sang about the America Maggie traveled to and her father fought for. And she likened it to what she sees today, all with their green Irish eyes.

Me Irish gran gazed at Miss Liberty with hopeful tears that gave her the strength to succeed beyond her station and fears...

My father looked at the sea with pride and grace, knowing that he fought valiantly for country and those who could not be replaced...

My Irish eyes want to see the world with their optimistic view, but my cockeyed glance of today's divide will mend my heart and soul to cleanse my green eyes anew...

The song was beautiful, poignant, and filled with emotion emanating from Peggy's sweet voice. The appreciative crowd burst into applause when she was done, filling her with joy. She gratefully smiled at Liam, who blew her a kiss.

Afterward, the band joined her as she played her version of a couple of old Irish folk tunes, and the audience sang and clapped along, just like they were in an Irish pub.

Everyone was happy with the party, leaving satisfied that they had made a new connection with each other that could spring up into understanding and maybe friendship.

In the coming weeks, Liam and Peggy noticed a different attitude when they ventured into town. People smiled and waved. They thanked them for the party and complimented Peggy's singing. Maybe in their little hamlet, they had started to close the gaps and make over the world anew.

About a month after the party, Kyle excitedly ran into the studio, interrupting a rehearsal, to make an announcement.

"Pay attention, gals and guys, as we unveil a new star in our rainbow spectrum… Peggy Mac!" He grinned and held up Peggy's album cover for everyone to see.

Peggy gasped as she saw Liam's beautiful portrait of her in the yellow fields of wildflowers raised above her, ingrained forever.

With tears of joy billowing in her eyes, she took the album cover from Kyle as everyone cheered.

"We did it, kid!" Kyle smiled.

Then Liam came in with his arms full of champagne bottles, handing them out to everyone. As they popped the corks and saluted her, she kissed Liam with abandon. It was her dream come true.

Alive with enthusiasm, she could hardly go to sleep that night. The top of the Wanderer was open and she stared at the stars as Liam slept. She had one more important person to thank.

Dear Maggie,

I can't believe it. I have an album and Kyle says "Irish Eyes" could be a great hit and it's all thanks to you. In these last few years, I felt the link to you and my roots grow so much. And I'm able to look at the world differently than before. I was so restless and wanted more.

Now thanks to Liam and your memory, I'm at peace. I still want to change the world, but now I know that it's not just an empty dream. It is possible.

Chapter Eighteen

Woodstock

Spring 1969

About six months later, Peggy trudged into the Rainbow Studios office, tired and weary from her most recent tour gig and overheard some men in Kyle's office talking loudly and excitedly about their plan for a huge summer concert.

"It'll be amazing. We're going to convert a farm field into a giant outdoor concert bigger than anybody's ever seen. We can hold about 50,000 people and invite the biggest acts in folk and rock music," one man's voice said.

"A lot of them live around here anyway, so it wouldn't be a big deal, but we need a house band and some publicity. We thought you could help with that. We heard you had a huge gathering a while ago and befriended a lot of the locals," the other voice added.

Peggy was so beat, she plopped down on the couch outside the office, barely noticing what they were talking about. She just came back from another month-long tour playing in coffeehouses and clubs in the tri-state area. Even though she loved playing in The Village back in the day, this was work—30 days, 20 clubs on the road, just her and Liam in The Wanderer.

While she was able to spread her peace message to a lot of people, she still didn't feel she moved the needle any further. Sure, she had an album and her song was played on the radio some, but in the massive abyss of music, she thought of herself as just another player.

She caught her breath and went down to the studio to see her friends. After a bit, Kyle came in and told everybody that they were booked to be the house band for a big outdoor concert that was taking place nearby.

"These goofy guys have a handshake deal with a local farmer and want me to set up a few of the artists we produce and get them to play at this crazy outdoor concert. They plan on having 50,000 people. I can't even imagine it. Who in their right mind would come out into the cornfields and listen to music? But if it works, it could bring in some cash. Who knows?"

"Why would big acts perform in a cornfield?" Chuck asked.

"Exactly. I don't know how I'm going to sell this to any of our talent. Maybe some local talent, since they don't have to travel. Can you believe they're calling it 'Aquarian Exposition: 3 Days of Peace & Music'? Ray, help me call a few people and see if we get any takers. I have a feeling we're gonna get hung up on a lot."

Ray exited, shaking his head while an equally frustrated Kyle stopped on his way out and patted Peggy on the back. "Glad you're home, kid. Heard you did well on the road."

"It went well." Peggy faked a smile and said briefly.

After two weeks manning the phone, Kyle was able to put together a few small opening bands, but the elusive headliner that would attract sales was slipping through their fingers.

He gathered everyone to ask for help. "Look, I know some of you guys have been around and have some contacts. I told those guys they have to throw money at the big acts, but they're doing this on a shoestring. Does anybody know anyone who would play at this thing? I have a feeling it's gonna go down in flames, but I want to give it the best chance I can. These guys are so enthusiastic and committed to this—they won't take no for an answer."

Then the phone rang in Kyle's office and he ran to answer it. He came back a few minutes later with a look of relief on his face.

"That was them. They finally listened to me and committed to forking over some real money. They got Creedence. It should be easier to reel in some more acts now. If anybody knows a group, let me know," he said, and retreated back to the phone in his office, while the band looked at each other and shrugged in shock.

"Well, guess this thing may actually happen," Ray said.

"Creedence just came out with an album. That will help get some interest," Chuck added.

That first booking broke the dam, and they started booking more and more big acts for the festival. Kyle's phone rang off the hook with acts who formerly turned down the gig and now wanted to be in on it. There were still holdouts like Dylan, but other acts like Richie Havens, Joan Baez, Janis Joplin, and Jefferson Airplane were in. Even Jimi Hendrix said yes.

The more she heard about this event, the more interested Peggy became. It would be an opportunity to meet and sing backup with a lot of enormous groups, including several people she knew from The Village, like Stephen Stills, who recently left Buffalo Springfield to form a new band with David Crosby from The Byrds and Graham Nash from The Hollies.

Peggy saw the concert guys go in and out of Kyle's office many times. Anytime she overheard their interactions, they appeared over the moon with enthusiasm. Kyle, however, always came out looking for a hit afterward, when he shared all the hassles they were going through—dealing with zoning boards, security, food, vendors, stage construction, sound, parking, and everything in between.

"I'm sorry I ever got mixed up in this, but these guys are a centrifugal force of perpetual motion. This is going to happen no matter what," he sighed and inhaled a joint.

In April, when they got the approval for the August concert, it started looking like it was really happening.

"Ticket sales are going well," Kyle reported and each day he seemed a little more positive about the concert. By July, he appeared to be looking forward to it.

But then in July, Peggy went to his office and heard his end of a phone call.

"What? When? Where? Are you kidding me? Man, I gotta split." He hung up the phone and smacked his head face down on his desk.

"Kyle," Peggy said. "They're waiting for you in a session."

"Peggy, I've done a lot of difficult things in my life. Growing up was a challenge and then I never thought I'd be able to start the studio and make it happen, but it did. I even thought this goofy concert would finally work out, but I just got a call that they lost the venue and now they're going around from farm to farm in the area trying to find another." Kyle lifted his head and leaned all the way back in his chair.

"Oh, wow, what happened?" Peggy said.

"Apparently the ads in the newspaper and on the radio are generating buzz and have freaked out the people in the town, who are not interested in tens of thousands of hippies descending on their little Hooterville." Kyle plunged his face flat on his desk again.

"Sorry, can I help or get you anything?" Peggy asked sympathetically.

"Yes. Drugs. Fast." He lifted his head up. "But not now, I've got to go into town and see if I can get a farmer to help them out. I put too much work into this for it to go belly-up now."

For the next few days, Kyle was gone and Chuck and the others led the sessions on their own. Kyle was so wrapped up in the concert, he paid little attention to Rainbow Studios or her career. Peggy was relieved he didn't book a bunch of those one-night tour gigs again, she needed a rest. But she was concerned that her debut album may be a forgotten memory.

She was looking forward to the festival, but at that point the Woodstock gig was no big deal to most of the group. They thought it would be a good time, but would prefer to have Kyle back producing their sessions—and sane. His involvement and all the hassle surrounding it made him crazy and carried negative vibes that swept throughout the whole studio.

A few weeks later, Kyle came back looking solemn and grateful.

"We finally found another farm, thank God. This thing is definitely gonna happen, guys, so we need to start practicing some of these songs."

From that point on, the concert was front and center on everybody's mind. Peggy even got a call from Maxi and Ravyn and planned to meet up with them during her breaks from being on stage. That night, before they went to bed, she told Liam about the call.

"Liam—Maxi and Ravyn are coming to the concert. It'll be wonderful to see them again."

"Great, call back and tell him to look for The Wanderer. That'll be easy for them to see. They can stay with us," he said.

Peggy's forehead wrinkled in confusion. "OK, it will be cozy, but I guess we can fit four in the van. We just have to remember to tell Ravyn she can't bring any men. They'll have to find another place to do that. There won't be room!" she laughed.

"Maybe they can use the farm fields," Liam laughed.

***

For the next few weeks, Kyle acted both bothered and excited about the concert. The band sessions were going well, and it was all coming together.

Finally it was time to go set up on Max Yasgur's farm near Bethel, New York, about an hour away.

The band packed up tents and supplies, along with sound equipment and instruments in several vehicles. Liam and Peggy and their trusty Wanderer would lead the way.

Liam gathered vegetables from his garden and some pots for cooking up stews over a campfire. Even though he wasn't a musician, his job as chief cook, bottle washer, and gardener made him an honorary member.

They got there a week before the concert would start on August 15. When they arrived, the place bustled with activity. Workers dug and re-dug the wet farm fields after record rains, busily setting up the staging and fence to surround the venue and erecting stands for food and medical areas to take care of injuries and bad trips.

As they all pulled in, they noticed a small group of tents already assembled in what was supposed to be the parking lot.

"Are people here for the concert this early or maybe those are workers?" Peggy wondered.

They parked just inside the partial fence and all got out and walked to Kyle, who was walking around in a tizzy. In the last six months, his hair thinned from his constant nervous habit of pulling it from his forehead, yanking it on the crown.

"I'm glad you're all here at least. This concert is going to kill me," he frantically complained to them. "You can bury me in the field. I'll be OK with that. It'll be peaceful."

"What's wrong?" Peggy asked, patting him on the back to soothe his nerves.

"Look around. Everything's wrong. It's a swamp here. The workers are starting to look like the Creature from the Black Lagoon because of the mud. Nothing's done. The only thing even closely under control is the Hog Farm. We hired their commune group to handle the freakout and medical tents. They're the only organized ones, so we gave them the security detail because the New York cops dropped out and the last minute. Damn state politicians."

"Commune people know how to take care of others—it's what they do," Peggy reassured him.

He nodded and turned to look at the parking lot and pulled on his hair again.

"Did you see people are already starting to arrive? Every day more and more keep coming?"

"We saw the tents and were wondering. Why would people arrive at a concert a week early and campout?" Peggy asked.

"Many don't have tickets and think they can hear the music from here for free or get in somehow. I don't know. It's crazy. We sold over 50,000 tickets, but now they're talking about a couple of hundred thousand people showing up with or without tickets. I have a really bad feeling about this whole thing," he said.

Liam put his arm around Kyle's shoulders.

"Kyle, you're going to hurt yourself, man. Just go with the flow. What's going to happen is going to happen."

"Liam's right. But just in case it doesn't, I think we need a truth circle." Chuck waved to everyone as he and a few members of the group went over to convene a circle and pass a joint.

Peggy looked around concerned and shocked at the state of the concert venue.

"Liam, in just a few days, a couple hundred thousand people will be here. This is crazy. Do you think this is going to get all done?"

"Come on, Piggy, you know how it works. The universe dishes out reward or punishment at its will. We only ride the roller coaster it creates. At least we can get ourselves set up. Let's find a place for our camp," Liam got in the Wanderer and drove to find an out of the way clearing.

The next day, the 600 portable bathrooms and some of the food vendors arrived. The stage was making progress and the fence was nearly up, so everyone felt more confident they would be ready by opening day, but there was still much to do. Even the musicians pitched in to help set up the sound. Peggy was relieved that it would all come together and Kyle wouldn't have a heart attack or spontaneously combust from the pressure.

But as they all looked out on the horizon, they spotted more and more tents and people showing up in vans, in cars, on bikes, and on foot all day. The parking lot was nearing half-full and the concert was still three days away.

That evening, Maxi and Ravyn arrived and found The Wanderer camp.

The four huddled and hugged just like they used to do in The Village when they all lived together. It was a glorious reunion.

"We made it. The road coming here has more people and cars than you can imagine. It looks like they're fleeing the homeland," Ravyn wryly commented.

"A lot of them don't have tickets or any money. They're just coming because they want to be here. We interviewed a few as we came up. At a grocery store in town, an old lady told us that people feel bad for them and are giving them sandwiches and letting them fill canteens from their hoses. I'm so glad I'm here. This is gonna be the story of the century," Maxi explained, nearly giddy from the exciting vibes.

"This is the way socialism is supposed to be. No one worried about money. Everyone helping others. It will be a beautiful experience. And I see a lot of strapping handsome men. My goal is maybe 10 conquests in the next five days. Two per day. Definitely can be done," Ravyn declared.

That night, they introduced Maxi and Ravyn to the rest of the studio group and ate Liam's fresh salad and farm vegetable stew. They sat by a campfire for hours, talking and having a great time. Ravyn had her eye on Chuck all night, eyeing him… and eventually followed him into the woods.

Peggy smirked and almost giggled when she saw them. They were perfect for each other—she knew they'd have a good time.

The next morning, Peggy and Maxi ambled toward the concert gate and saw the workers taking down the fence they had just put up. Kyle paced back and forth in a now typical harried and intense manner.

"Why are they taking the fence down?" Peggy asked.

"There are too many people without tickets already. This is going to be a disaster. Those guys want this to be an embracing environment with no violence—they don't want people crushed up against the fence or trying to take it down themselves and getting hurt. It's going to be a freebie now," he said, frustrated, wiping his brow with a bandanna.

Karla ran up to the group holding a transistor radio. "Guys, you're not gonna believe this. Cousin Brucie on WABC just announced on the radio that the concert will be free. And the news reporter says that people are flocking out of the city to come here. I'm worried. Listen…"

"Sullivan County is now a parking lot. Anybody who tries to get here is crazy. Police have closed the thruway to try to cut it off from more people getting on to come here."

They glanced over at the parking lot and noticed there were no cars coming in anymore, but droves of people on foot wearing knapsacks, backpacks, and whatever else they could carry.

Then they overheard some people walking by them.

"It's like the whole city is on its way to this concert. The streets are like a parking lot, man. We just left our car on the road a mile back. Some people said they ran out of gas and just left their cars there on the road too."

They all looked at each other, astonished.

"This all just became a different ball game," Peggy said, worried.

"Far out—sounds like it's going to be wild," Maxi said with excitement.

"I'm definitely not going to survive this," Kyle groaned. He walked off with his head in his hands, pulling on his hair.

"Poor Kyle," Peggy sympathized. "This has been a real drag for him from the start. I don't know if he's going to have any hair left after this is all over."

Maxi grabbed her arm, smiling. "Don't you see what this means? This is our time to show the world that our way of peace, compassion, and harmony works. All they see of us is our protests. This could be a shining moment where we explode on the scene and say… 'This is our generation. You don't like the way we dress, our music, or the way we act and feel. You don't understand us, but we're getting it done our way and it's working.'"

"Maybe you're right. When have you seen a couple of hundred thousand people crammed into an outdoor space without an incident?" Peggy scanned the area as far as she could see.

"I'm so glad I brought my camera. This is going to be a career-making story," Maxi enthusiastically took pictures of everything in their sight.

"I only hope you're right. Let there be peace," Peggy said still uncertain.

They were on the precipice of something, but she didn't know what

---

Another morning dewed the already soft landscape. Liam woke first, exiting The Wanderer to get breakfast started for the group and immediately stuck his head in the van, wound up.

"You guys have got to see this!" he shouted.

Peggy, Maxi, and Ravyn rubbed their eyes of sleep and hustled outside.

It was beyond belief. In the new day's sun, all they could see were people. The festival was finally going to begin, and the entire concert and far into the distance were filled with wall-to-wall people.

The parking lot overfilled into the nearby fields with tents, lean-tos, cots, sleeping bags, blankets, and people roaming around everywhere.

Slowly the rest of the band joined them, each staring in shock at the scene.

"Well, didn't you all wanna play for a small city?" Chuck laughed and grabbed plate of food.

Before breakfast finished, Kyle sat down at the campfire and poured himself a cup of coffee from the pot Liam laid on the fire, gulping it like lifesaving medicine. "Gather around, everyone. I don't want you to panic, but the organizers now estimate 400,000 people for the next three days."

The group was stunned staring at him unable to utter a word of reply.

"I know what you're thinking, and you're right. We don't have enough food. We don't have enough bathrooms. And I don't even know if we have enough space for all these people," he said with his head down and then filled another cup of coffee and downed it with renewed enthusiasm.

"But the organizers are really psyched and I've decided that I'm going to let the universe take it where it goes. The music is going to be even more essential to keep the peace. We're determined to give this small city of people the best experience they've ever had, and hopefully we'll come out the other end thinking the same."

Peggy stood up, breaking the silence. "Right On! How can we help?"

Kyle gave her a tight-lipped smile. "We need to get things started earlier and we have a few hurdles to jump. The only road coming into this area and to the town is completely jammed with cars for miles. So that means the bands can't get in that way. We were up all night on the phone and were finally able to secure a couple helicopters to get the bands in here, but it's going to take a while. So, you guys have just become the featured players today. Chuck, Peggy, everybody, I need you to sing and play everything you know until we can get someone here. I'm not saying it's going to be easy, but fill up with coffee and get on the stage as soon as possible for a soundcheck. It's up to us to keep this going." Kyle walked off before anyone could respond, leaving them all speechless.

Maxi looked around, seeing the terror on all of their faces.

"You guys, this is a great opportunity. You have a front-row seat to everything going on at the most happening place in the world right now. And you get to be part of the solution. This is something you're gonna be able to tell your grandchildren."

"If we live through it," Ray said.

Liam stood up and raised the coffee pot into the air.

"Maxi's right. This is a once in a lifetime chance. You're the backbone for what could be the greatest achievement of our generation. Now let me fill up all your cups and I'll keep them coming. We all have work to do."

They drank up and assigned tasks. The band went on the stage, set up all the equipment, and scrawled a set list on a scrap of paper. They knew they might have to fill several hours of music, starting in the early afternoon.

Liam pledged to keep the coffee brewing and their energy up, as he and Ravyn began preparing vegetables and trying to figure out how they could still feed their group and help provide food to the others.

While Peggy worked on the music with the band, Ravyn and Liam went to talk with the Hog Farm organizers, Wavy Gravy and Lisa Law, about the food plan.

Peggy went back to the camp to get a cup of coffee and found Liam and Ravyn gathering vegetables.

"How's the music going?" Liam asked her.

She signed in reply. "There will be music, that much is sure. I just hope the groups come soon. What are you doing?"

"The Hog Farm is preparing an organic muesli concoction of oats and wheat in brand new garbage cans - enough to feed an army. They have some vegetables, but I thought we could spare some of ours to help the effort," he replied and filled his arms with boxes of vegetables and walked away.

After living in a commune for two years, Peggy knew firsthand that communes knew how to take care of people with no money on a big scale. She was confident the food problem would be solved, but less certain she was ready to perform for a mass of people for an unknown period of time.

She crawled into the corner of the Wanderer by herself and wrote in her journal.

Dear Maggie,

I'm seeing this with my own eyes and I still can't believe it. There are 400,000 people out there waiting for the experience of a lifetime. I believe in karma and a benevolent universe. I'm trying to align my positive chakras and hope everything turns out OK. But I'm terrified.

What if they don't like the entertainment? I do not want to go down in history as being responsible for a riot.

I'm wearing your vest and Grandpa Mac's tartan skirt with your broach on it. I'm going to sing Irish tunes and I need all of our ancestors to shine on me today. I'm betting on the luck of the Irish. I'm going to believe that it's true. I have to.

Liam returned to the van and saw the door open. When he found Peggy curled in a ball in the corner with a scared look on her face, he crouched beside her, putting his arm her and held her tightly.

"I don't know if I can do this. Sing for this many people? What if they boo me?" Peggy's voice trembled a little in fear.

"Piggy, you're just getting cold feet. This is an extreme situation, no doubt. But you were ready to sing for 50,000 people, so why not 400,000?"

He kissed her firmly until he felt her body soften and ebb with ease and then gently pulled away.

"Your singing is beautiful and soothing. You transport people into a place deep in their soul that connects on every level of being." He grabbed her shoulders and gazed deeply into her eyes as if transferring his confidence and energy to her. "You made an album. You've toured and sung in front of countless others. You can do this. This is what you always wanted... to make a difference."

Still doubtful, Peggy sighed as she saw a peaceful sea of blue pooling in his bright eyes. She kissed him again, long this time, to inhale his vibrant pink aura. Then she slowly left the Starry Wanderer and walked to the stage. She wasn't sure, but with her confidence increasing by his infusion of love and light, Peggy knew she could go on, for better or worse.

When she approached, the group was locked in a healing circle, holding hands and passing a joint to ease their nerves. Peggy took a quick hit and a few cleansing breaths, trying to remember the yoga breathing she learned in the commune, but her nerves made her mind draw a blank.

Kyle joined the circle and took a quick hit.

"OK, guys, this is it. Someone's gonna announce you as The Rainbow Crew. Feel the crowd and tap into their energy. The acts are on their way. It may be only a couple of hours. This is going to be amazing."

Kyle's demeanor changed overnight. She didn't know if his karma or psychedelics improved his mood, but was glad for him... for all of them.

As the promoter welcomed the swelling crowd to the Woodstock Music and Art Fair, people clapped and cheered with a raucous thunder that reverberated and echoed in everyone's soul. He promised that they were going to have a weekend they—and the world—would not forget.

The band gathered hands and walked onto the stage together. This was it.

They seamlessly got into place. Peggy stood next to Jasmine and Karla and caught her first real glimpse of the audience.

It was a sea of humanity, with hundreds of thousands of eager faces in all sizes, shapes, and colors ready and willing to be entertained.

The band decided to do a few driving rock songs together as a group to get the people in the groove. As Jimmy clicked his sticks to count them in, Peggy gripped Karla's hand, took a breath, and began to sing.

Just a few bars in the crowd began clapping, cheering, and dancing to the rhythm. It was working.

Then Chuck sang a few of his songs with the group backing him up. Peggy knew she was up next but tried to stay present in the moment.

When he finished, she grabbed her guitar and carried a stool up to the front of the stage.

She sat down cross-legged and inhaled the crowd's energy. She was filled with an overwhelming sense of peace and happiness. She was ready.

"I wish every single one of you could see what I'm looking at right now. It's simply out of sight. We are the generation who will change things. We believe in peace, happiness, and harmony for all, and each of you is showing the rest of the world that we're right. My Irish great-grandmother came to this country for opportunity and freedom. Here are my versions of some wonderful Irish folk tales that she loved. Join me in this celebration of life and love."

As she finished speaking, a wave of cheers floated over the ocean of people and swept her up in their glorious force. In that second, she connected with the audience on a level she never achieved before. Maybe it was the circumstances or the number of people, but peering out at the smiling faces and swaying bodies, she was riding on a contact high no one could stop and nothing could duplicate.

When she finished her set, she bowed and waved in gratitude for the applause, as the announcer came out and then resumed her place beside Jasmine and Karla.

"Woodstock Nation, give another hand for Peggy Mac," he said. "And keep your appreciation going for Richie Havens."

Richie Havens, a singer Peggy had seen many times in the Village, was the first act to arrive, since he lived nearby. The band would back him up, and energized with the love from the people, Peggy was ready to sing as long as she was needed.

Havens sang for a couple hours, then Indian guru Swami Satchidananda stood in front of the assembly with the glowing amber backdrop of the sun descending into the horizon.

"America can lead the world and spirituality. Through the sacred art of music let us find peace that can cover the whole world. Let us not fight for peace, but find it in ourselves."

Peggy heard the overhead ticking and clicking cadence of helicopters bringing in more musicians like Greek gods delivered on gossamer wings.

As the sun set, one by one, artists took the stage and were received by the welcoming and grateful crowd. Sweetwater, Bert Sommer, and Tim Hardin followed in succession. Then the band took a break as Ravi Shankar began to play.

Around 10 o'clock, it started raining. But amazingly, it was a warm and cleansing summer rain. No one moved, so Ravi and his sitar continued, never faltering.

The Rainbow Crew finally took a much-needed break, but Kyle came back to the Wanderer camp and asked if a few people could go and accompany a folk singer-songwriter named Melanie.

"I know you guys only had an hour or so of rest, but she's all by herself and wasn't on the roster, so she's doing us a favor. The string band that was supposed to play refuses to go on in the rain. It's a lot to ask—but any takers?" Kyle asked, with his face begging.

Without hesitation, everyone stood up. It was a magical moment and they were willing to be part of every second.

After several encores following Melanie's impromptu set, the band went back to their encampment while Arlo Guthrie and his band entertained the wet, sleepy audience.

As the rain ceased, Peggy and Liam moved into the audience around 1 o'clock in the morning to see a very pregnant Joan Baez take the stage.

The blue hue of the smoky stage lights shone as the heavens' few twinkling stars blanketed the sky above. The ascending sun's glow spotlighted the singers' sweet tones washing over them like a lullaby rocking them all to sleep.

Despite the long day, filled with the good energy of the moment and the high of performing, Peggy walked past their Wanderer encampment and led Liam into the woods to the bank at the edge of the water.

With the moonlight shining, she took off her clothes and waded into the water, beckoning him in. Their wet bodies pressed together and they kissed, hugged, and intensely made love in the trickling edges of the lake, swimming in the comforting love of their warm lips.

Peggy remembered their first time together and when they met. They knew every part of each other's body, every button to push; but in the morning mist rising off the warm water, she knew it was different. This was more than a typical lovemaking. She didn't know how, but when she awakened in his arms on the water's edge, she felt an unfamiliar inner warmth that encompassed every fiber of her being.

She kissed Liam awake and when she saw the flutter of his eyelids; she kissed him again.

"I don't know how I know," she told Liam, touching her bare stomach, "but I think we just made a baby."

Without a word, he smiled and held her, kissing every inch of her body, rolling into the wet, welcoming water, making love once again.

On day two, the band played backup for some acts, but on others, joined in on the experience with the crowd.

The Hog Farm passed around the muesli and granola while everyone miraculously shared everything they had with others.

Jugs of wine and water traveled from person to person, along with blankets, clothes, food, and some drugs. Selfless sharing became the order of the day.

Some walked around in various stages of dress, blanketed in smoke, meeting and greeting others, while others trekked into the farm fields together in the practice of free love and came out arm in arm with smiles on their faces.

The lake became a popular skinny dip watering hole for bathing and refreshing, almost baptizing one's soul.

Standing and sitting shoulder to shoulder, parents cradled and fed their children, suckling milk as other children sucked their thumbs, running around freely bare, gleefully playing.

As Peggy and Liam observed the scene, they felt as though they were back in the commune. Everyone helped each other. It was a unique peaceful and harmonious vibe reverberating all around.

Maxi roamed, too, interviewing anyone who would talk to her, scribbling notes in her notebook and taking pictures, certain she had the inside scoop of a lifetime.

Ravyn moved within the crowd looking for her next sexual experience. Peggy noticed her coming in and out of the fields with men and women in small and larger groups.

The midday musical landscape began with the band filling in and backing up anyone who was there and ready to play. Lesser-known groups like Country Joe McDonald and the fairly new West Coast group Santana filled the afternoon along with others like John Sebastian, who was recruited from the audience to play with a borrowed guitar.

Chuck and the other guitar players stood backstage mesmerized by the amazing nimble fingers of Carlos Santana on the guitar.

Day passed unceremoniously into night and the sun ebbed into the clouds of darkness as the alchemy of musical genres fed the wanting crowd.

Groups like the Grateful Dead and Creedence Clearwater Revival continued to hit the stage upon arrival and play into the night, without warmup or rehearsal.

In the wee hours of the morning, Janis Joplin and Sly and the Family Stone offered nonstop music to anyone who was awake.

Peggy arose in the middle of the night and noticed Liam was gone. Wrapped in a blanket, she found him outside listening to The Who perform their entire rock opera *Tommy*. The two huddled together and watched amidst the rose- and purple-colored hues of the rising ball of the sun as Roger Daltrey appropriately sang "See Me, Feel Me." It seemed as though he was ordering the sun's ascent.

Liam put his arm around Peggy. "You missed Pete Townshend smash his guitar on the stage to wake people up. But if this were an experiment in the evocation of all the senses offering peace through music, it worked.

Take it all in. We'll be able to tell our children and grandchildren about this experience."

"It's a beautiful idea of the world coming to life. I wasn't sure at first, but it all worked. I'm glad we're here to see it. I wish it could always be this way," Peggy kissed him and looked up as the sun rose and smiled on a new morn.

The last day brought a strange and treacherous turn to the festival. After the morning rose with Jefferson Airplane, hours later torrential rains opened the heavens and poured on the music-goers after Joe Cocker performed. People climbing the towers of scaffolding were ordered to stop and they halted the music for safety, but no one left. Peggy and Liam sat in the shelter of the van. Later in the afternoon, Maxi and Ravyn came in, drenched to the skin.

"Come on out, guys, everyone's sliding around in the mud and dancing in the rain," Maxi said.

"It's a gift from God," Ravyn added.

But they opted to stay dry while some of the others joined the mud ball.

A harried moment reared its head when the portable bathrooms overflowed an unpleasant odor leached into the air and added to the mess, one more thing to add to the piles of goods and bads that made up the weekend.

The rain finally ceased and the performances continued well into the night, with notable bands like Blood, Sweat & Tears and Crosby, Stills, Nash and a surprise of Neil Young joining them into the dawn.

Peggy looked through the open skylight of the Wanderer to see purple-blue haze shadows in the darkness turn to amber and rust as the sun rose in a kaleidoscope of colors.

At first light, the crowds began to dwindle, but everyone in the Rainbow Crew sat together listening in awe as the much-anticipated Jimi Hendrix stopped the world on its axis by shredding the national anthem on his guitar.

"Wow, you'll never hear anything like that again. It was worth the wait," Chuck said.

"I guess it was all worth it in the end," Kyle added as they admired the final musical note.

Along with the other hundreds of thousands of people, with the festival over, the Rainbow Crew packed everything up but waited until dusk for the masses and parades of cars to clear the way.

Peggy and Liam hugged and bid a warm farewell to Maxi and Ravyn as they drove out for the city, back to The Village.

By dusk, every field was devoid of people and only the mounds of garbage remained. Kyle stood with the promoters and the Rainbow crew surveying the 600-acre landscape with the farm owner, Max Yasgur.

"Max, you've now proven to the world that a half-million kids can get together for three days and just have fun and music and nothing else, and God bless you for it," one of the promoters said.

Finally it was time to go back home to Rainbow Studios. As Liam drove the Starry Wanderer down the roads, navigating around people and the cars abandoned on the shoulder, joining the camaraderie of caravans, they saw a sign with the Woodstock logo—a dove standing on a guitar neck.

"That's appropriate," he said. "Like the guru said, peace through music. That's what just happened."

Peggy squeezed his hand and went into the back of the van to take out her notebook and record the intense emotions surging through her.

Dear Maggie,

I just experienced several magical moments of my lifetime. The festival came and went, but we will all remember every detail forever. It was honestly the most invigorating and enlightening event I've ever witnessed.

It cleared a path devoid of all the strife in the world, showing me and everyone else that peace is a way to allow people to live in harmony. Differences don't have to become divides—we can all just get along. Maybe this will give generations to come a roadmap that can lead to a new evolution of society.

And I think Liam and I may have made a greater contribution than expected. I have a wonderful feeling that in the wake of the overwhelming lovefest, we sliced a piece of it ourselves and created new life.

I can't wait to bring a baby into this world. It will have happiness. It will be loved. And it will be taught every lesson I learned from those who came before me, but it will be given the freedom to mark its journey, wherever it leads. And if it's a girl or a boy, I would like to honor Caroline by naming him or her Carol either way.

Chapter Nineteen

Grandma Piggy

Spring 2001

"I think we'll be able to find some good stuff for you for your hippie costume," Peggy said to her granddaughter, Jackie, as they climbed the attic stairs in Red and Suzy's house.

"Why are your old things in G-Grams attic and not in your house in New York," Jackie said.

"We came to Chicago for a while after your mother was born and our house didn't have an attic. Neither does our apartment at The Dakota. And somehow, I always believed they belonged here. All our family treasures resting in one place," Peggy said, looking around the attic."

"That's nice. Here, what about this old trunk?" Jackie asked, and she blew the dust off an old steamer trunk.

"No, that huge thing was G-gram's. Not mine." Peggy chuckled and kept looking through the attic, moving boxes and furniture out of the way. "I just had a small trusty old suitcase. Here it is."

Peggy grabbed an old brown suitcase, quickly wiped the surface, and lifted it on top of the steamer trunk.

When she opened the latches, revealing a trove of old clothes, Jackie cheerfully rushed toward the case.

"Oh, I like this vest," she said, picking out the first thing she saw. "And this headband is cool." She held the faded leather braided headband up to her forehead. "This is hippie, right?"

"I guess most people would consider it hippie," Peggy stared at the headband and smiled. "For me, it was much more. It was freedom."

"Hey, is this you wearing the same headband?" Jackie asked, picking up an album cover from inside the suitcase.

Peggy smiled, remembering when Liam painted her portrait.

"Yes, it was my first album. And your Poppy painted this picture." She beamed.

"You kind of look like me, Piggy," Jackie remarked.

Peggy looked at Jackie. With the family red hair and green eyes, the strong resemblance stayed in the family. From Maggie to Red to her and then to Jackie.

"Yes, you carry the family genetic code and traits. It's an important legacy. But it usually skips a generation. Your mother got your Poppy's blonde hair," Peggy said, admiring Jackie's hair.

"But if you want to see real hippies, take a look at this." Peggy picked up a scrapbook from the suitcase and sat in on an old chair. Jackie stood next to her looking on.

Leafing through the yellowed pages, she pointed out a picture of her and Liam sitting on the ground.

"This is Poppy and me at Woodstock."

"What's that?" Jackie asked with a blank look.

"It was a huge outdoor concert in 1969. Maybe 400,000 or even 500,000 people attended. No one really knows, but it changed my life. Your mother was a Woodstock baby, along with many others."

Peggy turned to the pages lined with newspaper clippings about Woodstock and a Life cover that called Woodstock the greatest peaceful event in history. Other papers wrote of it as an example of the hippie ethos illusion of infinite possibilities.

"Here's a special edition at a paper I used to work at, written by a friend of mine," she reminisced, pointing to The Other coverage featuring Maxi's story and pictures called Song and Soul: The Anthem of Woodstock.

She read a section out loud to Jackie. "A half-million hippies and young people descended on this community who feared mass destruction and the demise of civilization, and the only thing that happened was a transcendent communal experience. In the end, Woodstock wasn't just about a concert with sex, drugs, and rock and roll. It was a spiritual experience that blended people with love, sharing peace and harmony and offering proof that a new way of life and freedom could change the world and a hope that it does. Right on!"

Peggy set down the scrapbook for a moment and stared out into space. "It was Maxi's big break. She wrote about what we saw and the people we met, but she also wrote about what it all meant," Peggy explained. "It led her to the New York Times and eventually a Pulitzer Prize for her reporting on protests." Peggy chuckled. "She's still trying to change the world."

"Oh, I've heard you talk about her and somebody named after a bird," Jackie exclaimed.

Peggy laughed. "Oh, yes—Ravyn. We lost track of her. The last time I saw her, she was doing experimental theatre in New York."

"Did you ever make another album, Piggy?" Jackie asked, looking at the Irish Eyes album cover.

"No. After Woodstock, making records wasn't important to me anymore. I made my album and said what I needed to say. And I sang and played on many artists' records that began some amazing careers. I never wanted to be famous, just play my music." Peggy said.

Jackie glanced at Peggy's album again. "I like your album. It must be fun to play in front of people."

"Yes, it is. Even though I didn't record again, I never left my music behind. Over the years, I performed at The Village clubs once in a while, just for fun, but then the music changed and many of the clubs closed. I still sing whenever I get a chance. In Ireland, there are summer festivals that really enjoy new and different takes on old songs. And I'm very content singing for my family. Your mother, when she was young, and Poppy… and you," Peggy explained.

"That's too bad. I think your voice is so pretty. I remember you singing to me when I was a little girl. I still love to hear it," Jackie smiled and Peggy kissed her on the forehead.

"Passing the music to another generation is enough for me." Peggy put away the scrapbook and album.

Jackie pulled a tie-dye shirt over her head and added the vest and headband.

"How does this look?" she asked.

"It's like looking in the way-back mirror. What if we sewed some flowers on your jeans and we'll get some for your hair too—then it'll be perfect for a school

dance." Peggy admired Jackie lovingly, like an image from the past reflecting back at her.

"This is so cool. Some kids are just coming in store-bought costumes; I can say everything I'm wearing was from Woodstock—authentic 1960s," Jackie said, proudly modeling in the mirror.

"But remember that vest is nearly 100 years old. It's a family heirloom. It belonged to your great-great-great-grandmother Maggie. She was a seamstress who came to America from Ireland. In fact, I have another family treasure for you." Peggy walked over to the corner of the attic and picked up her old worn guitar case painted with rainbows and flowers all over it.

"Wow, it's like a painting," Jackie said, running her fingers over the case.

"Yes, your Poppy used to add to the designs when the mood suited him," Peggy laughed. She carefully removed the guitar from the case and handed it to Jackie. "And if you're interested, I can teach you how to play this."

Jackie's eyes grew wide as she took the guitar. "Wow, really? You think I could play it?"

"Yes, your G-gramps taught me, and I'd be happy to teach you my songs and some of our traditional Irish songs that he passed down," Peggy said.

"Like those ones you sang to me when I was little about Tír na nÓg and Too ra loo la!" Jackie sang and danced around a little.

"Yes, you have a rich heritage from every member of your family. You come from seamstresses, bricklayers, painters, singers, mechanics, war heroes, and even Irish royalty on your Poppy's side," Peggy told her.

"I know. Poppy is always doing goofy voices and telling everybody he's a count, like Dracula!" Jackie laughed.

"Well, not like Dracula, but he is a real count and I'm a countess. Maybe this summer your mother will let us take you to Donegal Manor and you can see it for yourself. That is, if she doesn't have you signed up for too many camps and things over your break," Peggy said with disapproving sarcasm.

"I'd like to come, but I think I do have soccer camp and 6th grade prep this summer," Jackie looked down, disappointed.

"It's really beautiful. We ride horseback through the rolling hills and vast countryside and swim in the lake on warm days. When your mother was little, she used to love our Irish summers, especially high tea in the solarium every day. But when she got to be a teenager, she didn't want to leave her friends. G-gram and G-gramps come with us every summer. They walk in the gardens and G-gramps picks flowers and gives them to her, just like when they were first dating. Someday it'll be your home too," Peggy said.

"And then I'll be the count!" Jackie proudly stated with her hands on her hips and her chin up in the air.

"Almost! You'll be the countess... I think. I don't necessarily know how that works when a girl is the heir. We'll have to find out," Peggy said. "Maybe Poppy knows. But he never cared about titles anyway. He just likes connecting with our ancestors and keeping family traditions alive. I'm happy you're interested in these things. It's nice to have somebody to hand things down to."

"Yes, like here in the attic. It's full things to look through - like an adventure through time," Jackie said.

"That's a really great way to put it, honey." Peggy stood up and turned around, fondly scanning the attic while remembering decades past. "I used to spend a lot of time here looking through all the boxes and steamer trunks, practicing my guitar, and singing alone. It was my own secret place."

"Jackie, it's time to go!" a woman's voice called up the stairs.

"I guess this means you're off. Don't keep your mom waiting. I'll bring the guitar to my house back in New York. When you come over this weekend, bring your jeans and I'll help you sew on those flowers and we'll start our lessons."

"Thanks, Piggy. You're so cool," Jackie said, kissing her on the cheek and running down the stairs.

"Don't forget to say goodbye to Poppy, G-grams, and G-gramps before you go."

Peggy waved goodbye and began picking up clothes and putting everything back in its time vault. She returned everything to its place in the suitcase and looked around the attic, quietly reminiscing about each treasure. She was so entranced in her memories, Liam startled her when entered the attic; she hadn't even heard him climb the stairs.

"So I hear Peggy Mac rides again," he laughed, kissing her. "Jackie told me about the guitar."

"Yes. It'll be fun to teach her. And you know, she's right. This attic does tell the story of our family. It holds all the precious memories of generations gone by so that youngsters never forget," she said. "And despite what our daughter thinks, I think that our ancestry is in good hands with that little girl. Hopefully she'll carry the torch. By the way, you need to talk to your daughter about letting Jackie come to Ireland with us this summer."

"Why me?" Liam grinned and grabbed her around the waist.

"You know darn well why. She likes you better," Peggy said, hugging him.

"And who could blame her? You can't turn down the count of Donegal!" he said, kissing her again. "I'll try. Now, before we go back to The Dakota, do you want to go to the pub for Guinness stew?"

"In a while... lock the door. I never had a forbidden tryst in my parents' attic. Another adventure to add to our list."

Liam walked down the stairs to lock the door.

Before Peggy closed the suitcase, she touched the leather-bound notebook.

"Don't worry, Maggie—just like your red fiery hair, your legacy will continue in this family, too."

What Happens Next?

In the final volume of the McIntyre saga, a disaster causes a family tragedy, bringing new perspective and giving an opportunity for healing and growth.

And Jackie travels to Ireland for the first time and immerses herself in the land of her ancestors on a journey of enlightenment and discovery offering new friends and a chance at first love, all in the magical landscape of the Emerald Isle.

CLICK FOR DISCOUNTED PREORDER

A Timeless American Historical Romance Series

Sign Up for sneak peeks: https://suzanneruddhamilton.com

About the Author

Thank you for reading this book. I like to tell stories about women with heart, hope and humor. Life is full of all three and you need to have each to thrive and survive, much like all the people in this book.

I encourage everyone to make their own path in life, no matter what age. I did, but it took a long time.

I spent my first career trying to find my bliss in journalism, public relations, real estate, and marketing. Now I'm enjoying my second career—writing. I write in many genres for all ages, but I always try to tell stories of everyday life experiences in a fun-filled read. Originally from Chicago, my husband and I, along with my computer, are happy transplants in the warm and gentle Florida breezes.

Please let me know what you think with a review on BookBub.com, Goodreads.com or Amazon.com.

I value the opinions of my readers and will always strive to entertain and give you a good feeling after the last page is read. Feel free to reach out to me on my social media channels and sign up for my newsletter to get weekly short stories, bonus materials, name and book cover reveals, contests, giveaways, exclusive sneak peeks, and updates on new releases.

I love to hear from my readers. You can sign up for my newsletter, read free short stories, get sneak peeks on new books and get some behind-the-pages information at www.suzanneruddhamilton.com.

You can also follow me on social media at:
Instagram @suzanneruddhamilton
Facebook @suzanneruddhamilton
Youtube @suzanneruddhamilton
Tiktok @suzanneruddhamilton
Pintrest @suzanneruddhamilton
Twitter @suzruddhamilton

My Other Works

Welcome to my world. I write cozy mysteries, women's fiction, historical romances, books for middle grades and young adults and children's illustrated books under a couple derivatives of my name, listed below. My books are clean and friendly for any audience. If you want to read more from me, here are my works. All novels are available in paperback and eBook on Amazon.com and Kindle and soon to be available as audiobooks through Amazon.com/Audible – click on books to link to series. I also write plays for the performing arts: *Hollywood Whodunnit*; *Death, Debauchery and Dinner*; *Dames are Dangerous*; *Puzzle at Peacock Perch*; *Sounds and Silence;* and the musical *Welcome Home*.

Cozy/Detective Mystery:

Secret Senior Sleuth's Society Series

*Beck's Rules
Mysteries*

Romance:

*A Timeless American
Historical Romance Saga*

First Sight:
Contemporary
Love Stories

Women's Friendship Fiction:

The Little Shoppes
Women's Friendship
Fiction

Middle Grade/Young Adult:

Growing UP girls books by
Suzanne Rudd

Children's Picture Books:

How an Angel Gets It's Wings by Suzanne Rudd

Acknowledgements

A big shout out and thanks to all those who shared their stories of The Village, Woodstock and the 1960's with me. It's a time that seems so recent, but still more than a half century ago. I feel priviledged to chronicle that time inside the fictional world of this book to preserve its special nature and share it.

To my safety nets, my editor and cover designer for hopefully making me look good.

.... And a special thank you to my friends and family and writing friends for their continued support of my author career.

Printed in Great Britain
by Amazon